To My Fr
From Lord B,
`Fair Winds`

MW01598631

YAKUTIAN
MAGIC

Michael Murphy
April 24, 2025

MICHAEL MURPHY

 FriesenPress

One Printers Way
Altona, MB R0G 0B0
Canada

www.friesenpress.com

Copyright © 2025 by Michael Murphy
First Edition — 2025

All rights reserved.

No part of this publication may be reproduced in any form, or by any means, electronic or mechanical, including photocopying, recording, or any information browsing, storage, or retrieval system, without permission in writing from FriesenPress.

This book is a work of fiction. It contains factual names, characters, places and incidences. The precise words and details are the product of the author's imagination and used fictitiously. Any resemblance to actual events, locals or persons, living or dead is entirely coincidental.

For information, contact Michael Murphy.
www.mmurphyauthor.com

ISBN
978-1-03-832545-7 (Hardcover)
978-1-03-832544-0 (Paperback)
978-1-03-832546-4 (eBook)

1. FICTION, FANTASY, HISTORICAL

Distributed to the trade by The Ingram Book Company

DEDICATION

To God in heaven. His son, Jesus Christ and the Holy Spirit.

Author's note

The pronunciation of Yakutian Magic (Yah-qu-shun)

THIS IS THE SECOND NOVEL
IN THE FAIR WINDS TRILOGY

ACKNOWLEDGMENTS

I would like to thank my wonderful wife, Tanya.

She has supported me from the first page to the last page of this novel, with both editing and typing my story. Hand in hand we have travelled along this path together.

Special thanks to Brett for the cover design of Yakutian Magic.

I would like to thank my sons and friends, who have always been there to encourage my efforts. Special mention to Terry, a lifelong friend. He brought clarity to my work with his critique and valued comments.

I would like to acknowledge the incredible efforts of all the brave men and women in history who pioneered opening Siberia, along with the merchants and traders who have traveled "The Silk Road."

CHAPTER 1

The early morning had Ragnar standing on the familiar rough-planked floor of his boarding room above the hotel saloon. His friend Uraan had secured the room in the Old Crow Hotel after Alexander Baranof had placed Ragnar in his care. Looking at his sparsely furnished living quarters, Ragnar reflected on how they had been his home for almost a year, all while healing from the gunshot wound to his chest.

Most travelers would consider it very meager by any standard, but he had come to welcome its simplicity after a while. A small wooden bedstead stood in one corner, not more than a cot really, with cut straw laid over as bedding. On the other side of the square room was a modest but practical table and chair, silently residing beneath a round window from which he could view the outside world. A large clay pitcher and water basin rested on the table, used daily to refresh himself. A crude nail tacked to the wall held a towel. Now standing on his two feet, there was nothing else of note to see here, and he felt more grateful than sad at leaving it behind.

He presumed Baranof had continued with his ship and crew from the Russian town of Petropavlovsk and then sailed south to Canton to conduct his fur trade business. Ragnar was speculating, of course, but knowing Baranof's nature and obsessive appetite for wealth, he felt it was a good guess.

"Put those thoughts in your wake." He spoke to no one. "That part of your life is over for you."

His near-death experience on the island beach of Saint Mikhail's, Alaska, had almost claimed his life. He also knew the encounter had taken the wind out of his sails for good. He had resolved not to go back to a sailing life. All he really wanted and thought about was returning to his homeland of Norway. It was time to move on.

Ragnar's thoughts now turned to Ayaana's foretelling, to her tarot cards almost three years ago. It was then, in this very same hotel, that she had foreseen "gathering clouds" in his world, with a life-changing event yet to unfold. The weight of her words still lingered, adding a layer of intrigue to his decision to leave Alaska and return to Norway.

"It feels like another lifetime. I wonder how Grigori and his brother Mikhail's lives have played out. I'm sure they're fine," he muttered. "That lad Grigori was a quick learner and very resourceful. Well, it's all in the past, and there's nothing more for me here." Ragnar shook his head and ran his fingers through his hair.

He reached for his woolen sailor's bag and slung it over his shoulder, wincing regretfully in pain. The wound he carried had not yet fully healed.

"Slow and steady as she goes, mate." He then adjusted the sack correctly.

Exiting his room, he walked downstairs into the Russian kabak, looking for Uraan. Crossing the floor of the public house, Ragnar nodded in acknowledgment by tipping his hand forward in farewell to the proprietor, who, upon seeing him leave, called out, "Fair winds, my friend." Then he returned to his customers' demands.

Hearing those words brought a flood of memories back to Ragnar, and a smile creased his face. He felt good opening the front door. Then he crossed over the threshold into what would hopefully be the start of his final journey home. Uraan sat waiting on a two-wheeled ox-drawn cart laden with hay.

Ragnar paused momentarily and raised his face skyward to feel the heat of the midmorning sun warm him before calling out. Too many endless winter nights sailing and living in the Arctic had given him an appreciation for one of nature's most simple gifts—a sun that gave up its heat to the land.

"Uraan," he cried out, seeing his friend.

"Hoy, Ragnar," was Uraan's quick reply. "Are ye ready about?"

"Aye, we can be away any time now."

"Arr. But before we leave, my daughter Ayaana wishes to say goodbye to you."

"Well, I would also like the same and to thank her for helping me recover this past year."

Ayaana stepped out from behind the cart. Seeing him well, she gave a genuine smile his way. "I see you are ready to travel the long road to your home," she said thoughtfully.

"I am, and thank you for your comforting words, Ayaana. As always, your voice puts me at ease. Traveling this day would not have been possible without your medicine and help."

He briefly regarded Ayaana, trying to understand the person behind her dark beauty. She was a healer by nature. He knew only a few men would seek her true essence. Most would desire more from her. They would seek to own and possess her body and soul. She was a unique young woman; her inherent and natural qualities were to care for and support those in need. Beyond these were her deeper attributes, which connected her spiritual self between two worlds, making her a shaman of the Yakutian people. Few would see beyond her physical form, even fewer her mystical powers at work. Ragnar had seen and felt both.

Now, he stood before her, remembering the shortened days and long winter nights in this northern realm while she worked her healing magic toward his eventual recovery.

"I don't know where to start to thank you."

"No thanks are necessary. This is karma in life. Your father saved mine, and I am now able to help you. It is a full circle for our families. In Yakutia, we believe in karma."

"Still, I feel I am in your debt, as I will not be returning here."

Ayaana looked at him carefully before speaking sincerely. "Take this talisman with you. It once belonged to my grandmother, and now it belongs to you." Then she placed it in his hand. "This journey will not be easy to accomplish; it will take you on a long and dangerous path. It begins at the mouth of the Amur River, then to the Road of Bones and beyond. Perhaps this ring, known as the Eye of the Raven, will aid you, though I cannot say. I only know its influence is strongest under a full moon at night."

Ragnar studied the ring and held it between the tips of his fingers. It was a lustrous oval of red onyx, ringed in black, with a smooth, domed surface. The underside was perfectly flat, and four silver talons held it precisely in its setting. Its modest size reminded him of a human eye.

"I am just a sailor and traveler passing through your land. You are a shaman, and I will take your word for it. It's special to me, Ayaana. Thank you. I will wear it for good fortune, but I will also keep it as an heirloom to be passed down through my family, God willing."

Slipping the silver band onto his left index finger, he reached out, hugged her, and said goodbye. There were no more words to be spoken between them. After only a moment of silence, they both felt and understood each other.

Ragnar then stepped up and sat on the wooden bench beside Uraan, who was waiting quietly, holding tight the leather reins that controlled the harnessed ox.

"Are you ready, my friend?" Uraan asked.

"Aye, as ready as I will ever be."

"Well, stow your gear behind the seat and get comfortable; we've got at least a full day's travel ahead of us. As we discussed earlier, you'll board a ship that takes you across the Okhotsk Sea, and then you'll disembark at the mouth of the great Amur River. This is where your journey really begins.

"But first, we go by land to the other side of this bay. There, you are expected to join a crew of seasoned men, sailing a swift carrack to a small village and your destination." After saying such, Uraan gave the tremendous horned beast a snap of the reins, commanding him forward.

As their two-wheeled cart lurched and creaked forward in motion, Uraan continued speaking. "That's quite a gift my daughter has given you. I know it has a special meaning for her. It comes from her mother's side of the family. Many in that bloodline before her have been shamans for our people.

"I believe Ayaana will be a great shaman and healer one day, as she is still young and learning the craft. Her second sight was revealed to her at an early age. First, appearing in her dreams and now, as you have experienced, through her tarot cards."

"I think of her gift as a great honor, and I am humbled to have received it," Ragnar replied sincerely. He then again admired the black-ringed stone on his finger. "It will always remind me of her, you, and the kindness of the Yakutian people in this remote and faraway land."

Uraan acknowledged Ragnar's compliment on his family and people, nodding before responding.

"Yakutia is a remote region only a few travelers like ourselves know of. Most Sakha people, as we call ourselves, are fiercely tied to the land. Our traditions and culture are old. Most of our people never travel, as family and village come first whenever decisions need to be made.

"I am only one of maybe a dozen Sakha men to have traveled and sailed the great seas. Most would prefer the ground beneath their two feet, as opposed to a ship's wooden deck rolling on high seas. But I was restless in my youth. No amount of discipline could keep me from wandering farther away from my village and responsibilities.

"One day, a small band of darkly bearded and strangely garbed men entered our village looking for hunters to aid them in replenishing their ship's stores. When the request came, the village men learned they would be away from their families for days at a time, and no one volunteered. I was a youth then, but still a capable hunter.

"All Sakha men and some chosen women are trained in hunting skills from an early age. They then use their great bows to support the villages with fresh meat for sustenance.

"Much to the disappointment of my family, I willingly and with purpose volunteered to help these outsiders, if only to learn more about them. It wasn't long before they accepted me as one of their own. These foreign men quickly realized my hunting skills and knowledge of the surrounding land were valuable assets. After only a few days of hunting together, their dogsleds were full of salted meat in wooden barrels, ready to fill their ship's stores.

"They called themselves Russians and, as such, spoke a crude dialect similar to my own Yakutian tongue. All were big men, at least two hands taller than myself, and dressed from head to toe in long bear coats. At night, over our fires, they told me wild tales of sailing blue and green oceans in their great ship to the most distant and strange lands. How the charms of exotic and beautiful Nubian women on distant shores could not be resisted, even by the strongest sailor. Of their prowess and fearlessness in ship-to-ship battles at sea.

"At that time, I felt like an equal to these men. Maybe I was being a little naïve, not having yet proved myself in combat, but I was keen, and they could see my enthusiasm.

"Ragnar, that one week with those people changed my life's course forever. I was determined to set sail with them, no matter the cost. Of course, my family was very unhappy with my decision to leave them and our village.

"Eventually, all their arguments for me to remain had been used to no avail. My mother wept, and my father remained silent as I boarded their ship. When casting a long look back their way, I said goodbye." Uraan then went quiet, reflecting on that long bygone day.

"How long were you gone before your return?"

Their cart, jostling along the dirt road, seemed to shake Uraan out of his momentary isolation, and he pondered Ragnar's question.

"Five years and five more months at sea brought me back to my home shores. What now seems like another lifetime. My near-death encounter with your father was my final great voyage across the brine. That last desperate sea battle, fighting bloody pirates on the north coast of darkest Africa and being rescued by him from shark-infested waters. It gave me an even deeper sense of my own mortality and more of where I belonged in this world.

"After his daring rescue, helping me escape from a black, watery grave, I knew a lifetime at sea was not my calling. What I valued most, Ragnar was calling me back to my family and village."

"The words you are saying to me are also my thoughts, Uraan. Now, at this time in my life, all I want to do is return home, strike my colors, and surrender my past. I want to reach out and feel like I belong somewhere. I don't know why the call of the sea is lost to me. I feel I am done." He lightly touched his still-tender chest wound.

Both men went silent and watched as the day broke open nicely, with a red-sky morning in early spring. They traveled first west, then south along the bay's curved eastern shoreline. The road they followed was well-worn, defined by a rutted cart trail. Obviously, this was a result of frequent travel between Petropavlovsk and the fishing village they were headed for.

Ragnar noticed that the road rose sharply above the white, pebbly shoreline and Avacha Bay, as it was known. It was shaped like a horse-shoe, ringed by high stone cliffs, and overlooked a natural harbor with a narrow entrance. He could see and hear the cries of thousands of sea birds everywhere below them, especially gulls, puffins, and many others that use these cliffs as a rookery. Below, on a sandy shore, four Kamchatka brown bears fought amongst each other for dominance. Just offshore, seals and sea lions sunned themselves on low tidal rocks. At the entrance to the bay, three large, spired rock columns jutted out of the water, standing in defiance of the natural order of the sea.

"Do you see, Ragnar? Those 'Tri Bata' at the entrance to the bay?"

"Aye, if that is what you call those giant stones."

"It is. The Sakha people believe a great winter storm was sent long ago to destroy this village and all its people. Three courageous brothers sailed out to the bay entrance to challenge the gods. Seeing their defiance, these same gods, in anger, turned them to stone. That is why, to this day, our harbor never freezes in winter; they still protect us."

"An interesting tale, Uraan. I will take it with me and tell it to my sons and daughters," Ragnar said with a wry smile. "Perhaps, in the retelling, I think I would say to them, 'The men of Yakutia were to be so greatly feared that should any woman go to your village looking for mates, they should beware the gods who may turn them to stone.'"

Both men laughed at Ragnar's response.

Uraan, with a slightly more severe tone, replied, "Well, just remember there are powerful forces at work in the world that cannot always be explained away. Both a man's good intentions and another's evil deeds can harm you if you are not careful. Keep an even keel in your travels, my friend, and your path will lead you home."

Their cart moved through white patches of snow resembling soft bits of fabric among new spring green grass, awakened from winter's rest and reaching for the sky. Ragnar perceived their early demise from the warmth of this day's morning sun.

"What is the name of the guide you spoke of earlier? Who will help me reach the northern Silk Road of the Mongol?"

"Your guide's name is Modun Teresov, and he is a very old friend of mine. We spent many years of our youth learning to hunt. His reputation today, I hear, coming out of Yakutia, is that he is an even greater tracker. Few men know the land and woodcraft as he does. If anyone can help you navigate your way to Mongolia and the Silk Road, it will be Modun. I sent word to him months ago and asked he meet you at first spring in the village on the mouth of the Amur River."

"How will I know him, Uraan?"

"Well, he looks like any Yakutian man and probably dresses a lot like me. He might be garbed in the common winter attire of our people. A cap and waistcoat made of horsehide, with leggings and boots from the reindeer. The great bow of the Sakha hunter that he carries will be an especially identifying feature for you. In truth, he will look a lot like me, although not as handsome," he said with a sly grin.

Ragnar laughed aloud at his brazen words, responding equally in return.

"So, when did you become a Yakutian princeling, my friend?"

"Well . . . in our land, we say, 'An old stallion cannot rest until all the mares rest in peace.'"

Ragnar nodded, slightly surprised to hear Uraan talk this way, knowing his wife, Ayaana's mother, had recently passed from this world.

"My wife was very good to me in our time together," Uraan said, "but after her spirit departed this realm, she left three unmarried sisters for me to care for. I'm still unsure if they're a gift to me or her final revenge upon me. Time will tell."

"You old sea dog," Ragnar replied, feigning shock and then laughing aloud.

"Even in my elder years, life can still be good. I believe I made the right decision to return here, and I think you are hearing a call within yourself to return home. It is the way of a traveler to follow his heart's song.

"In truth, your life journey is not yet complete, my friend. You have cheated death many times in your years at sea, Ragnar, and your gods have not abandoned you to a saltwater grave. Ayaana and I believe there is more to you that needs to be spoken of."

"Thanks, Uraan. Your words assure me I've made the right decision to return home over land rather than by sea. I couldn't bear the thought of a two-year journey across treacherous ocean waters. My heart told me the road home across your land could, with some luck, be achieved in one year's travel.

"If your friend, and now my guide, Modun, can take me to the Silk Road of the Mongols, I will hire out my services to protect one of the many caravans traveling west to Istanbul. Even if I reach the Caspian Sea, I can find my way home from there. My Viking ancestors mapped the inland sea routes across eastern Europe. This navigational knowledge has been passed down from every sailing father to his son for generations. It is our way, Uraan. We are world explorers and chart makers."

With a sarcastic laugh, Uraan replied, "I don't think any spider webs are under your boots, my friend. It is not in your nature to remain still enough for any spider to begin spinning."

"You're probably right."

Both men looked ahead and beyond the horned beast that pulled them up along the road they traveled. As the day wore on, they spoke of their trials in life, of their daring and courage in sea battles long days ago. They were content together, as men would be. Uraan painted more colorful stories, particularly of the harbor wenches he had encountered, whom he was always making promises to but never returning their way.

Although a good storyteller, Ragnar struggled to match Uraan's tall tales of rutting his way across the seven seas. Instead, he respectfully yielded to his elder friend. "Uraan, I know you as a brave and loyal friend. But if the mast that you carry in your breeches is as tall as the tales you tell, then surely all the saddened women you have left behind are damning you to hell."

Both men roared in laughter like two drunken sailors at these words while their cart trundled along the road they followed. By midday, the sun had passed its zenith and rapidly descended in the sky, evidenced by the long shadows cast.

"Let's stop and set a fire for the night," Uraan suggested. "Darkness will surround us quickly, as will tonight's chill. We're not far from our destination, and the ship carrying you tomorrow morning isn't going anywhere without you aboard. If you gather the wood, I'll tend to the ox and our provisions."

"Aye," Ragnar said, gladly stepping off the cart and stretching his legs.

Sitting around their fire later that night, Ragnar asked, "Do you see success in my goal, Uraan?"

"I do, but it is a long journey, my friend. Modun will only go as far as the land of the Mongols. After that, you will be on your own. His knowledge of the land comes to an end there."

"I see," Ragnar reflected.

"Your thinking of using the riverways as much as possible is good and sound. You will travel far this way on your journey."

Lying on his back and seeing a black velvet curtain behind the myriad points of light, Ragnar witnessed a raven flash overhead, westward across the sky. "Did you see that, Uraan?" he asked quietly.

But Uraan was asleep and oblivious to his voice. Soon, Ragnar slept under this blanket of stars.

The following day, Ragnar woke to the smell of mint tea brewing in a small pot Uraan was preparing over an open fire. Seeing Ragnar awake, Uraan started, "Our fare is not much, but it's hot, and along with some smoked salmon, sour cream, and berries, it'll be enough to start our day."

"If it warms my belly, I'll not complain."

Sitting up with his bowl of food and cup of tea, Uraan said, "Over that southern rise is a bay where your ship will be anchored and waiting. We should arrive in about two hours' time. This is also where our paths divide, leading us each back to our homes, my friend."

"God willing," Ragnar replied, knowing full well it would take more than just a little luck on his part.

"Aye, and God willing."

The two men broke camp in silence, rolled up their bedding, and loaded their gear onto the cart before continuing along their trail. Shortly after that, they stopped for a moment when they crested the rise. They looked across and below to the bay and the waiting ship, an upgraded carrack by design. Ragnar could see it resting and remarked that the three-masted craft had one square sail, two triangular lateen sails, and a stern rudder.

"She looks a little old school, Uraan."

"Not to worry. She's built Portuguese strong, I'm told, and seasoned Russian sailors man her crew."

"Well, that's encouraging. Good! Let's go meet her captain and crew, then."

Uraan snapped the reins to move the beast forward.

The two men arrived on the sandy beach in a small, sheltered cove at the very tip of the Kamchatka Peninsula. It was a natural harbor, the cliffs behind them shielding the cove and preventing strong ocean winds from gathering any strength. The waiting ship Ragnar was to board was built for speed and maneuverability in open waters, a carrack. She wore triangular sails like veils, allowing her to sail forward into the wind.

Uraan lit a beach fire to let the ship's captain know they had arrived. In time, a small rowboat approached. It beached near where they stood, and a sailor approached the two of them, asking for Ragnar Olaffson.

Uraan spoke first. "Well, our journey together is now over, Ragnar. I'm sure you'll have a tale to tell when you reach your homeland." He reached out his hand in friendship.

Ragnar gladly accepted his gesture, and the two gripped arms fast, like kindred souls born of the sea. "Thank you for all your help in my recovery, friend. It's a great debt I can never repay. Fair winds to you and your family."

"Aye." Uraan nodded. "Fair winds for you as well."

Rowing to the waiting ship, Ragnar watched one last time as Uraan receded from his view like a tide before a red sky.

Ragnar arrived at the ship's side, and a rope ladder was lowered to him; deftly, he climbed up, then stopped suddenly when his hand grasped the deck rail, remembering that for luck, his right foot must always touch down first to avoid disaster. Assuredly, he stepped aboard.

"You're Ragnar Olaffson?"

"Aye."

"I am Captain Solokov. Welcome aboard."

CHAPTER 2

Tucked inside the small unnamed cove, Ragnar stood on the bow of the Portuguese carrack. He faced south, waiting for an eastern rising sun. Without turning about, he recognized the boot steps of Captain Solokov approaching.

"Your thoughts this morning, Mr. Olaffson?"

Ragnar paused. The air was cool. His breath was frosty.

"It'll be challenging, Captain, given our current conditions. We'll be mostly drifting inside an ice flow with minimum steerage without sails. If we're caught in an ice jam, we'll be crushed with nowhere to turn. And there's a fog comin' in, courtesy of today's sun warming the ice and waters. I still can't see more than three ship lengths ahead."

"Aye. I do not see many choices. We can wait here until the ice passes, which could be days long. Or raise anchor and try to slip through the ice with the least possible damage, then set all sails."

"I'd agree, Captain, and I'll give way to your decision."

"Aye. I want to navigate these waters and keep moving. If an ice jam occurs before us, we could be locked in for a month, and a lot of unexpected trouble might come our way. Also, your contact in the village of Tyr might not wait a month."

"Good, I can work the foresail for you. And keep an eye on the waters and signal the pilot manning the tiller."

"Sounds good, Mr. Olaffson."

Captain Solokov turned to a group of men standing around the capstan, waiting for their order to raise the anchor. "Anchor aweigh!" he bellowed.

Hearing the order, Ragnar immediately joined the men, eager to be on their way.

Back on the bow, Ragnar had a bird's-eye view of the ice flow drifting around them, part of an early spring breakup. The broken ice was mostly contained to the shoreline. Still, overnight, a sizeable south-moving pack had quietly surrounded their position, catching them like a prize in an ocean surface drifting net.

"An easy starboard hand on the tiller," Ragnar called out to the pilot, who was standing atop the rear quarterdeck.

Captain Solokov repeated the order, and the bow nudged left, bumping a large chunk of ice with a sounding crack.

This'll be a challenging task, Ragnar thought. *Trying to reposition the ship and guide her into open waters without breaking her apart.*

He looked away from the ice flow for a moment and regarded their overall position. It was hard to evaluate with so much fog over the water. Staring past the stern, Ragnar's eyes widened, with surprise and shock. Emerging from the river fog was, at first sight, a ghostly apparition, then the solid manifestation of a sizable three-masted Chinese warship. All red sails unfurled, and she bore down on their position with speed.

"Captain Solokov, two points starboard off our stern," Ragnar pointed out, alarmed.

Solokov was stunned when he turned. The advancing ship, with all sails open, appeared as a threatening Komodo dragon with gills flared menacingly.

"What is to do, Mr. Olaffson? Can you get us away from here and free us?"

"If we do nothing, we're damned. She flies a black pirate flag. I say we cut and run for it. Damn, the ice pack. Set sails, Captain."

Hearing Ragnar's urgency, Captain Solokov ordered all hands to ready about and set all sails with haste. "Quickly, men, stop what you are doing; everyone up the ratlines and unfurl all the sails. Hurry."

The sound of war drums began emanating from the pirate ship that spanned across the water between them. It sent a shiver up every man's spine.

With full sails, the hull of the carrack hit the ice hard, but their passage was true. Ragnar was leading them along a dangerously icy path. Every seaman on board suddenly heard a loud crack, and a shudder ran the length of the ship. Ragnar yelled to the captain, "We're only 100 feet away from harm's way! Fly her apart!"

Ragnar pointed wildly to open waters ahead. "Now, Captain. Breach the ice wall now!"

With a final gasp, the carrack lunged forward, breaking free of the ice chain holding her back. The ship's bow plunged deep into dark waters and moved to position ahead of the Chinese pirate ship.

Too late.

Multiple grappling hooks shot from behind, fastening to the carrack's rear quarterdeck. The warship, twice the size of the carrack, acted as dead weight, stopping her forward motion.

"Damn, Captain, we're dead in the water."

As the warship pulled alongside, black arrows flew across all decks as warning signs. No sailor was harmed, and two black arrows struck deep into the foremast Ragnar stood beside, narrowly missing his head. Now, more grappling lines fastened along rails mid-length, and the two ships were forcibly rafted together.

"Since no one has been injured or harmed, I think we might be at the mercy of our Chinese captors, Captain. Let's find out what they want."

"We don't seem to have much choice here. Every man, stand down and raise the sails before we flounder," Captain Solokov ordered. "We will soon learn what the devil wants with us."

A crush of heavily armed Chinese sailors boarded the carrack, surrounding Captain Solokov and Ragnar Olaffson.

Cheng I Sao was fully aware of her physical beauty and attraction over men. It had always been so. Lying on a divan in her ship's cabin, she reflected on her earlier youth. She had been known as Shih Yang while working as a Cantonese prostitute and living in a world devoid of any human compassion. There, she met and then married the notorious pirate Cheng I. Everything she'd learned then served her position perfectly now, for both power and wealth.

Her earliest memories were of monsters in a dark room, cruel and unusual sexual deviants willing to pay large sums of money for their indecent abuse of her. At first, she did not understand why their behavior was so merciless. After many red sessions with these strangers, her will to live ever so slowly waned and almost broke. She was reduced to the most basic suffering and pain imaginable and remembered herself lying naked on a wooden floor at night, crying for mercy. Her mind was scared and lost in a dark place, knowing that no one would come to aid her.

At this moment, she realized that for her very survival, she would have to embrace the wickedness of these men, not resist them as she had in the past. She needed to learn what motivated their lust and role-play with them equally. What drove them to such cruelty they often displayed so openly? With a newfound awareness and knowledge, her life force returned.

She discovered the men sent to her for their pleasure were wealthy and powerful merchants, money lenders, and politicians. She joined with them in their impure behavior, and in time, she viewed men as weak creatures, slaves to the shameless goat between their legs. They thought of themselves as the masters. In truth, she fed their souls even darker abuses, slowly bending them to her will. She would intoxicate them with her wanton lust before making their most carnal desires reality. She knew firsthand that many men of power carried a great burden of guilt, and they needed to release this weight from their conscience.

These weak men sought a mistress equal to themselves in depravity. With Shih Yang, they were not disappointed in her skills with the bamboo cane, striking their bare buttocks and the lash across their backs.

"Men are to be used for my entertainment." Her gaze held the red-stained pole in the center of the room and the iron ring attached to the top. There, those wealthy men, with their hands bound above their heads, learned to dance a different way, contorting their bodies as she, their dark mistress, administered richly deserved pain.

A soft rap on the door brought her back into the present. "Enter," was her single uttered word.

Two eunuchs had been standing outside her chamber, barring entry with crossed spears. They now stood at attention, allowing access. When her ship cabin's doorway opened, she watched as a large, handsome, white-haired man was prodded forward at spearpoint toward her.

Ragnar took a moment to gather in his surroundings. The air he breathed was heavily scented with lavender and opium. This room made him uncomfortable, and his eyes watered slightly. His vision had to adjust, peering through the smoke-filled room. A eunuch unbound his hands, and the door quietly closed behind him.

"You do not need to worry here, Northman," Cheng I Sao said, her words a long hiss to his ear.

Taking a few cautious steps forward, Ragnar halted, only to stand before a woman of exquisite beauty. She reposed on sable fur, covering a sizable ornate divan. She wore a gown of the finest silk, completely sheer and like a second skin, revealing her shapely and youthful form in every detail.

"Do you know who I am?" she asked.

"I know you're a pirate," Ragnar replied angrily. "You're holding me, our captain, and the ship's crew captive. For what?"

She laughed at him. "Yes, I am a pirate, Northman. My married name is Cheng I Sao, and I am feared by many along China's coastal shores. Where I go, the waters run red."

"What do you want with me?"

"I am not sure yet. You are the sail master, are you not?"

"Aye, I am."

"You almost eluded the best sailing men of my fleet. If not for the ice flows in this bay, you would have escaped my trap. Perhaps I will force you to work for me."

"I am no pirate but I see you as a sea devil incarnate."

"Silence, White Hair," Cheng I's voice spat back like black venom as she partially raised herself from the divan. "I could have you killed for your insolence. You do not know me and what I am capable of doing. I have experienced a cruel and unusual life. Do not persuade me to teach you the pole dance of the red dragon," she said, indicating with her hand the blood-soaked post behind him. "You would not like it much."

Turning, Ragnar saw the attached iron ring overhead and chose to remain silent.

"Where are you from?"

The question surprised him. "I have been sailing most all my years. The sea is my home, but if you are asking me where I was born, it is a land called Norway, a place I desire to return to."

"Desire?" Cheng I Sao queried with interest. "Now, that is an interesting choice of words. As a woman, I too have desires, carnal urges of the most erotic kind with a man such as you." Her fingers played lazily through her lengthy black hair.

Ragnar stiffened, caught off guard by her words. Such explicit advances didn't shame her at all. "I thought you to be married."

"My husband, Cheng I, is an old mule and cannot satisfy me any longer. I am young and beautiful, and I have certain needs that only a younger, more experienced man of the sea can give me. Will you be the one, White Hair?" she asked seductively.

"What if I refuse you, Sea Witch?" he replied, wavering on his decision but moving closer to her.

"I would be forced to kill you and your mates, then burn the ship you sail just for this insult."

"And what of your husband?"

"He and his ships will be here in two days' time. If he finds you here alive, he will personally cut off your head and throw your body into the sea."

Ragnar weighed the choices before him. Although Cheng I Sao was beautiful, her eyes revealed a wickedness that told him she could not be trusted. "Do you live by the pirate's code?"

"In a manner," she replied with a wicked smile.

"Will you give me your word the ship I sail, her captain, her crew, and I will be free to leave?"

"Only if you can satisfy my yin. Then yes. Come here, lay beside me, and be my yang, Northman."

Perhaps it was the present danger he was in or more the heavy opium in the air he breathed, but Ragnar slowly and purposefully undressed. He revealed a lean, muscular body for Cheng I Sao to savor.

"You are an adulteress," he whispered, lying down beside her soft and shapely form.

"I am, and of the most shameless kind," she readily admitted.

Ragnar moved to kiss her cheek, and she turned to receive his lips. Her breathing grew heavy as he pressed his knee between her inner thighs. She received him eagerly, gasping for air, knowing he was more than needed. Gently, as a ship in harbor, he rocked back and forth, calming her with words as a good lover would.

Feeling comforted, Cheng I Sao's mind drifted back to her other life as Shih Yang and another northern man with whom she had fallen in love. The last she had seen of him, he had given her his love and promised to return, but sadly, he never returned. A single tear rolled down her cheek, and she pushed the memory away.

Early the next morning, Ragnar quietly dressed himself beside Cheng I Sao, who continued to sleep soundly. Looking down at her porcelain beauty, he regretted leaving but knew she was married to another man. He did not belong here. Ragnar turned away and stepped outside the ship's cabin, onto the quarterdeck, and into this morning's salty sea air.

Breathing deeply and filling his lungs, he made his way to the Russian ship rafted alongside, looking for Captain Solokov's midship.

"You old sea dog!" Captain Solokov called out when Ragnar approached the gangplank. "So, have you negotiated our freedom this past night?"

"Aye, Captain. It wasn't easy, but we're free to leave. We should make haste as well. There is, I'm told, a hell-hound not a day's sail from our position who will sink this ship of yours if I'm still standing on it."

After hearing the urgency in Ragnar's voice, Solokov replied. "Aye. Set all sails, men, and make ready," he ordered as Ragnar jumped aboard to lend a hand.

Eager to be away, Captain Solokov directed his crew, "Let out the forward sail."

Ragnar had already begun to pull on the flying jib line as the command was given, and more hands arrived to help. The sail rode up with haste along the spar at the ship's bow. Just as swiftly, the craft lunged forward as it gathered more wind for speed.

"I thought you said you earned us safe passage, Mr. Olaffson," Captain Solokov remarked to Ragnar sharply.

"Nay, Captain, I obtained freedom to leave from our captor. Our safety is not any concern to our host, sir. But I wouldn't want to be seen on the horizon when her husband arrives if you know what I mean."

"I think I do, Mr. Olaffson. As initially planned, we will steer our course south by southwest rather than points west. Then, at dusk, we turn back directly northwest and sail up the inside passage west of Sakhalin Island. In dark waters, we will play a little game of cat and mouse while sailing to the village of Tyr on the Amur River."

"I like your way of thinking, Captain."

"Good. With some luck, we will sail free of them from light into the dark."

CHAPTER 3

It was late afternoon when Ragnar arrived in the harbor town of Tyr. Having said goodbye to Captain Solokov, he picked up his woolen bag and walked up from the beach. It was, surprisingly, a busy fishing village, remarkable by its remoteness in this part of the world. He knew only a few would have heard of its name and even fewer still of its location.

The sky revealed a gray day, and the clouds told him rain would not be far off. Knowing this, he was not sorry to have accepted Captain Solokov's gift for saving his ship and crew from Chinese pirates: a great coat made from the hide of a Russian bear. Although heavy and cumbersome, rain could not penetrate the thick hide, and any moisture would flow over its fur like water off a duck's back. "Not a bad exchange for one night's work."

As Ragnar entered the town, he searched seriously to find his Yakutian guide, Modun. He knew the man would be elderly and look perhaps a lot like his friend, Uraan. A man with sun-baked brown skin and a leathery, wrinkled face. Not too tall, but solidly built and dressed in Yakutian clothing. But where? After searching for this man for some time, to no avail, he turned to finding a place with food and lodging for the night.

A local merchant told him of an inn just outside town at the end of the main road, so he proceeded in that direction. He came to a large wooden building, one story high, with a thatched roof. It was also elevated on stilts 5 feet above the ground to prevent being washed away if the river delta flooded in spring. Judging by the sounds inside, the raucous crowd was as familiar to him as at any seaport he had ever visited.

He stepped forward when suddenly the front door burst open, quickly followed by a man falling on his back and groaning. Ragnar stopped and looked up at the porch entrance, where a large, muscular woman stood. She had black hair and was breathing heavily. If indeed it was a woman.

She cursed loudly at the fallen man, with a few choice words in more than one language. Looking very capable of handling herself, he noted as he passed by she was as tall as him.

"Friend of yours?" Ragnar asked in a cynical tone while walking past.

The angry woman glared at the back of Ragnar's head, clenched both fists and growled. She watched him walk away and into the tavern.

Ragnar strode over to the bar, spoke briefly to the proprietor, and ordered food with drink to be brought to his table. While he sat and waited, he gazed about the room, seeing a lot of men and some women in the establishment—a real mix of races, with Chinese being the greater numbers. However, Turkish, Russian, and even Yakutian were evident as part of this diverse crowd. Their traditional clothing identified each group. He saw dice games and gambling in one quarter. In another, a small group of Chinese men sat facing each other in a circle, passing around a pipe. *Most likely opium*, Ragnar thought with disdain.

From the corner of his eye, he watched as a prominent dark figure approached silently on his left. He did not indicate acknowledgment but subtly moved his right hand onto the hilt of a hidden dagger in his sailor's boot. When the person stood still before him, Ragnar looked up.

"You can take your hand off that knife. I'm not here to kill you, stranger. I hear you've been asking for a Yakutian named Modun." She sat down across from him.

"You walk very quietly. I didn't hear you approach me," Ragnar responded as he recognized the woman he'd passed in the doorway again. Not so angry as she was earlier, but more relaxed and confident in herself. A dark beauty, but hard.

He had not seen many like her, with black hair falling past her shoulders and held in place with a tan-colored leather headband. Her eyes were ebony, as were the brows that crested them. She had a small hawkish nose with full lips below. Ragnar also noted a nasty vertical scar, which ran straight down over her right eyebrow to the center of her cheek. That mark alone told him she was not to be treated lightly.

"It's a practiced skill that I exercise every day," she replied, looking straight at him. "My father was a renowned hunter and tracker for the Sakha people. He had no sons, so he taught me all his woodland skills for as long as I can remember. He has since passed away, and I am the last of his line."

"You look Turkish to me, and your great height is uncommon for Sakha."

"My mother was Turkish-born." She answered arrogantly, with serious intent and unwavering eyes. "Now tell me, stranger, why do you seek a man named Modun?"

Ragnar felt less wary of this bold woman sitting before him but was still not fully trusting. She had exposed a little of her past and spoke as an equal in a man's world. She had the same confidence he could admire in any warrior.

"My name is Ragnar Olaffson. A friend arranged for me to meet him in this village in early spring. Modun is the name of the man who would be my guide through northern China and to the Silk Road of the Mongols."

"My father was the man you are seeking. He sent me here in his stead as his dying wish to honor a friend named Uraan. I will lead you there, Ragnar Olaffson, but I hope you brought some coin for our journey. It is a long way."

"Aye," he whispered so as not to draw any attention. "Silver coin, as requested."

"Good, I'm hungry, so you can buy me my meal. My name is Sayiina Teresova." She drove the pointed end of her hunting knife into the wood table, leaving it standing as an exclamation point for all to see. "We will leave in two days after more arrangements can be made." Then she called out for more *koumiss*.

On the second day's morning, Ragnar waited and watched outside the inn as Sayiina approached. She sat assuredly atop a horse, leading another behind her. When she stopped in front of him, she asked, "Can you ride?"

"It's been a while, but I know how," he said as he mounted the steed.

"Good, we've got a three-day ride to the next village." She handed over the reins. "I lead, you follow, and we will get along. And don't be staring at me when we ride. My instincts always let me know if I'm being watched. You should be more concerned about the many Amur tigers that reside near this river road we follow."

"Aye. You can be the captain and I the mate, if you want. The last woman I spoke with wasn't as hospitable as you. She wanted to cut off my head."

"I like her already. What was her name?"

"She called herself Cheng I Sao."

Sayiina scoffed, then laughed at Ragnar. "You sailing men are all the same to me; just swagger and brag," she said, shaking her head.

"I don't lie, and I am not trying to play a trick on you."

"Really!" Sayiina said with scorn. "Cheng I Sao and her husband are two of the most feared and vicious pirates sailing these coastal waters. If captured alive, no one would escape her red hand without some form of retribution for their release. So, what did you give her for your freedom, Ragnar, son of Olaffson?" she asked mockingly.

"Well, to be honest, I convinced her when I gave up my pride for one night," he responded.

"Now that's a good story," she said with a mirthful grin. "Sakha men are good at telling stories of their prowess, but yours might be one for our shamans to retell. I wouldn't travel those waters again if Cheng I learns of you. You won't have any pride left after he's done with you."

"I have no such intention."

At that, Sayiina urged her horse to an easy trot following the great Amur River south. Ragnar followed suit.

CHAPTER 4

After a full second day of travel, Sayiina and Ragnar dismounted on an isolated beach along the Amur River.

"We'll camp here tonight," Sayiina instructed.

Ragnar was removing his saddle when she called his attention to her. She stared over her mount about 100 yards upriver and indicated with her hand that he do the same.

"Do you see that creature?" she said, scarcely breathing in disbelief.

He looked to her bearing and was as stunned as she was. Emerging on their side of the river was a great white ape.

"What do you make of that?" she whispered. Confident they were hidden behind a random group of large standing rocks, much like a stone garden.

"Something I would let pass by. Why invite trouble our way? White apes should be avoided and not challenged, Sayiina."

Without moving her eyes from the creature, she replied, "That's not an ape. It's too tall and walks more erect, like us. That is a Russian *menk*, or what others call a yeti. Our fireside tales speak of great hoarded treasures within their caves. I would find this out and track it to its hidden location. Cover me."

Ragnar crouched in a stealth position.

"This action is very dangerous. Do not take this path, Sayiina."

The beast, shaking ice-cold water from its fur, was immense. It was easily 7 feet tall, barrel-chested, with long, muscular, hairy arms and legs like tree trunks. Ragnar surmised it might be unnatural to this world, perhaps a pre-human race, the last of its kind. Whatever it was, it had to have superhuman strength to swim across the river against the current.

"Sayiina," Ragnar implored, "this is foolish. You are chasing a child's dream, like smoke from a fire."

"I'm a Yakutian huntress, and it's my nature to search out new things. Will you follow and cover my back?" she demanded a second time.

"I don't think I have a choice here. Without you, I have no guide." Annoyed, he withdrew a long Yakutian spear from his saddle sheath.

"Good. From here forward, we only use hand signals to communicate. When we make our way into the beast's lair, do not hesitate to kill it if attacked. We will only get one chance."

Reluctantly, Ragnar agreed but had many misgivings as to her recklessness. The wise choice was to let the creature pass by. He was learning that Sayiina was a strong-willed and determined woman. Once her mind was set, she was hard to deter.

Securing the horses, they crouched to move where the yeti had left the riverbank for the forest. After five minutes of tracking, Sayiina lost the trail. They stopped to identify their surroundings, looking about for any natural sign. Forty yards ahead was a frozen waterfall, about 12 feet high over the face of a rock bluff. Sayiina signaled they investigate and, without a word, led the way.

A faint but distinct odor of sulfur hung in the air. It reminded Ragnar of the hot springs in the city of fire and ice, Petropavlovsk. Some people there called it "The Devil's Breath." He thought it might be an evil omen.

Sayiina moved silently from the face of the frozen falls to the far-left side, then disappeared. A short moment later, she reappeared and motioned for him to follow quickly.

When he reached her position, Ragnar saw the secret opening behind the ice. If it were summer and the water flowed, the entrance would not have been noticed at all.

Sayiina led him down a series of flat stones, crouched, and quietly waited for their eyes to adjust.

They stared into a large cave. The air was more pungent now, and his eyes watered. The whole area was lit by random, penetrating shafts of light from above. A small stream of opaque water steamed its way through the cave. Ragnar felt it must have been sourced from a natural underground hot spring.

A slight sound to his left caught his attention. Peering deeper into the cavern, he perceived the outline of the white beast squatting before a massive pile of bones—mammoth tusks, reindeer antlers, and even human skulls. The sight caused a chill to run up his spine, and he knew death might be before him.

The character of the whole room presented an eerie aspect. Shafts of light painted the walls of the black cave gray. Rising mists of steam followed above the streaming water. The tremendous hairy beast sat on its heels, much as a pit warrior would sit before trophies of ruined victims and skeletal remains.

The creature was casually rubbing a stone between its thumb and forefinger. It didn't look up and seemed unaware of their presence. The acrid smell would hide any trace of their body odor.

Sayiina signaled Ragnar to remain ready at his position. Before he could object, she was gone, silent as day to night. He turned his gaze back to the beast, which continued to rub the stone. Suddenly, a large rock fell near Ragnar, and the beast's red eyes looked up in his direction, finding him . . . alone.

The beast howled in defiance and outrage that something would dare enter its personal domain. Eyes not moving from the beast, Ragnar reached to grapple the spear he'd set down when crouched, only to find it now jammed beneath the stones.

The creature took three steps toward him, stopped, and then roared, baring its fanged teeth. Its mobility and speed shocked Ragnar, knowing it wasn't natural. Again, it called him out in a primal challenge, echoing throughout the chamber. With no response coming, it charged Ragnar.

At that exact moment, Sayiina leaped mid-air, thrusting from a concealed position above. Both of her Yakutian long knives lifted over her head, poised to strike as she descended on the back of the yeti, driving both points deep into his muscular shoulders. She had missed her mark for the first time in her life, having aimed to pierce under his arms and into his heart.

But the beast was lightning fast, and now it screamed horrendously. Wounded, it reached behind, grabbed, and threw Sayiina over Ragnar onto the stones above like a rag doll. She remained still.

The hairs on Ragnar's neck were raised from the great danger he was in. The white beast, blind with rage toward its enemies and screaming in pain, lunged forward to kill them.

Ragnar knew running away would be futile. He might only gain a few yards, and then what about Sayiina's fate? No, there would be no retreat for him this day as both hands gripped hard to raise his Yakutian long spear. Time momentarily slowed in Ragnar's mind as he watched the white beast's fury. Unheeding, it rushed toward him and lunged straight into the partially raised lance Ragnar held. In an instant, it had pierced the beast's heart and exited through its back.

Unmoving, the beast lay dead beside him. Ragnar, standing stunned, realized the outcome of the confrontation. It was over. He heard Sayiina moving behind him and turned to aid her.

"Where do you hurt?" he asked, helping her into a sitting position.

"It hurts to breathe. Did you really kill the beast?"

"I did—more by luck than anything else. I held the lance with a steady hand. It all happened so quickly. I was determined not to run but to stand my ground."

Sayiina didn't immediately respond. Her thoughts were trying to process what had just unfolded. After a few moments, and with great humility in her voice, she trembled.

"Ragnar Olaffson, I am ashamed of myself for having put you in harm's way and failing to kill the beast. Never before have I been unsuccessful in a kill, and rather than retreat, you saved my life by standing strong.

"I am forever in your debt." Her eyes lowered with her admission. "No man has ever shielded me from certain death. I've never met a man I would consider as brave as me. Most men would have fled and left me to die, but not you. I've never had a reason to say thank you till this moment. From this day forward, I will not lead, nor will I follow. My bow is yours as we travel this path together as equals."

She looked up, hoping for his acceptance of her apology.

"You've done nothing wrong to feel remorse for, Sayiina. Dying in a cave with our skulls mounted on sticks is not what our gods have planned for us. I look at what just happened, and I wanted to save myself as well. I'm not a perfect man, and I accept your apology and would welcome being your equal."

Sayiina let out a sigh of relief. "Can we leave now, Ragnar? This place smells horrible."

"What about the yeti treasure you were seeking here?"

"I think you were right, calling it a child's dream. I should have listened to you at the start. There is only death here, as I both smell and see it."

"Just one moment, and we'll leave. I want to scout something."

"Where are you going?"

"Over to where we first saw the beast, at the pile of bones. Call it a sailor's hunch if you want, but I will be right back."

Ragnar went to where the white ape first squatted by the stream. He was looking for something small . . . something . . . there! He spotted the stone about the size and shape of a robin's egg and picked it up. Two more he spied, lying in the black sand, and retrieved them. He put all three safely into an inside pocket of his linen jersey.

"We can go now," he said, helping her stand.

She reached for his hand for support and grimaced in pain from the effort to raise herself. "I think I have some broken ribs. It hurts to breathe."

"There's nothing else for you to do other than rest a few days. I'll look after things until you can ride again."

"The gods have put me at your mercy." She groaned and trudged up the stone steps to the outside world.

"Aye, that is the way the winds blow, lass. It truly is a change in our fates."

"What were you doing down in the cave?"

"I'll show you in a couple of days. More important is for you to heal."

They passed the frozen waterfall, and he lifted his face skyward, smiling at the red-setting sun. "Good things are coming to us, Sayiina. I can feel it in my salty bones."

"Why do you say that?"

"There is an old mariner's saying that foretells a man's fate. 'Red sky in the morn, a sailor be warned. Red sky at night, a sailor's delight,' which means a storm has passed us by."

Sayiina looked first to Ragnar to see if he was mocking her, then skyward to the red sky as she hung onto him for support. "You have good karma. I think your gods favor you. Please help me to where the horses are tied. I will sit and listen to your wisdom all night and not say a word."

Laughing, Ragnar replied, "That would be a first."

She laughed with him but quickly stopped when she realized laughing caused sharp pains across her injured back. "I hurt everywhere."

"We're both lucky to be breathing."

Together, the two of them hobbled out of the forest and onto the river's edge.

CHAPTER 5

On the riverbank, Ragnar sat at the fire across from Sayiina. He didn't really look at her, but he could feel her watching him. He was tending to tonight's meal, prepared on a spit. On the other hand, she just sat there quietly, very much unlike herself since the incident in the cave two days before.

He poured a little water over the meat to tenderize, and the flames and smoke flared up and licked their evening meal. The sound of it crackled and sizzled nicely to his ear. Breaking the stillness between them, Ragnar asked, "What are your thoughts, Sayiina? How do you feel?"

"I still hurt, but I can breathe easier each day."

"Good. Give it time. Tell me your plans to take us to the Road of Bones," he encouraged.

"If you wish. But first, I must tell you I'm struggling within myself over the event in the cave."

"We are both survivors, Sayiina, each in our own way," he said softly. "Knowing our strengths and weaknesses makes us who we are. Everyone must learn from their past to become a better person. What occurred there was for a reason. Understand this, then share our two destinies on this road we travel together."

Sayiina sighed deeply, relieved to hear the sound of his voice. She felt no longer alone. When she heard Ragnar's wisdom, she knew he was a kindred spirit, and something deep inside her stirred. She drew in strength from his words like no other before him. She blushed, hoping this northern man would not see her this way.

The red flames of their open fire partly disguised the flush on her face when she calmly replied, "The way to the Road of Bones is long. It is, in fact, as far as my knowledge travels. In a few days, we will reach the town of Khabarovsk and have to change how we travel."

"What are you saying?"

"At this place, the road ends. Here, river travel is the swiftest way for us, and still, it will take a half moon to get to where we want. In my condition, I will not be of any help to work the oar against the current."

"I see," Ragnar replied thoughtfully.

"The Road of Bones is the gateway you seek to the Silk Road in Mongolia and beyond." Sayiina went quiet, looking at Ragnar.

"Is it the only way?"

"No, but it is the safe and sure way. Otherwise, we would have to cross into China, and I cannot speak the language. For 2,000 miles west, this river we follow is the great barrier between Russia and China. There will be many villages along its shores to renew our supplies when needed."

"And you say you cannot work an oar. That's not good. I'm going to think on this a little more. Can you ride tomorrow?"

"I think so, with your help to throw the saddle on."

"Good. We leave for Khabarovsk tomorrow morning when we are both ready."

After finishing their meals, Ragnar cleaned up the campsite and threw the scraps into the flowing river to avoid attracting night scavengers. Looking behind, he watched as Sayiina settled in for the night. She favored her back in her movements. He knew she would have many restless nights ahead, but she would heal eventually.

Intentionally, he slipped his right hand into the inside pocket of his sailor's jersey, touching the three stones. With the thought that now would be a good moment to show her, he purposely walked back to their fire and sat down beside her.

"You asked me why I went back down into the cave, Sayiina."

"I did. Did I miss something?"

"As I said, call it a sailor's hunch." Pulling out the stones, he displayed them in the palm of his hand. "I found these lying in the sand near the bone pile."

Sayiina stared at them with fascination as though held by a spell. They were the size and shape of three smooth robin eggs. They appeared a soft gray until the light from their campfire crossed over them. There, reflecting back, was a quick flash of blue-white light.

Watching her expression closely, Ragnar offered. "Choose one to your liking. By the time our journey is over, you will have earned it."

Sayiina reached out her hand and chose the smallest of the three. "What manner of stones are they?" She held it up before the fire, entranced by it.

"I am not 100 percent certain, but in the hands of a true artisan, I might find the truth of my suspicions."

"What do you mean?"

"I believe these stones are raw, uncut, and unpolished diamonds."

Sayiina gasped at the thought that it might be true. "That would mean . . ." she began, then stopped and stared in disbelief at Ragnar.

"Yes, they are each worth a king's ransom or more," he said, completing her last sentence for her. "Perhaps those bedside tales Yakutians tell their children have some truth to them."

Sayiina clenched the stone in her hand tightly, then threw herself on Ragnar, planting a kiss on his lips. She immediately regretted it and groaned as a sharp pain crossed her back for her effort. Lying over him, she looked him in the eyes. "You, I will follow to the end of time if you ask me."

"Perhaps you will, and I wouldn't stop you. But right now, my shoulder is hurting, and I can't move when you're on top of me like this, Sayiina. So, we can't go anywhere." He laughed.

They struggled to untangle themselves to sit up, and both felt a charm when they did.

"Be sure to put your stone someplace safe," he told her as he watched their fire slowly die out.

Lying on her back with her eyes closed, she smiled slightly, knowing his gift to her was safe.

"You know, Sayiina, you kiss good. Have you been practicing?"

"There is an old Yakutian custom my mother taught me. The first kiss you give freely to a man. All the others he must earn."

"Oh! That is wise advice your mother gave you. I will do my very best to earn your next one," he said, smiling in her direction.

Sayiina did not stir but took comfort in his words and the sound of his voice. Tonight, she knew this man beside her had already earned a second embrace and much more.

Ragnar gazed at Sayiina as her breathing grew deep, telling him she was sleeping. He turned his head to the night sky just when a star flashed westward across the cosmos before closing his eyes. It was a good sign.

Early the following day, Ragnar was first to rise and made a small fire to boil water for tea. Sayiina awoke at almost the same time and watched him make everything ready.

"After tea, we should be on our way to Khabarovsk."

"I agree."

"How is your wound this morning?"

"I hope the worst of it will be over by the time we reach the village."

"Perhaps it will," he encouraged her. "But first, I am concerned about our food supplies; we are getting low. Perhaps you could teach me how to use your bow, and I will do the hunting for us."

"I would like that, but it requires a lot of practice."

"Well, time is on our side, and the road is long. I can always practice when the horses need to graze during the day."

Ragnar saddled up both horses for them and then put out the fire. Mounting their horses, they looked at each other, and he asked, "Are you ready to set sail, lass?"

Sayiina, with a grand salute and with great sarcasm, replied, "Aye, Captain, anchors aweigh."

They both laughed and set out, traveling south alongside the Amur River.

On the morning of the third day's travel, Ragnar declared they were officially without food.

"Well, we either keep riding on empty bellies to Khabarovsk, which you tell me is another day, or we stop and hunt for our next meal."

She looked at him as a true son of the seven seas. Fearless and brave beyond measure but really out of his element on land. She shook her head at him. "You sound desperate, Ragnar Olaffson," she said with feigned sincerity.

"I'm more frustrated than anything else. I've got a purse full of coin with nowhere to purchase goods. Hunting for what we need might take us off course all day."

"I've never gone hungry a day in my life," she replied, dismounting. "Take the horses, follow me off the trail, and I'll teach you a Yakutian hunter's secret. Oh, and bring a lance with you."

Ragnar complied, following her into a small open area in the woods. He saw she was studying the grassy area, where it ended and the forest began. She stood perfectly still when she found what she was looking for, motioning Ragnar to do the same. Then she took the spear from him and pointed its blade downward.

He watched quietly, hearing her make a series of clicks with her tongue and teeth. To him, it was a chittering of sorts but unmistakable. Amazingly, when she stopped, a large hare approached from the treeline and halted right before her. Without hesitation, she drove the blade into its neck.

"Quick, painless, and the best way, Ragnar." Then she passed it over to him.

Again, he witnessed her success for a second time, providing this day's meal.

"The land provides for all we need. Together, we will never go hungry," she said as she walked back to the horses.

Ragnar was impressed. "How can you call the forest creatures to you?"

"It's part of my magic. I put a spell on those creatures so they would do my bidding."

"That's not possible, and you're lying to me."

"Careful now. Perhaps I will put one on you when you sleep and make you tend to all my needs and wants forever."

Still puzzled over what had just happened, Ragnar followed behind her, now deep in his thoughts.

Up front, Sayiina had a big grin on her face. Without turning around and revealing her happiness, she asked Ragnar, "So . . . are you preparing our meals tonight?"

CHAPTER 6

The morning air was crisp as the two rode alongside each other toward the town of Khabarovsk. Even during early spring in this northern part of the world, winter was reluctant to let go of its grasp over the land.

"How much farther?" Ragnar asked Sayiina.

"Probably three or four miles along this way. It's been long since my father and I traveled here together. I can tell you it's where the two great rivers, Amur and Ussuri, meet. They join hands to flow into the sea."

"You mean a natural confluence, right?"

"I do. Call it what you like. I see it as two streams of life with a common destiny."

Sayiina suddenly stopped and dismounted.

"What's wrong?"

Kneeling, she put her hand on the ground and looked back before standing. "I think there are riders behind us. Let's move off the road and see who it is. We aren't running away from danger, just being cautious. I don't like surprises."

Ragnar agreed, and they moved to conceal themselves and their horses in a dense nearby grove of maple trees. After a few minutes of waiting, three hard-looking horse soldiers of unknown origin came into view, heavily armed with lance and sword. Tethered and riding at the back were three young Yakutian women, hands bound behind their backs.

Seeing this, Sayiina lunged forward, wanting to aid the women, but Ragnar held her back.

"Now isn't the time. You're injured, and to free those women will require stealth, not just an open fight. It's too risky for us to try this here."

Knowing he was right, Sayiina stopped, but she still glared with hatred toward the soldiers.

"Who are those men, Sayiina?"

"Cossack mercenaries. They do the real dirty work of the Russian government, who are expanding their influence in this area."

"Are they slaves to be sold at a market?"

"No. Their village was probably first burned, and the fleeing women then abducted, mostly for chattel and rape." Furious now, Sayiina clenched a fist. "They might be housed in a camp but more likely kept locked up on board one of their ships in the town's harbor. The local government wouldn't openly approve, of course, but would look the other way if a private agreement had been reached."

"I see. Let them pass this time. Maybe they won't be so fortunate if our paths cross again."

"Thanks, Ragnar. Sometimes, I'm impulsive, even at personal risk. It's my nature."

Ragnar and Sayiina rode toward Khabarovsk in silence, each within their thoughts.

"We need room and board for a few nights. I am sure we can find a kabak to stay in or a place to have a hot bath. What do you say, Sayiina?"

"I'd also like to bathe. Too many days in a saddle, along with camp-fire smoke, can produce a distasteful scent unless you like that sort of body odor."

"Can't say I've noticed anything different about you, Sayiina."

"Really! Well, you have changed." She laughed. "Might be we both smell bad. You just haven't smelled your own self yet." She urged her horse to trot away from Ragnar for some fresh air.

The two entered town that afternoon with lots of sun in the sky. Ragnar looked about, noticing it was a bustling place with many different people going about their business. Shops on both sides of the main road sold food and services to the public. All were open for business. Soon, they found a livery stable, stopped in, and dismounted.

"Sayiina, would you get our horses tended to here, then get us rooms for three nights' stay somewhere nearby? I want to find and talk to a specific tradesman. Preferably a boat builder whose shop will likely be down by the riverside. I'll be back in a while and meet up with you at the hotel. I'm sure you won't be hard to find."

He gave her a few silver coins and walked toward the docks not far away.

It wasn't long before Ragnar found the shipyard he was looking for. A group of tall buildings attached to each other. They were wood framed with wooden roofs, but the front and back of each structure were wide open, with no walls. This was to help facilitate indoor work on larger riverboats. He stopped a young boy carrying wood planks inside and asked, "Do you know where I might find the local shipwright, lad?"

"You'll want to talk to Master Pavovich. He's over there."

Then, he pointed to a large man working beside a small craft and continued his tasks.

Ragnar walked over and observed the man inspecting some slight detail of his work. This craftsman's fingertips brushed along the boat's starboard side, much like a painter would regard each stroke of his portrait on canvas.

"You look like you know boats," Ragnar remarked.

The big man looked up as though distracted by Ragnar's voice. "I should. I've been building or working on them since I could hold an axe. Who are you, and what brings you into my shop?"

Ragnar wasn't surprised by the abrupt response. He appeared Russian, and many Ragnar had sailed with were also very blunt in discussions with strangers. The man was tall with broad shoulders, muscular arms, and big hands. His blond hair and blue eyes were distinct, but his whole aspect was not that of a brute but of an intelligent presence that drew people to him with respect.

"You're correct. I'm not from here. I'm trying to make my way back home, God willing. My name is Ragnar Olaffson of Norway. And yours?"

"Petr Pavovich of Crimea. You look like a man who has traveled far and seen much. What do I know that you might need?"

"I know your waters and have sailed your Black Sea, Cossack," Ragnar replied evenly. "I have also sailed with a great shipwright named Yuri Kozachenko. A man so innovative, many thought he could make sailing ships weep for his sure hands on deck."

"I know that name," Petr countered brazenly. "We are brothers of the same steppe. You are comrades?"

"Five years together at sea. We lived and fought side by side as brothers against our enemies. Alexander Baranof was the ship's owner, and me, its sail master."

The shipwright went quiet in thought, then privately confessed, "The Cossacki have few friends in these waters, but many enemies are waiting, Sail Master Olaffson. I would like to count you as a kindred traveler and friend far from home. How can I help?"

"I need a rivercraft built for me. Something different."

"I have many strong and sure boats available for sale. I've made them myself."

Looking around, Ragnar scrutinized much of the inventory that Petr held in his large workshop.

"I need something a little less common. I see here that you have only to assemble the parts you already possess."

"Show me what you mean." He handed Ragnar a flat, square piece of soft slate with a stylus.

Ragnar began to illustrate on the slate what he had seen and learned while traveling the southwest waters of Polynesia. At the same time, he showed Petr how his existing watercraft could easily be modified to accommodate the unique design before him.

"The sail cloth I will purchase, cut, stitch, and install once the spars are ready. I'll also need an oarlock placed on the stern portside for steerage here." He pointed at the diagram. "What do you think, master shipwright? Do you see what I see?"

"Aye, and I've never seen anything like it. It just might work. Where did you learn of it?"

"There are people in the South Pacific who inhabit many islands. They use this type of watercraft for fishing and transporting materials between their islands. They're very swift, and the lateen sail you'll help me install will allow me to travel upriver against the wind without tacking."

"Impressive," Petr acknowledged. "Where will you take this craft?"

"To the headwaters of the Amur."

Petr nodded without speaking, then asked, "How will you pay me for my work?"

"I have silver coin, but I also have two horses with saddlery I want to include in the purchase."

"And when do you want to complete our business?"

"I will assist you with this task every day. Then hopefully, on the third, set sail."

"Good, I accept your offer. The final price we can discuss when the task is complete."

Petr reached out with his open hand to Ragnar, who accepted it, and the deal was struck.

Sayiina went into the streets of Khabarovsk after securing their horses and saddlery. Looking to find room and board for them, but also explore. She had a natural curiosity about the world around her, and in this market town, she could see it had a lot to offer.

"So many shops and so many people. I don't remember this many when I was last here."

But that was twenty-five summers ago when traveling with her father. She took her time browsing the many artisans' wares that lined the streets. Everything had a price for sale or barter. Weapons, armor, food, silk, and even fragrant bath oils. With all this teeming of people in one place, she felt alive. The strong scent of lavender came from a small open stall, so intoxicating it compelled her to enter.

"Come in, dear," were the feminine words directed to her from the back of the shop. "Please sit down. I am an old woman. I will not harm you. I have been waiting for you."

Sayiina walked ahead slowly. Following the sound of the voice, she found herself in a small cubical surrounded by softly colored curtains. There, she saw an old, blind woman sitting comfortably before an empty chair.

"What is your name?"

"Sayiina."

"That is a Yakutian name, correct?"

"It is."

"Sit across from me. Please give me your hands to hold. Perhaps I can foretell your future if you would like."

Sayiina did as instructed, sitting quietly before her.

"Your hands are strong, not weak. Are you a warrior of your people?"

"I'm a huntress and tracker of my people."

"I see."

Still holding Sayiina's hands for another moment, the old woman said, "You are in love."

Shocked at her words, Sayiina instantly pulled her hands away.

"Do not be surprised. I am a seer, but I cannot see everything. Come, let me touch your face."

Sayiina allowed her this personal request.

"I see you on a journey far from your home. How far you travel is in your control. But the more distance you travel, the greater control you lose. You are young and strong. I also see a child born to you in a new home, so do not be afraid to follow your heart along its natural course. That is all I see, child."

After paying the seer for her visions, Sayiina smiled and stood to leave. When the coin from her hand touched the seer's hand, a dark image appeared to the old woman. With her eyes shut and back stiffened, she begged, "Wait, child! You are in immediate danger. Be aware dark forces are waiting nearby."

Now worried, Sayiina responded. "Thank you, old woman. I am aware how life can be cruel, and I hear you. There's no need to remind me." Looking over her shoulder, Sayiina's fingers gently touched the hilt of one of her knives.

She left the tent, angry and in deep thought.

Back among the busy crowd of people, although stressed, Sayiina continued looking for a place to stay over. She could see farther down the road a two-story building, usually indicating rooms to let on the upper floor. Walking toward it, she wondered if Ragnar was having any success on the waterfront.

While entering the building, three Cossack soldiers of fortune intently watched her every move.

"Perhaps we should let this one go," Olek said softly to Marko. "She doesn't seem weak or timid like the others, but very capable of defending herself. It's obvious she's alone."

Marko spat back, "Did you lose your manhood somewhere? We're three blades to her one. Follow the plan. You and Vadim go in first and position yourselves behind or near her. Try not to draw any attention. On my word, grab her wrists and bind them. She'll fetch us a large price on the Chinese slave market after her spirit is first broken by all three of us."

Olek and Vadim hissed, "Yes," at the thought. All three mercenaries eyed her with evil intent.

Sayiina stood at the bar in the busy public house, trying to get the proprietor's attention. It was raucous, and unless she shouted, she was going to have to wait for her turn to be served.

Marko saw his opportunity and moved to stand next to Sayiina. With his meaty hand, he grabbed her buttocks roughly and pulled her against him.

"You come home with me tonight, whore," he growled.

"Don't touch me, swine. I know your face, slaver." She snarled in contempt.

"I am Cossack. I take what I want."

"I said, let go!"

"Or what, bitch?" he said as he released his hand, only to grasp her breast. The man squeezed hard, causing Sayiina to fall back.

Feigning great pain while executing a master's sleight of hand, she withdrew her Yakutian knife from its sheath and drove it through the back of her assailant's other hand, pinning it to the wooden bar.

"Or this." She sneered openly.

Marko screamed in pain while blood ran freely beneath his palm.

"Move, and you will never use this hand again," she said as she ever so slightly twisted the blade.

"Kill her!" Marko yelled to his two comrades. "Kill her now!"

But Olek and Vadim hesitated, knowing that open murder of anyone would implicate them and put their own lives at risk.

At the moment of this vicious quarrel, Ragnar walked into the public house, looking for Sayiina. He grasped the circumstance instantly, seeing the two mercenaries with blades drawn and pointed behind Sayiina. He grimaced at the sight of the Cossack's bloody hand skewered to the countertop.

Ragnar slid behind Marko, pulled his head back, and placed his knife across his throat.

"Is this how you want to end your days, Cossack? At the hand of a woman and your northern enemy? No honor here today for you. Tell your men to leave now."

Marko felt the knife at his throat and cursed the man who held it. "Leave here now," he told his men in shame. "Another day, you will pay for my humiliation, Northman, you and your witch."

At that, Sayiina withdrew the bloodied knife from his impaled hand, allowing him to leave while grasping it and joining his friends outside the kabak.

"Are you all right?" Ragnar asked.

"I am. They're the mercenaries we saw on the road earlier. I hate them."

"Aye, I recognized them the moment I walked in. I'm sure the feelings are mutual now. Your message was delivered and received. Did you get us rooms here?"

"No, not yet."

"Good, let's find lodgings elsewhere. Someplace closer to the waterfront. People there seem more like us. Besides, I'd like some sailor's ale made by sailors' hands. I saw some being sold on the beach, and I'm sure there'll be rooming houses nearby."

"Did you have any success securing a ship for us?"

"Oh yes, and more. Although, I had to sell our horses in payment. Sorry."

"What?" she cried out. "You're supposed to keep this partner of yours informed."

"Well, I thought we might discuss it over a few ales to see which way the wind blows, lass."

The sun slipped closer to the horizon as the two walked down the main road toward the waterfront. Ragnar looked at Sayiina. She appeared angry, so he remained silent.

Sayiina, noticing Ragnar's silence, asked, "What is sailor's ale in your world?"

"Water, molasses, and young spruce needles, boiled and fermented."

"Ugh. I'll pray every night that you give this up," she said in distaste.

Ragnar laughed. "You might be praying for a long time."

"You're probably right. Forget it. Let's go have an ale."

"Aye. Tonight, you lead, Sayiina."

CHAPTER 7

Ragnar and Petr worked together intently, assembling the watercraft Ragnar had sketched out the day before. Unnoticed by both, Sayiina stood nearby, watching them at their tasks. They stopped to see her standing there only after she cleared her throat.

"Can I be of any help?" she asked.

Ragnar turned. "Petr, this is my guide and partner, Sayiina."

"Ahh." He nodded in acknowledgment of her, then gave her a genuine smile. "Welcome here. Might you be the woman who held Marko and his two dogs to heel yesterday at the public house?"

"If you're talking about the Cossack slaver, it wasn't me who spared his life. Look to Ragnar first. I would've killed him or, at the very least, split his hand like cleaning a fish."

Petr replied to Ragnar after hearing those words. "I like her. Does she have a sister?"

"Sorry, my friend, you're not in luck. She's one of a kind."

"I see. Strong women are hard to find."

Ragnar rolled his eyes. "Strong women are also hard to control."

Petr turned back to Sayiina. "The rumor in our town today is that a dark-haired woman challenged and defeated Marko Dragovich. I know him to be an evil man and not one to be made an enemy of. Many fear him and his men but are now encouraged by your results."

"He will not have a second chance with me. He is a *mudak*."

"Really, Sayiina? Shithead? Some might consider your choice of word too nice." Ragnar smirked. "But it's a good comparison."

"Marko won't show himself for a few days. He'll feel too much shame from the stares of everyone here. In my shop, you're welcome." Then he grinned at both.

"If you want to help, Sayiina, I need a net woven from this rope." Ragnar's hand indicated a spool nearby. "I'll show you the weave we need if you be ready, lass."

"I am."

For three days, they worked as a team. During the day, Sayiina and Petr witnessed and marveled as Ragnar demonstrated his knowledge of sailing crafts, surpassing Petr's skill for innovation. On the last night, they stood by the river and looked at their handiwork floating before them. Petr admired the craft and was pleased to be a part of its construction. Sayiina just shook her head, not believing she would be crazy enough to ride on it.

Ragnar knew this 20-foot vessel was an exact duplicate and smiled.

"Does it have a name?" Petr asked.

"The people of the South Pacific call it a 'catamaran.'"

"Let's call it *The Cat*," Sayiina announced, surprising Ragnar.

"I like that. It reminds me of you, Sayiina. Let's declare it and pour some ale on its bow," Ragnar suggested.

"That's a good idea. I'll go and bring us some right now."

Upon Petr's return, he gave each of them a mug. Lifting his for a toast, Ragnar declared, "To a safe journey!"

"And a sure one," Sayiina echoed.

"Aye, fair winds to us all," Ragnar finished.

Each, in turn, spilled some ale onto the bow and then drained their mugs.

"Well, it's done for now. I'll see you away in the morning," Petr said, leaving the two standing on the beach.

"Come with me into town, Ragnar. I want to have our palms read. There's an old woman there who's a seer and can predict a person's fortunes."

"Oh really? I'd like to meet her."

Sayiina was excited to revisit the seer and, this time, introduce Ragnar. She hoped the woman would see their destinies as one. Leading Ragnar straight to the same tent as before, Sayiina found a young girl selling flowers and spices at the entrance.

"Is the seer in the back?" Sayiina asked politely.

"There is no other here," the girl replied, frowning at the question.

"She was and read my palm only three days ago, right here in this very shop."

"I am sorry, there is no one back there." She indicated with her hand. "I am the only one attending. I sell flowers."

Angry now, Sayiina pushed her way through to the back and flung open a curtain, gaining her entrance. There, placed on the same familiar table, was a vase containing fresh-cut lavender and nothing more. Stunned, she turned away and stormed out. As she brushed past Ragnar, she was muttering words such as "mage," "dark magic," and "witchcraft."

He followed her. "Sayiina, slow down. Why be angry?"

"I'm telling you, there was an old woman here three days ago who read my future, and now there's no one."

"I believe you. People come and go through our lives all the time. What she said to you is all that matters. I hope it was pleasing."

"It was, and you're right. But because she's no longer there, I'm frustrated," she said. "Forget I mentioned it all. Let's buy supplies for our journey. We'll make our own fortunes tomorrow."

"Aye."

Walking beside her into the market, he threw his arm around her waist.

Early the next morning, Ragnar and Sayiina walked down to the river. Petr stood waiting for them under a large willow tree near where the catamaran was tied. "How far will you travel this day, Ragnar?"

"Hard to say. With this light morning breeze, we could go far. Our first destination is the next fort town upriver. I can't say we'll arrive there tomorrow, but it's possible with a couple days of good wind. *The Cat* is very swift, and I'll take all advantages I can on this riverway. Marko and his men might come around soon enough, asking about us and what you know."

"I've had those same thoughts. They're the worst kind. Mercenaries, blades for hire, and the reason most people resent Cossacks being here."

"What will you tell them?"

"You bought one of my boats and are paddling upriver to the next town. There won't be any mention of *The Cat*, of course. He's not clever enough to comprehend it all. But make no mistake with him. He's your enemy for life. A ruthless man capable of terrible things, even before he kills you. Do you know what I mean, northerner?"

"Aye, torture, then death."

"Good then. Show no mercy when the time comes. I'm certain he'll give chase until he tires. But for how long, I don't know."

"Thanks, Petr. Good friends are difficult to find, and I'll count you as one. If you're ever in Norway, look for me in the south. Somewhere in or near Oslo and her waters. Farewell."

"Wait!" Sayiina interjected. "Before we go anywhere, Yakutian people have a tradition I need to do before we depart."

With that, she removed a strip of cloth from her belt and tied it to a branch of a willow tree.

"With my people, this gesture is considered a good luck charm for travelers about to embark on a journey." Once securely tied to the tree, she said. "Okay, now I'm ready."

Ragnar instructed Sayiina to sit on the outrigger to stabilize the boat. Doing as directed and unfamiliar with her role, she awkwardly worked her way across the netting to sit, perched like a bird on a limb. Ragnar sat in the main hull and slowly unfurled the lateen sail. Just as quickly, it caught wind and shot forward, thrusting them into open water.

Holding tight so as not to fall over, Sayiina was thrilled. She felt the wind in her hair and a rush in her heart as they sped away. Freed from the earth beneath her feet, she was exhilarated, experiencing something that made her feel more alive.

Ragnar watched her closely and was pleased as he piloted their catamaran upriver. The wind lifted and blew her long black hair, giving her a semblance of a raven hovering above water at his side.

"You know I'm still angry," she feigned. "You sold my horses for this 'cat.'"

"I really had little choice, and there isn't any room for them on board. Unless you'd like to give up this ride with me?" he responded wryly.

"Never! This unchained freedom is priceless. Take me away, sailor man," she cried out. "We'll ride the wind together."

Over the next few days of sailing, Ragnar taught Sayiina how to operate both sail and rudder in unison. She sat in his arms as he imparted knowledge from a lifetime at sea. Sayiina listened carefully and asked questions when in doubt, for which he always had the answer. Occasionally, he passed the controls to her, almost as a test. Or maybe he was allowing himself to trust her. She knew he didn't let many get too close in his world. A sailor's life was not easy, never having a permanent home or partner. Perhaps he'd had lovers, but not one true love.

Each day, they grew closer. Every day gave her hope she was the one for him.

CHAPTER 8

Marko Dragovich was the only son of a Cossack smuggler. His father had been publicly hanged twenty years before in his home village in Crimea. Marko remembered the day well and would never forget being forced to stand before the gallows with his mother to bear witness. He'd felt a great shame at the moment of his father's death. His crime, Marko was told, was dealing in the contraband trade of weapons for drugs. Only a boy, Marko, had been too young to understand the reasoning behind his father's fateful end. What Marko did learn very quickly was that daily living soon became survival for himself and his mother.

Marko was larger than most of the village boys his age. His mother claimed his size was hereditary from the male lineage of her family. If true, then Marko decided his penchant for violence came from his father's side, as she was notably submissive to the will of men.

Growing up without a father for guidance, Marko learned early the hard lessons of theft and bullying at the hands of the local magistrate. In time, intimidating smaller, weaker boys became routine, which didn't go unnoticed by the older boys of his village. It wasn't long before they recruited him to do their dirty work. For coin, of course. If there was no coin to profit from, Marko received other things as payment, such as men's wives or daughters. He didn't care about others and their welfare. Why should he? No one cared for him or his.

The older boys taught him all the tricks of a smuggler's trade. After several years, there was no one better than him. His reputation as a young man was increasing in stature. One to be feared, or at the very least be given a wide berth. During this time of success, there was a violent anger deep in his core, constantly growing and becoming more apparent to others. At first, they saw small outbursts, but over time, these grew to larger, more aggressive exchanges with other rogues.

One night, some select merchants requested his services at a clandestine meeting, not wanting to attract the attention of any magistrates. They had illegal crates of Russian flintlock rifles waiting to be transported to a nearby ship. They assured him that all the usual port authorities had been bribed. His task was only to deliver the contraband and return with some Turkish antiquities they wanted in exchange. Their payment of silver coin in advance sealed the arrangement, and because he had dealt with these men previously, he accepted the undertaking.

Marko had only one weakness during his notable success as a smuggler: he had carved deeply into the town's commerce and didn't see that his lawless work negatively affected their profits. Some merchants were now furious.

These same men had secretly met to scheme his removal from their town. Their plan was simple. They only had to entice him into a single trade with minimum risk to him and at the usual pay rate. Once he accepted their assurances they had bribed the port authorities, they would only have to wait for his capture and elimination. No one wanted their names implicated, of course. So, the actual bribes would go to the local magistrates, who would now limit their investigation solely to Marko Dragovich. Without him, profits would be up, and their competition in the black market would be down.

Marko arrived on the secluded beach at the prearranged time. It was a moonless night; clouds overhead hid the stars from view. Everything went as planned as he eyed the small watercraft moving to his location. Like any other secretive meeting, he had dressed accordingly, wearing a black, full-length cape and cowl for concealment, which blended with his surroundings. Only a long, gleaming knife, belted low and tipped forward on his right hip, was carried for additional protection. If the exchange went wrong, he would run under the cover of darkness rather than fight and risk capture.

A forever memory was when the boat, quick and silent, beached. Four caped men disembarked, each carrying a large vase in their hands.

Marko cautiously moved his wagon toward their location, then signaled to them with his right hand to approach. When they were within striking distance of him, they stopped. Then, as one, they dropped their vases, pulled back their cowls, and revealed their true identities as military police. Instantly, Marko knew he had fallen into a trap, and his odds of escape were four to one against him.

The foremost soldier drew his sword to strike, but Marko was the quicker for his youth, pulling out his long knife. In a sweeping arc, he sliced the throat of his assailant. Once again, his success came as his adversary was caught unprepared to defend himself and parry his swift left-handed attack. For this same reason, Marko had been able to draw first blood on more than one occasion.

Seeing their captain crumple to the sand, the other three soldiers were momentarily stunned. Their shock gave Marko just enough time to turn heel and run for cover in the nearby forest, where his horse waited. Racing away, he knew he could not return to town. There would be a bounty on him and likely a death sentence for slaying an officer. So, he fled on horseback, leaving his pursuers behind. Riding south and not stopping at any place too long, Marko reached the southern province of Georgia.

Once there, he enlisted in the Russian military. Here, he would secure food, shelter, and, more importantly, buy himself time. He couldn't hide forever, but he could run. The tsarist government was recruiting young Cossack men as soldiers willing to make the arduous trek to eastern Siberia to protect its sovereignty. It was an opportunity he couldn't overlook.

The army would be a means to his goal. They would provide his basic needs for his continued escape from crime. In return, through strength of arms, he would be the exact soldier they needed to subdue all dissenting people whose land was now occupied. Of course, he wouldn't let this new military life get in his way. He would continue to enrich himself illegally by any means possible. He was, by nature, a Cossack freebooter, not a regular military man. He couldn't abide by the necessary discipline nor care about the fighting man beside him. Marko's attitude was "every man for himself."

The incident, a day he would never forget, was more than two years behind him now and 5,000 miles away. He had eluded his captors' reach by hiding in plain sight in eastern Siberia. Surprisingly, he had also risen in rank. Not so much as to draw attention, but just enough to intimidate smaller and weaker people. Other than the previous week's incident inside the kabak, he was enjoying his new life as an enforcer of the hated fur tribute, which the tsarist government forced all families to pay. He enjoyed the status that came with this type of law work, especially relishing the hate and fear in the eyes of men and women when he called to collect what was due.

Sitting astride his horse, he halted his reminiscence, carefully assessing the big man working on the beach. Marko wondered how much trouble the man would give him. The man was a Cossack like himself and would not be easily intimidated. Marko wanted answers to the vicinity and perhaps the destination of the white-haired northern bastard and the Yakutian witch. The two had injured his hand and shamed him publicly. He looked at his still-healing left hand. Better if they'd killed him when they'd, their opportunity. Shame fed his hatred toward them. Not since he was a boy watching his father hang had he felt that way. He nudged his horse forward to the big carpenter, then stopped.

Petr glanced up when he heard horses approaching. He was working outside his shop and, seeing his visitor, Marko Dragovich, intentionally put down his saw, reaching for his long-handled axe instead. A grim, unsmiling man twenty years Petr's junior, Marko looked the epitome of a fully armed Cossack warrior with two mounted henchmen behind him. He was just as large and muscular as Petr had been when in his prime.

Marko's head was shaved in traditional Cossack style, leaving a long black forelock on the top left side. The open, collarless, sleeveless vest looked like an afterthought to cover a thick, great, barreled chest.

Leather braces protected his forearms. Very loose-fitting red trousers were gathered at the knee, topping black leather boots. A wide red sash, wrapped multiple times around his waist, held a pistol and a long knife. His bandaged left hand held a coiled whip while his right hand rested on the hilt of his sheathed saber.

Petr saw a ruthless Cossack mercenary, a man with no honor, staring coldly and unwaveringly at him.

"Do you know me, woodcutter?" Marko asked in a demeaning tone.

"I know who you are, Dragovich. What do you want here?" Petr demanded as his meaty hand squeezed his axe handle a little tighter.

"I will ask the questions, not you. I'm looking for a white-haired Northman and a tall Yakutian woman traveling together. My informants tell me they came by this way as early as yesterday. What business were they doing here with you?"

Petr glared back at his countryman with disdain. All Cossack boys and men were taught to respect elder Cossacks in all dealings. Obviously, customs meant nothing, and Marko felt he was the law of this land.

"Again, I will ask you, what was their business here with you?" He snarled and leaned forward in the saddle.

Petr watched as the two henchmen shifted restlessly on their mounts as if to make ready a quick assault at the slightest sign. He knew refusing to answer would ignite the violence these men craved. It was simmering in their villainous eyes. He had seen that look before. Knowing when to bend to the wind and not let pride stiffen his resolve was an inherent strength of his character. It had kept him alive these latter years when others much younger had died.

"You and your men do not intimidate me. I am also Cossack with the blood of many men on my hands, and I know our old ways." He seethed. "I will answer your questions to see you leave. The two you are looking for purchased a boat from me. They left in it yesterday morning, heading upriver."

Marko ignored the first insolent remark from the carpenter. He would pay for those words another time. Instead, he asked. "What kind of riverboat did you sell?"

"A 16-foot two-man fish boat, the only kind I make besides barges."

"And you say they're working their way upriver against the current?"

"That's what I saw," Petr answered.

"And their destination?"

"They talked of the next fort village and wanted to know the distance. I told them it would be maybe five days of hard rowing if they stayed away from the middle of the river and kept to the shoreline."

"Were they traveling heavy or light?"

"Light. They had few provisions. It seemed to me they would hunt to feed themselves. That's all I can tell you about them."

"I don't trust you, old man." Marko spat the insult out. "You're clever enough to have survived many years, but I'm not as simple as you think. My life has not been easy, and I can sense when someone is lying," he admitted, and his now contorted face did not shield the truth of his words. He raised his voice angrily, revealing his true self to Petr.

"How were you paid for the boat?" he demanded. "How much money? Tell me now!"

"I accepted," Petr replied, unmoved by Marko's undisciplined display of anger, "their two horses with saddlery as payment."

"Good," Marko snapped in a high-strung pitch. "I will take them as my payment, and you will say nothing to the authorities."

"How dare you, you *mudak*. You hide your true face behind a soldier's veil when you are a common robber."

Petr's words had hardly been uttered when Marko stood in his stirrups. He uncoiled and released his whip, sending the lash out with a crack just inches from Petr's face. The sound caused his horse to rear up, releasing a great neigh and gnashing its bared teeth.

Petr braced himself, gripping his razor-sharp axe with both hands, awaiting their attack. All three men dismounted. The two backup soldiers, with swords drawn, approached him cautiously just steps ahead of Marko.

In a more reasoned but still malevolent tone, Marko said, "You can live today for the price of your horses, or I can return with more soldiers. If required to do that, I'll have you arrested for harboring fugitives. I'll arrange to have your freedom, which you value so highly, taken from you. Choose now. Either way, I leave today knowing those horses are mine."

Petr's blood raged, keen to engage and kill these men. Marko's words goaded him to strike first. It's what they wanted most. Again, common sense prevailed in Petr's thinking. It would be near impossible to best three young, heavily armed trained Cossacks, thirsting for blood in open battle. When he lowered his axe in symbolic submission to Marko Dragovich, Petr hated his actions. Hatred glared from his slit eyes and pursed lips.

"You will regret this insult to me, Marko," Petr challenged, knowing he was beaten but still unbowed before him.

Marko saw the look in his eyes and smiled. Petr was just like all the many others before.

"No." Sounding like a drunken lord over his subject, Marko said, "I am Cossacki. I take what I want, not you. You won't even fight for what is yours, old man. I think you will regret more the insults you have spoken to me.

"After I have captured and returned the two criminals I seek, I'll visit you again. Only this time, I won't give you any choices. You owe me, and I will collect my due. Olek, Vadim, take the horses and saddles," he ordered. "They'll bring a good price at the market."

With one last look of scorn and contempt for his beaten adversary, Marko pulled the reins and spurred his mount away, kicking up dirt into Petr's face.

CHAPTER 9

For more than 200 years, the Stroganov family had built a long and deep history with Siberia. In Russia's high society circles, their name was always foremost whenever imperial expansion was discussed. Indeed, this family had been financing Russian conquest east of the Ural Mountains since 1580, as Vasilii Stroganov had been told. Many people called them pioneers for their efforts, while others saw them as nation-builders. He knew all of this and more than most.

His family's history started in the Ural Mountains as merchants, landowners, industrialists, and (in time) statesmen. He saw his fore-fathers as both financial and political opportunists. They saw the big picture, investing their family's fortunes over centuries and not merely years. Their collective vision had made them very wealthy business-men with strong ties to the royal Romanov family. In return for their continued support, the Stroganov family was allowed to own armed troops, exercise military campaigns against Siberian rulers, and have duty-free trade with Asian nations. Building fortresses and founding towns was a natural consequence of expanding into Siberia.

Vasilii liked to think of himself first as a veteran soldier with a disci-plined mind, then as a seasoned administrator for his family's interests. He had enlisted into the Russian Imperial Army, partly as duty but also to test his strength and courage in a wild frontier. Unlike many other Russian army officers, he had come up through the ranks. He hadn't used his family connections to ascend quickly to his current stand-ing of major and commander. Building this fort town on the Amur River was an accomplishment he was particularly proud of. He viewed his efforts as a legacy to Russia. He had brought law and order to an uncertain and untamed borderland. Unfortunately, with this came the heel of the Cossack.

He stopped his train of thought while standing rigid before the open window. With shoulders square, hands clasped behind his back, he focused solely on the word "Cossack," which conjured both fear and hatred by most of the people. Particularly the Indigenous men and women along the Amur River, who were forced to pay the *yasak*, or fur tribute, to Imperial Russia.

A soldier's orders were not always easy to follow. A warrior class was necessary and used as a civic militia when dealing with locals. They could be both brutal and cruel, but they were clever enough not to exterminate the people. To do so would remove their power. Their real goal was to subjugate a race. No better group of Cossack militias could enforce the law. In return, they received large parcels of land and tax-free status. For this, they became the tsar's most loyal people.

Vasilii had served his country for ten long years in an active military career filled with much personal sacrifice along the way. He wished to retire as major and ranking commander of this fort. Even after five years at his post, he still didn't feel at home. For him, in this remote part of the country, the summers were too short, and the winters were seemingly endless. He longed for the Ural Mountains, the seat of the Stroganov family.

Six months had passed since he had drafted a letter of resignation to his commander. He knew another year might go by before his replacement would arrive, and he could put this chapter in his wake. In the long wait between, he would perform his duties as best possible. Dealing with Marko Dragovich was a necessary task.

Vasilii could lightly hear Marko grinding his teeth while the man waited restlessly behind him. Knowing this, Vasilii purposefully prolonged the wait.

"I want them brought back alive," Vasilii said with authority, more to the window than Marko.

It was insulting to a Cossack not to be spoken to directly, almost dismissively, which Vasilii used for effect. He did so intentionally, reinforcing who was in command here. Although Marko Dragovich was physically larger, Vasilii had no fear of him.

Vasilii had learned the hard way of a soldier, having killed many men in numerous campaigns against Russia's enemies. First, Tartars, then the Chinese, and now Indigenous people trying to free themselves. Unhappily, they bore the yoke of unyielding change. He knew Marko and all men of his ilk only too well, having witnessed their depravations, rape, and violence during war and conquest. Marko was like a chained beast, easy to control but never one that should be cut loose. This was to avoid the damage and chaos he would inflict on the military order he maintained in Khabarovsk, Russia.

Turning, Vasilii faced his Cossack law enforcer. "What do you need in order to capture and return the two fugitives?"

If ever there was a fiendish hate in a man's eyes for all to see clearly, Vasilii was witnessing the living proof on Marko's contorted face. His right hand gripped the hilt of his sheathed saber. His bandaged left hand held a coiled whip called a *nagaika*. Vasilii watched as Marko worked hard to get his emotions under control before replying.

"Twelve men, a river pilot, and a boat."

"Really? All that to capture two outlanders who escaped your grasp?"

"I want justice!" Marko demanded, raising his voice to Vasilii almost insubordinately.

"Careful with your tone of voice, Cossack. I, too, want justice, but not the same kind as you. I cannot allow commoners to assault the tsar's imperial soldiers and openly escape. If that were to happen, we'd all become targets. With no fear of retribution, we lose control. I'm also considering letting them go, only to perish on the tundra. No one can survive the winter for long without prepared food and provisions in the frozen wasteland."

"They're not like most of the timid people of Siberia," Marko said. "They don't fear much. They make their own way in life and are resourceful."

"Not unlike a Cossack, eh? I'd have to agree with you on your assessment. Few men and no women I know could best you with a blade. Looking at your wounded hand, I think they probably let you keep your life and weren't worried about your paths crossing again."

At this last remark, Vasilii could see Marko's sword hand visibly shake as he gripped the hilt even harder.

"Do you understand my orders, Marko? Bring them back alive, and they'll be publicly hanged for everyone to witness. As a reward, I'll allow you to personally put the nooses around their necks."

Marko's hooded eyes briefly strayed over the commanding officer's shoulder boards, knowing the gold star bordered by red pinstripes made him a senior officer. Vasilii's reputation as an excellent soldier and field commander had earned him a lot of respect from the men of this fort. To not obey would put him in prison. Marko reluctantly conceded by nodding. "I will follow your orders, Major Stroganov."

"Good then. But not with your men. I need them here to maintain order. You can have eight regular, fully armed grenadiers, our best river pilot, and my personal two-mast Koch. It's the swiftest on the river."

"What!" Marko exclaimed. "My men are without equal at ambushing. I need them for success."

"Find another way to capture them alive. Every soldier here is tried and capable. You know this," he spoke sternly. "Hand-pick your crew; when ready, I will personally see to your departure. How many days ahead of you are they?" Major Stroganov asked.

"Three, maybe four. They travel upriver in a canoe."

"You should be able to overtake them by the time they reach the next fort town of Aigun. More than a week's travel by paddle.

"Keep me informed. That is all."

Marko turned, dissatisfied, and muttered to himself, keeping his voice low so as not to be overheard, "We'll see about your damn orders. More than a few have *accidentally* met their end on a river."

The next morning, Vasilii met Marko on the river's shoreline to finalize the orders he had given.

"You have two weeks, Marko, to catch these fugitives alive and bring them both to imperial justice. I see you've chosen some excellent soldiers for your charge and my pilot, Vladimir. Good."

Marko stood listening quietly, showing none of the emotional rage that boiled inside him. He saluted the major, acknowledging his superior rank and command. Turning with the other soldiers, he stepped into the boats, waiting to ferry them to the anchored ship.

Vasilii watched Marko and his men take their leave. His best judgment told him Marko Dragovich could not be trusted. Even among his countrymen, Marko was the worst of his kind. *This mission will be a test of his loyalty*, Vasilii thought. *To fail my orders will, at the very least, result in imprisonment, with a maximum penalty of death.*

"We shall see."

Marko's time in Russia's service might come to an end. Perhaps the two outlanders he pursued would not show mercy a second time. Either way, he would be tested.

CHAPTER 10

Ragnar and Sayiina arrived at their destination by noon on their third day of sailing. Since departing Khabarovsk, this was the first fort town up the Amur River. Sayiina marveled at the great distance they had traveled in so short a time.

"I can't believe we're already here. Petr told us it was a seven-day journey, and we've completed it in half the measure. It's as if the wind literally picked us up and put us down at our chosen location."

"Well, in a manner of speaking, it has. Just not literally, Sayiina. No one owns the wind, and it has no home. We're fortunate our sailing has been fair to us these past couple of days. Were it much stronger or even a storm, we would've had to wait it out. *The Cat* would easily collapse in rough waters.

"No, our timing's good. She's a boat built for speed, not comfort," he said with a smile. "Did you want to go into town now or later?"

"Now," Sayiina replied quickly. "I'd like a hot bath and a room tonight."

"First, we'll need to secure safe harbor for the boat. Let's sail past the fort and village, then look for a shipyard along its shoreline. We need a shipwright who will help us secure coverage for *The Cat* tonight."

"Over there, Ragnar?" She indicated the location with her hand. "Is that what we want?"

"Aye, it looks like a yard. I'll guide us that way. We'll beach right on the riverbank, then drag *The Cat* ashore before finding the owner of this yard."

A few minutes later, they were pulling the catamaran onto land. When they looked up, they noticed a burly, bearded man approaching.

"He might be the shipwright, Sayiina. He's sure not a soldier from the fort, judging by his clothes."

"That is a very unusual craft you're sailing, stranger," the same man said in Russian. "We don't see any like it on this river, and I'd know. I've been building watercraft for these waters going on twelve years. Riverboats, barges, even a few of the sampans the Chinese love so much, and I've never seen one like yours."

"You're right. She's one of a kind. Are you the town shipwright?"

"Da. Artem Orlov's my name. And yours?" he replied evenly.

"Mine is Ragnar Olaffson, and my partner is Sayiina. We want to shelter our vessel here for the night. Do you have coverage in your yard?"

"Can you pay?"

"Aye, I've got coin."

"Well, stop your struggling then. My horse will pull your riverboat off the beach and into my shed. Just show me where to tie on a rope line, and the rest will be easy," he said with a friendly grin.

Ragnar agreed and supervised the rope tow into the boat shed. Satisfied that no damage had been done, he turned to Artem. "Thanks. I don't want to have her looked over too closely by the authorities. They might impound it for inspection. Can I have your word it won't be found out? We're just staying the one night, then moving on tomorrow."

"Of course. Everyone here on this river knows my word is worth its salt," he stated.

"You're a different-looking couple from the people who live here. No offense meant, but you're a white-haired Scandinavian, as I can guess. Your clothing suggests a sailor to me, but not government navy issue. So, you're no deserter. More a seafarer, to me. Your black-haired companion looks Turkish, with olive-colored skin, correct? Where are you two from?"

"My people are Sakha," Sayiina said proudly.

"No insult from me," Artem replied. "Everyone here is either Russian, Cossack, Chinese, or Mongol, that's all. You'll be noticed and watched. What brings you here, if I may ask?"

"We're just passing by. We saw the fort and thought we might stay a night. To set our feet back on land and clean up. Tomorrow, we continue upriver."

"How far upriver?"

"As far as it'll take us. After that, it's our own business."

Artem stared at the two of them in disbelief. He knew there was nothing at the headwaters of the Amur River, even though it had been years since he'd been there. He shrugged, knowing they would return when they learned this truth.

"The moorage'll cost you one coin, and I give you my personal guarantee it's safe here," he said, reaching out with an open hand for payment.

"Good. Now, where can we find a bath and a room for the night?" Ragnar asked.

"There's a public house inside the fort, but I'd stay away from that one. Too many Cossack soldiers in the garrison, and they'd ask you a lot of questions. There's another on the outskirts of the village that surrounds our fort. Though not as clean and disciplined a clientele, if you know what I mean. More of a gaming house, if you like that sort of entertainment. Plus, they serve the best *koumiss* anywhere on this river."

"What?" Sayiina exclaimed loudly. "This place sells fermented mare's milk? Don't lie to me!"

Artem laughed at her remark. He was big and not without some girth, too, which added to the volume of his voice. "I might be called many things, but never a liar. I go there myself at times for the *koumiss*. Watch out for the card games."

Hearing the word *koumiss* made Ragnar groan inwardly. For him, it was like drinking warm milk and whisky. Just an awful combination that brought back some bad memories.

"In what direction and how far away?" Sayiina asked with some anticipation in her voice.

"Well, if you walk east, past the village market in a straight line, you'll see two farmhouses at the end of the road. The one on the right is owned by an old and irritable farmer named Boris. He's always complaining that he can't sleep well at night. He says it's because of the noisy whores and drunk patrons in the house across from him."

"Good to know." Ragnar then turned to Sayiina, suggesting they buy needed supplies in the market before finding a room. "This way, we can leave at first light tomorrow."

"Fine with me," she replied. "As long as I can sample the *koumiss!*"

At that, they left Artem and took their time walking through the market. It wasn't busy at this time of day. They saw a few soldiers who seemed to be arguing amongst themselves and some elderly women in traditional peasant wear moving into and near different shops. Ragnar suspected most of the people would be working their farms or helping out a fellow neighbor, not unlike a commune. Spring was a time for planting in this part of the world, probably harvesting just a single grain crop before winter arrived at the end of September.

Farming in Siberia was a hard life. Many of the men and women here were fleeing persecution of different sorts from Western Russia and tsarist rule. These people were a different breed. Their hard work and effort made them tough, resilient, and owing to no one but themselves. Hunting and trapping in the lean winter months kept everyone alive.

Ragnar paused his line of thinking and turned to Sayiina. "Let's buy enough foodstuff to last more than a week. We could keep sailing instead of stopping and foraging for food every few days, right?"

"Okay, what are you thinking?"

"Starting tomorrow, I want to put some distance between us and this fort. The authorities might detain us and *The Cat*. We can always stop for fresh water along our way."

So, the two spent some time carefully choosing and then purchasing enough dried provisions. They chose pan bread, wild berries, and salted fish for their continuing journey. Just then, the distinct *ping* of a hammer on an anvil caught their attention, and they turned in that direction.

"I also want to stop at that blacksmith's shop ahead," Ragnar said. "What do you think a farmer in these parts would really value, Sayiina?"

"Probably more land. But not being a farmer, I don't know."

"I bet that blacksmith up ahead would know. I'll take our provisions back to the boat and leave everything on board. Why not find yourself a hot bath? I'll be back in an hour and meet you at the 'smith's' shop."

"See you then," she replied and started toward the gaming house at the end of the road.

Ragnar turned back and headed to the shipyard with their supplies. When he approached the boathouse entrance, he stopped abruptly. He wasn't sure why—maybe a gut feeling or wanting to get his bearings—then he proceeded with extra caution. His line of sight took him alongside the boathouse where the catamaran was safely held. It was a large, strong building. A simple enough pole-framed structure with split wood siding. Not a perfectly built shed, evidenced by the gaps between boards. In Ragnar's opinion, it was not a tight ship.

He stopped just before the outside entrance and peered through a gap, watching Artem, who was very closely scrutinizing *The Cat* with a measuring stick—its length, width, depth, and the height of her mast. Ragnar was not too surprised at his curiosity. After all, Artem was a shipwright and tradesman. What did alarm him was when Artem walked over to a table nearby and started scribing its details on a leather skin. He folded it neatly and concealed it in a wood pile when finished.

Ragnar revealed himself and walked toward Artem. "Can I be of any help?"

Artem froze. He was completely caught off guard by Ragnar's sudden appearance. With a guilty look, he quickly tried to recover himself. "I didn't think you would return until tomorrow," he said nervously, moving a couple of steps away from the parchment.

"I thought I'd make ready now for an early departure tomorrow." Ragnar now eyed him suspiciously.

Artem moved closer to the catamaran, feeling Ragnar's stare on the back of his neck. Worried he'd been found out, he tried to keep an even tone in his voice, saying in a flattering manner, "You're a man just like me. Leave nothing to chance, I say."

Ragnar ignored the compliment, deciding not to raise any concerns he might have toward Artem now. He would deal with it tomorrow. *Let sleeping dogs lie*, he thought and began stowing their provisions.

"We'll be by tomorrow morning," Ragnar informed Artem with an easy attitude.

"Good. Not to worry. Everything's safe here."

With that reassurance, Ragnar waved and walked out of the boatshed toward the blacksmith's shop, knowing Artem could not be trusted.

CHAPTER 11

Sayiina watched Ragnar turn and walk toward the shipyard with their supplies. Everything they had purchased was contained in a large jute bag, resting easily across the back of his neck and broad shoulders. His manner of stride and the way his whole body moved would be seen by many as a swagger, but she saw it differently. Sayiina saw a man with total confidence in his physical strength who often relaxed under pressure. This came from a lifetime of experiences, both good and bad. Although just a few years older than herself, he had a youthful vitality. Not much, other than maybe a great storm at sea, could possibly discourage his spirit. She liked what she saw and expressed a rare small smile for anyone to see, surprising even herself.

Turning to walk through town, she passed the busy kiosks in the open market. A few, but not all, of the villagers gave a passing stare her way. Mostly, elder ladies grouped together for the day's idle gossip. Physically, Sayiina saw little difference between them and herself. The real difference was cultural. Their full-length patterned linen dresses with matching headscarves completely contrasted with hers.

Sayiina's clothes were cut as a man would wear. Knee-high boots, pants, and a long-sleeved shirt under a vest. Around her waist was a tightly wrapped sash securing two long knives. Across her back, she carried her Yakutian great bow with a quiver full of arrows. To these people, she probably looked more like a man than a woman, perhaps like another foreign mercenary searching for work.

That's fine with me, she mused. *I don't need their approval. I'm a Yakutian huntress, and I walk my own path.*

A short while later, walking to the outskirts of the village, Sayiina reached the end of the road. It was just as Artem had described. The house on the right was obviously a working farm. It fronted a field of early-growing rye, which, when harvested, would produce black bread. The nearest corral to the house held goats and two horses. She saw a second nearby, holding a dozen reindeer. These were the real working animals on the farm, used for plowing and hauling timber. In the midday sun, all their sled dogs were collared, tethered to stakes, and asleep. She had seen this sight before in her village in Yakutia, just different people using the same methods for survival.

She turned her gaze to the second house, sitting in the middle of the opposite field, not 100 yards away. It was a large, older, two-story wood structure in some disrepair. Perhaps a family's farmhouse at another time. Walking the dirt lane, she noted that the surrounding field was mostly wild grass interspersed with flax, wheat, and rye. Occasionally, a small patch of berries would reveal themselves, almost ready for picking.

Her preoccupation quickly fled as two peasant men approached. They had just finished relieving themselves from behind a tree and were close at hand. She could hear their conversation was Russian. Not surprisingly, their clothing was of dyed blue linen made from flax they had probably grown. It gave away their heritage with baggy trousers and jackets covering a collarless white shirt. The distinct Bast shoes from the plated inner bark of the lime tree completed their image. One man smiled politely and wished her well. The other, obviously more intoxicated upon seeing Sayiina, fell to one knee and declared his love for her.

"You're a dark angel sent to me in my time of need."

"Save yourself, man," she replied humorously. "I might be dark, but I'm no angel." Then she continued on to the converted farmhouse, now used as a public house.

It was busy inside; the clientele was mostly Russian and Chinese working-class peasants of all shapes and sizes. There were a couple of off-duty soldiers and, surprisingly, several women and young girls. Sayiina worked her way through the groups of people toward the bar and innkeeper. She still had to secure a room. Besides, there was at least one mug of *koumiss* she wanted to sample. Hailing the proprietor achieved nothing, and she resigned herself to waiting her turn. He did eventually come around to her.

"I need two things right now."

"Okay, say it," was his brusque reply. "I've got a lot of patrons waiting."

"First, I need a room with a bath for tonight. Second, one pint of your *koumiss* for now."

"*Koumiss,* I got," he said as he filled a cup. "Rooms I don't got." Then he passed her a full mug. "I doubt very much you'll find a room anywhere tonight. Look at my place here. It's full and will be all night, I expect."

Holding the unsampled drink in her hand, Sayiina frowned with disappointment. "Is there a special occasion occurring today?"

He was surprised at her question. "Do you not know that today is our Orthodox Easter celebration? Everyone in the village and on the farms will be in a festive mood tonight. It's a tradition in these parts."

Sayiina stood stunned and mute as she heard his words. For a moment, nothing seemed natural. She should have known, but her travels with Ragnar had changed her perspective on everything, and these past weeks had caused her to lose her sense of time. Sayiina realized she was living in his world now, alongside him. Together, they overcame obstacles and great dangers, yet she learned to sail as fast as the wind in his arms. She was giving freely and sharing her innermost thoughts with this man, who patiently, steadily was changing her world. She allowed him to guide them safely on their journey. And so engaged that she failed to remember this special time of year and the day of her birth!

The innkeeper was still speaking to her, and although a little bewildered, she caught his last lusty words. ". . . I'd be willing to share my bed with you. You're about my size." He stood there waiting and expecting a favorable response.

Lifting the mug to her lips and looking over its brim, she drained it. Then, before replying, she slammed it down hard on the bar. "I've had better *koumiss* than this and better offers to bed me."

With that, she turned and walked out. "Men . . . always thinking with their little head and not the one on their shoulders."

Having failed to get them lodging for the night, she decided to meet up with Ragnar. They would need to discuss their situation, and the thought of sleeping in a boat shed wasn't very appealing. Perhaps Ragnar would have an idea.

During this same time, Ragnar was entering the blacksmith's shop. It was dim inside, but everything you would expect to see was there. He saw various farm tools, axes, nails, fishhooks, and tongs. The smith had his back turned to Ragnar and was working beside his furnace with burned black leather gloves. The man worked a large pair of red-hot iron tongs, holding a piece of metal in the fire. The air had an acrid smell about it the closer he moved toward the furnace. So, Ragnar stopped and waited nearby until noticed. The blacksmith looked up from his forge, saw Ragnar, frowned, and then, turning, spoke thoughtfully, "How can I help you, foreigner?"

"You're correct, blacksmith. I'm not from these waters, but I suspect most people like us come from somewhere else. I doubt there are many secrets in this town."

"That be true. Again, how can I help you?"

"I want to impress a certain farmer living on the outskirts of your village. His name is Boris. Do you know him?" he asked as he casually looked about at some of the farm tools.

"I do," the smith replied. "Boris Bagrov's his name."

"All men have wants and needs, but I'm sure you know this. What would a farmer like Boris need from a shop like yours?"

The blacksmith laughed at the question. "He wants everything I have here. But if you're looking to bargain with that wearisome man, I can tell you he needs that spade over there against the wall," he said, pointing to it. "He's had his eye on it for quite some time. If you own it, he'll want to talk with you."

Just then, Sayiina walked into the shop, and both men turned in her direction.

"How did you fare at the public house?" Ragnar asked her.

"Bad and worse. The *koumiss* they serve is overrated, and no rooms are available," she said, sounding slightly discouraged.

Ragnar saw the frustrated look on her face and turned to the blacksmith. "How much coin for your spade there?"

"Three silvers, and it's yours, my friend."

"Deal!"

Sayiina was stunned by Ragnar's response and now curious about his intentions. "Really? Did you not hear me? No room, no bath, nothing. And you buy a shovel?"

"Well, now we have something to bargain with."

Sayiina was irritated and let Ragnar hear her frustrations as they left the blacksmith's shop. "What good is a shovel to us at this time? We leave tomorrow at dawn."

"Most people think of a shovel for moving dirt and such. This one, I think, would better serve us as leverage. This particular one is what farmer Boris desires most. Perhaps enough to give us a room in his home for a night."

"What? Bribery with a shovel?"

"Aye," he added breezily.

"That's dirty play and brilliant. I like it. Are you sure you're not even a small part Yakutian?"

"Not the last time I checked." He grinned. "Let's go visit Farmer Boris. Perhaps both of us might be able to charm him into giving us a room tonight. If not, we'll use the shovel as our reserve plan."

"Honestly, Ragnar, I don't think I'm the 'charmer' type," she openly admitted.

"Well, just smile at him once or twice when I'm talking with him."

"What? Do you want me to encourage him to think I'm available? I'm not that shameless, you know."

"Sayiina, we need a room for tonight. Some feminine luring from a Yakutian would be helpful."

When the two of them arrived at their destination, they were met by a stout older man and woman, both of simple means. They looked to be in their late sixties, but it was hard to tell. Their immediate appearance was of strong Russian descent, with deep lines and creases in their faces—a result of hard work when exposed to the elements and weathered over time.

"Is this your farm?" Ragnar asked politely.

"What's your name, traveler? I'll tell you mine," the man replied bluntly in a typical gruff Russian manner.

"Ragnar Olaffson, and my partner Sayiina. We want to talk to Boris Bagrov. We're told he lives here."

"Well, I'm who you are looking for. I'm an honest farmer, and I have no coin if you're thinking of robbing me." Then he turned his pants pockets inside out. "What do you want?"

Sayiina looked at Boris, the farmer, and gave him a big smile, as Ragnar had suggested, to try to influence the deal. Standing there, she felt pretty foolish, performing at his request.

"Why is your woman smiling at me like she wants to steal something?" Boris asked.

"Oh . . . uh, she just likes people," he stammered. "You're making Boris nervous with your smile, Sayiina. Why not speak with Mrs. Bagrov while I continue with Mister Bagrov?"

Mrs. Bagrov led Sayiina by her arm toward their farmhouse at this suggestion.

"Sir, we are looking for a room you might let out to us for one night."

"Tonight is the Orthodox Easter celebration. Any other night, I could offer you a bed to sleep in, but we're expecting many guests to arrive here shortly to feast and dance in celebration. I wish I could be of more help."

With his response, Ragnar felt he was a good, honest man. He reflected on Boris's reply, then spoke his own words a little more thoughtfully.

"Everyone has wants and needs. As I am sure you know, these words are seen as two very different things in men such as us. I have always thought they can be bargained for separately, at a fair price, between men. I do have something you might need with me." Then he revealed from behind his back the spade from the blacksmith's shop. "I'll offer you this for what my partner and I want. Are we in agreement, Boris Bagrov?"

Boris stared wide-eyed at the shovel, momentarily lost for words.

"You've got my shovel," he stammered in disbelief.

"Well, I do own it, although I don't need it," Ragnar said, holding it before Boris as if to lure him into the agreement.

"It's no secret in this town that I have wanted it for a long time. I need to speak to my wife before I can agree on what you need and what I want. Come with me to my house, and we can talk some more there."

Ragnar followed him into his home. Once inside, Boris excused himself to find his wife, and he gave Ragnar a moment to observe his surroundings in more detail. He saw a beautiful simplicity within its four square walls and wooden floor. A lounging cat ignored half a dozen chickens pecking into a wooden feeder.

It was a room large enough to hold maybe twenty people comfortably. In one corner was an open oven where all the heating came from. Inside was a large pot of stew, and its delicious aroma was brewing for tonight's guests. A large axe, along with a very worn-down shovel, rested against the front door wall alongside a stack of cut firewood. A wide wooden bench ran around three walls. He thought they could be used as beds. A large table with chairs sat beneath a window in another corner, framed in red and white embroidered cloth. Sitting on top of the table were wooden bowls, and a particular one Ragnar knew was called a *kovsh*. Its design, in the shape of a bird, was to function as the main serving bowl. A large, decorated distaff, used to spin thread from the flax they grew, stood neatly on its own beside a few spools of yarn.

It was a humble grace to be here and now. He felt it deep within, as calm waters on a gentle sea.

Mrs. Bagrov entered the room just then, smiling at Ragnar.

"How is Sayiina, and where is she?" he asked courteously.

"She's fine. I have shared some time and words with her. Sayiina is a woman who cares deeply. As a huntress, there are few her equal. She thinks she has found herself a mate in you, a seafarer. But who am I to know? My man works the land. Other men, like yourself, sail the seas." She sighed.

"Sometimes men don't know what they have until it's gone. Regarding Sayiina, I advise you, as a mother, to have no regrets. Live well together, and time will tell you what is to be. I have drawn a bath for her outside; she'll want more hot water now. She'll be here in a while." Then she turned to leave.

Now Boris entered the room wearing a wide grin, like a cat who had just caught a mouse. Looking innocently at his wife, he stopped abruptly.

"What have you been up to?" she demanded. "You look as guilty as a dark sin exposed to light."

"Oh, nothing, dear. Just waiting about for you," he said, remembering how he secretly watched their dark-haired visitor slowly undress before stepping into the bath.

"There is an old Russian proverb in Siberia we live by even now," Mrs. Bagrov shared. "Bring to the table all you can find in the oven. Although poor to our table, you and your mate are welcome to join our friends and neighbors tonight. You are pilgrims in need, sent by the Lord."

"You are a gracious woman. Thank you for your hospitality and kindness." Ragnar was very pleased.

"Well, that's all decided then." Boris declared. "You'll stay tonight. Do you know what the Russian drink *kvas* is, Ragnar Olaffson?"

"I've heard of it but can't say I know of it proper."

"Well, it's a working man's drink made from barley, honey, and salt. We've also purposely upped the punch, if you catch my drift. Come here with me over to the barrel, wet your tongue, and let's talk about that handsome shovel you won't need anymore." Then he smiled.

Boris filled a cup for Ragnar and passed it to him. A knock at his door drew his attention away, and he excused himself. Ragnar watched as three women and three men entered the living area. They were all talking gayly and in a merry mood. Boris was eager to welcome them to their traditional holiday celebration. More people were entering by the minute, and Ragnar realized the living room was full. Soon, eating well from the stew pot and drinking hard from Boris's cask of spirits had begun.

Many people thought Ragnar must be a pilgrim on a journey, judging by his appearance. They asked him where he was from and what news he had heard from Moscow. All this while Boris continued filling Ragnar's cup with *kvas*, never once releasing his hand from his new shovel. Boris drifted from one group of guests to another, proudly displaying his prize.

Ragnar felt among friends there, with a sense of belonging. He had been missing this for so long a time. It reminded him, more than ever, that he needed to get home. He was feeling the call for Norway, something he had seldom felt over the years.

Sayiina was not in the room, and he wondered about her whereabouts. At this time, Mrs. Bagrov appeared in the middle of the room, ushering her guests to clear the area.

"Everyone, please take your food and drink and sit along the benches provided."

Like everyone else, Ragnar cleared the way, trying to see Sayiina. He asked himself, *why isn't Sayiina here? Perhaps I will look for her.*

But before he could leave the room, Mrs. Bagrov came forward and asked him to stay a moment.

She walked over to a small group of men looking to her for instructions. One of those men, a barefooted guest, retrieved from his side a small flute. He tapped his feet and began to play. Beside him, another brought forth a violin and put it to his chin. He listened momentarily, then drew his bow across the stringed neck to match the flute's key. Next was a tambourine and wooden drum, keeping a steady beat. Finally, Mrs. Bagrov slapped two wooden spoons into her palm, producing a clacking sound of her own. Once the rhythm of the folk song was found, some of the women in the room sang its lyrics in unison.

Discretely, the guests nearest the front door parted, allowing Sayiina a grand entrance into the gathering's midst. Here, all eyes were upon her. For a moment, Ragnar wasn't sure it was her. From top to bottom, she was transformed, appearing as another woman, no longer the warrior huntress in leather and fur. He stared in disbelief at the change.

He put down his cup of *kvas*, thinking perhaps he had consumed too much and this was an optical illusion.

Her long black hair was braided in two lengths, with a blue ribbon attached to each. Around her neck, she wore a pale leather collar. The center of her throat held the king's jewel that he'd retrieved from the cave of the beast and gifted to her. She had donned an almost sheer white blouse whose folds barely contained her voluptuousness. A distinct slap was heard somewhere across the room; a male voice cried out, followed by a female's mild scolding. Sayiina wore a white linen skirt with blue embroidery, cinched at her waist and finishing just below her knees. On her feet, she no longer wore black leather boots but a pair of soft shoes laced to her ankles, accenting her pale calves. In this short moment, Ragnar took in her new image.

Still, the music did not die down even slightly.

Sayiina, standing there motionless, looked like the embodiment of Siberian womanhood in all her vitality. Her roaming eyes found Ragnar's and locked on him as he stood among the invited guests. With her hand, she beckoned him forward into the circle. He could hardly refuse such an invitation and was bolstered by many clapping hands nearby. He stood before her and gave a foolish grin, not knowing what to expect next.

"What are we doing together here?" he asked above the din of the revelers in the room.

"You need not do anything, Ragnar. I'm going to dance for you."

"I don't know how to dance," he admitted.

"Not to worry, my man. It was Mrs. Bagrov who suggested I dance for you. Something of Yakutian culture to catch your attention on this night. A dance no one has seen before."

She stopped talking and raised her hands above her head to signal the musicians that she was ready. The tempo increased, and now placing both hands on her hips, she slowly gyrated them in a circular motion. Her feet moved to the beat, and she circled Ragnar suggestively. Whenever she passed in front, she proudly threw back her shoulders, one at a time. Her large and robust breasts, swaying independently, were a clear show of her feminine virility, capturing every man's immediate attention. Still, the rhythm did not stop, and Sayiina continued to dance. At one turn, she shamelessly rubbed her buttocks against his own, causing some men, including even Boris Bagrov, to cheer her on.

Ragnar was suspicious of her intentions. "What are you doing, Sayiina?"

"I was asked to give a dance that no one had ever seen before. Are you not pleased with my performance?"

"I am, but it is very seducing and immodest for all to see."

"Good. It is supposed to be," she whispered in his ear and lightly rubbed her pelvis against his thigh. This caused many of the elder ladies in attendance to gasp and cover their mouths. Some were even pointing in shock, and still, the music continued.

"This is a traditional dance of my Yakutian people. It's always performed by eligible young girls wanting a mate. It's not Christian, but a pagan fertility dance. It is also the day of my birth, Ragnar, and I want to celebrate tonight with you. Let's live now for what this moment is. Tomorrow, we will be gone from here."

She stopped before him breathless and looked to him for an answer. He studied her face. Once again, this woman had stirred and aroused raw emotion in him. He pulled her in close and pressed his lips to hers. The assembled friends and relatives spontaneously erupted in good cheer.

"Aye, lass, tonight we sail across your ocean with love."

Someone passed two cups of *kvas* to them, and they moved away from the center of the room. Another couple took their place in a round dance, Cossack style. People clapped to the beat. Ragnar and Sayiina were watching a traditional Ukrainian dance, and they, too, cheered them on.

"You may have started some good trouble here. Something of a dancing competition among couples. I see it as a good thing."

"Well, my father always said, 'Trouble will always follow a bad temper.' With you, it's hard to be angry. Let's celebrate with friends this night and face tomorrow's troubles together."

"Aye." He slipped his arm around her waist. "We sail this night together."

CHAPTER 12

Sayiina was the first to open her eyes on this early morning, awakened by the sound of a noisy rooster publicly crowing dawn to the world. She turned to stare at her still-sleeping man, Ragnar, lying on the bed they shared last night, being not more than a thatch of hay inside a barn. She remained motionless, watching him as his bare chest rose and receded to a steady rhythm of deep breathing. He seemed at peace and, for the moment, herself as well while at his side. A wave of emotions flooded her as she recalled last night's celebration, her salacious dance culminating in their passionate lovemaking. What a night it was.

Sayiina sighed, looking at him thoughtfully, and realized she was in love with him. She remembered the words of the blind seer in the lavender tent, who had foretold this to her. Then she recalled her mother's words of advice about love. "Let the mate you choose come to you first; only then openly declare your love for him. When it comes to matters of your heart, be cautious, Sayiina." She would hold true on this council and not reveal her feelings to Ragnar. Like the good hunter she was, she would wait patiently.

She stood, stretched, and let out an early morning groan, and in doing so, Ragnar stirred, opened his eyes, and smiled her way.

"You're up early," he stated, noticing shafts of morning light were piercing through the room's pale gray hue.

"I am. Aren't you the one who wanted an early sailing this day?"

While dressing herself, she made ready by gathering their things for today's journey.

"Right, you are, lass. Let's make ready to set sail." Rising slowly, he stood before her. "But first, a kiss to remember last night." He pulled her in close for an embrace.

Sayiina smiled as she placed her hand on his chest in weak resistance to his advances. "You had more than your share of those last night, my man. Besides, I can hardly walk this day without being reminded of your amorous caresses. There will be time for more later. Let's gather our things and start out at where Artem's boathouse keeps our 'Cat.'"

Ragnar knew she was right. She was a very practical woman who, for the most part, liked to take charge. He didn't mind either; in many ways, it made his life simpler, less to worry about. So, he conceded and asked her, while readying himself, "Is this how married couples behave, Sayiina?"

"I don't know what you mean." Feigning innocence, she looked at him intently. "I've never been married . . . yet."

Ragnar stood, confused for a moment. "Ahh . . . should I know something here, Sayiina?"

"Well, it's a custom with my people that mating couples don't keep secrets from each other. Is there anything you might want to say to me before we head out?"

By the tone of Sayiina's voice, Ragnar was pretty certain she was trying to coax something from him. But he couldn't read her mind, so he left her question unanswered. "You're right. We should make ready. I want to be on the river by sunrise."

Sayiina realized Ragnar would need more time and thought. *When it comes to relationships, most men are clueless.*

After they had gathered up their belongings, they proceeded to Artem's, each in their thoughts. Ragnar felt a cool dampness on his skin. Looking skyward, he saw the low-hanging clouds appeared heavy gray, and his sense of smell detected moisture. Perhaps rain this morning. More fortunate, he noted, were the clouds drifting in an east-to-west direction. Exactly the way they would be sailing.

He turned to Sayiina. "How many more days do you see us on this Amur River?"

"Not many," she replied distantly. "As you are fond of saying, with a 'fair wind,' perhaps three to four days' sail. The next village will bring me to the end of my knowledge of this land and my obligation to you."

"You're speaking of your father's final request?"

"I am. Beyond this river, which Modun and I traveled so many years ago in my youth, I do not know. I can no longer be your guide to what you seek."

"I see." He retreated into his cold silence, continuing to walk the road to the boathouse.

As they approached, Ragnar motioned for caution, lifting his index finger to his lips. He wanted to scout the boathouse undetected for signs of activity. Once he was certain no one was inside, he told Sayiina of his suspicions about Artem.

"Having copied *The Cat*'s design on parchment in detail, Artem hid the truth from me by concealing it in a wood pile."

"Really? If you don't want to be found, leave no traces behind."

"Aye, lass, I agree. Let's drag the boat down to the river and stow our gear, then I'll snatch the parchment Artem hid."

Once on the river's edge, Sayiina prepared for departure, and Ragnar ran back to the boathouse, seeking the wood pile. A few moments later, Sayiina watched Ragnar sprint toward her, yelling excitedly and loudly, "Shove off! Make sail!"

Uncertain of the urgency, her question was immediately answered when she saw three armed soldiers in high pursuit. They crested the rise hard on the heels of Ragnar, distantly followed by a heavily panting Artem Orlov. With great effort, Sayiina pushed the catamaran into the water. She first heard a rifle shot boom, then felt the heat of a musket ball pass by her face. She leaped into the drifting boat, urging Ragnar to hurry.

With no moment to lose, he reached the river's edge, lunged into the ice-cold water, and leaped onto *The Cat*. The current pulled them swiftly away from shore, and Ragnar told Sayiina to stay low and paddle hard windward to elude their pursuers. A desperate glance behind told Ragnar, with some relief, that the four exhausted men stood spent on the beach. He had taken the wind out of their sails.

Certain they were a safe distance away, Ragnar opened the lateen sail to cut and run upriver and out of harm's way.

It was then Sayiina turned to him. "What happened back there?"

"I'm not sure. I can only think that Artem changed his mind about us and reported his findings to the fort's authorities. When I was spotted leaving the boathouse, the chase was on. We're really fortunate you had loaded up and were ready to go. A couple more minutes and we might have been captured and put in a guard house for questioning."

"Did you successfully get what you were looking for?"

"I did," he replied with some satisfaction, holding up the parchment for her to see.

"Good! You know, I didn't think you could outrun three soldiers half your age. I might put a wager on you for the next time." She smirked.

Ragnar laughed at her remark, knowing she was teasing him. "I could catch you easy in a foot race."

"Hah, only if I let you capture me."

"Woman, you are both a siren and a vixen to me, and I can't decide about you. You're like a storm inside," he said with a smile.

"I'll take that as a compliment. Sail onward, my man." She turned to face windward, away from Ragnar, and quietly whispered so as not to be overheard, "You still have a few days remaining to make up your mind."

Looking ahead, Ragnar expertly held fast the sail line and steadied the rudder. "Did you just speak to me, Sayiina?"

"Oh, I was just saying it's good to be alive."

"Aye, lass, you're right."

Three days of sailing from dawn to dusk, resting only at night, brought them close to their destination. The sun was setting behind their horizon, and another day was quickly coming to an end.

"Ragnar, soon it'll be too dark to see our way. Let's find a sheltered cove to put in."

"I agree. We should make land somewhere on that big river island up ahead on our port side."

Once there, they built a small fire on a sandy beach. As they sat across from each other, Sayiina spoke thoughtfully.

"If I remember correctly, we're very close to our destination. We shouldn't have to hurry. Let's look around tomorrow morning and even go hunting. I'm tired of our regular berries, dry meat, and hard-tack fare."

"I can follow you if you want. I'm sure there is much to learn from you." Ragnar purposefully avoided direct eye contact with her, as he knew she saw too much of him in these moments together.

Watching Ragnar carefully, Sayiina took notice of his change in mood. She noted his eye avoidance as well. *He's hiding something from me, I'm sure. But what?* Age and experience made him hard to read. He was different from the others. She had learned, at times, that a quiet man could also mean a thoughtful man. Her father once told her, "In some men, still waters run deep."

Now, trying to measure him and his change in tenor, she inquired cautiously. "Is there something you want to say to me, Ragnar? I sense a change has come over you."

"Nay, lass, all is shipshape. Tell me again, what might be the distance to your journey's end?"

Those last three words almost stole her breath away, and still, he would not look her way. Her body tensed, but her eyes were riveted on him as her mind was a whirlwind of emotion. She knew he already had the answer. *Say it*, she wanted to scream aloud. It took her every measure of control to give back a restrained reply. "We'll be there by noon tomorrow."

Watching him from across their small crackling fire, she sat unmoving. The silence between them was a cold, weighted burden, looking more like an opaque wall of destiny. It stood between them, waiting to be shattered.

Ragnar raised his eyes and met her gaze in the still of the moment. "Love isn't a word or feeling I'm much familiar with, Sayiina. It doesn't come easy for me to express at all. Perhaps the gods never intended me to have love in great measure, or maybe I slowly closed my heart to it over my seafaring years. Yet somehow, you have managed to open it, and I feel compelled to share this with you.

"I'd ask you to travel to the end of my journey as my partner and equal, though it be perilous. You're the only woman for me, and I'll never break my promise of fidelity for as long as our journey takes us and beyond."

Hearing Ragnar's words caused her to reel in joy. The words he uttered shattered the wall between them; once again, he had determined her fate. By doing so, he rescued her from a dark and uncertain return path; she would've had to travel back home alone.

"Ragnar Olaffson, I, too, feel the same as you. We're kindred spirits, you and I. For many years, I've traveled this land. Now, your waters have touched my shores. We've found each other."

She stood and crossed to where Ragnar was sitting. Kneeling beside him, she felt something inside, touching her very essence. Not since her mother's passing had tears welled in her eyes. As she touched his rugged face and gently kissed his lips, she whispered, "I accept your offer and would give up my life to save our love." Then she sat beside him before the fire's light.

Sayiina rested in his arms, and he held her close. He noticed a full moon rising in the night sky. A raven flew past it from nearby, starkly contrasting its luminary form. His mind's eye instantly revealed a black silhouette suspended in time above them. He smiled, taking this as a good omen for them. He quietly asked Sayiina if she had seen the same, but she had fallen asleep. Soon after, he, too, yielded to the night as another day passed.

Early the following day, a rising sun awoke them. Their fire had burned itself out, leaving a pile of ash in its place.

"I want to explore and go hunting this morning. Are you coming along?" she asked.

"Aye, I'll try to stay abreast." He grinned.

"Good, I like nothing better than an early morning hunt." She winked at him with a motion to follow, grabbing her great bow.

Within minutes, Sayiina found a game trail winding its way into the forest and rising steeply away from their camp.

After some time tracking, Ragnar became uncomfortable. He didn't like being too far from the boat, their only means of transport. "Sayiina, stop a moment."

She stopped, hearing Ragnar's voice and waited for him to approach, then showed him three paw prints that crossed over the path they were on.

"What is it?"

"I'm not sure."

"Is it a three-legged creature?"

"No, I suspect perhaps a wounded cat is nearby. We have also passed some unusual trail signs that have caught my attention."

"Really? When were you going to tell me about this?"

"Now you know," was her curt reply.

"How much farther do we follow this way? Until now, we haven't found any game, and I'm sure we can easily bow hunt geese along the reedy shoreline. Is this really necessary?" He sounded frustrated and looked back along the path they had walked.

Sayiina paused. "Maybe you're right, but I would like to continue a little more. I think it will lead us onto the rock bluff above."

"Aye, lass. To the cliff we go then, and no farther."

They stepped out of the woods when they reached the trail's end. Both were struck to find themselves staring at a large stone table placed between two square obelisks of great height. The three pieces stood in stark contrast to the natural world around them. Ragnar was awestruck. The forest had tightly encircled every side of the stones, preventing anyone from seeing the altar. From the river below, there was no question about what it was. Cautiously, the two moved closer to observe the pieces in more detail.

Almost at once, Sayiina stopped in her tracks, cautioning Ragnar, "This place has a dark past. I can sense it."

"How do you mean, Sayiina?"

"My people, as myself, believe all things contain a spirit. Animals, trees, water, and yes, even stone. They can be either good or evil in this world. My feelings are this is a bad place to be. We should leave."

As Sayiina was speaking, Ragnar walked to the stone altar. He could make out animals' shapes and strange runes engraved on its surface. Its antiquity and artistry fascinated him.

Sayiina watched a thick, low-hanging cloud moving unusually swiftly toward their position, enveloping the site. Despite warning Ragnar not to touch anything, she cautiously knelt on one knee, allowing her hand to contact the ground and confirm her instincts.

"Ragnar, we're in danger. We're being hunted."

Ragnar didn't hear Sayiina's last words. An unnatural force gripped his hand, moving it involuntarily over the stone tablet's surface. Spellbound, his mind was lost as in a cloud. His hand came to a rest on one of the animal forms. It was that of the leopard.

"Ragnar, stop what you're doing! That is not an alter your hand should rest upon. It's a sacrificial altar of evil intent."

She raced to his side to release his hand from the spell that held him. In doing so, an image of a cream-colored leopard flashed through her mind. Too late: she heard a low growl from behind one of the obelisks.

Instinctively, she loaded her great bow and pulled it taut. The air was heavy and damp, and she could not distinguish what was beyond a couple of feet because of the thick, dense cloud.

"Ragnar, arm yourself. We're in great danger."

His mind cleared, and he withdrew the two long Yakutian knives from his belt. He, too, could now hear the growl but not place the cat's location. The sound echoed around them in every direction, almost circling, looking for a weakness to attack.

Ragnar went into a defensive crouch, slowly walking back and away from the altar, both knives held out before him.

Sayiina stood tall, stepping warily, ready to unleash a kill shot. In an instant, she saw the face of a leopard breaking out of the mist to her left, coming straight for her. Its fangs were bared, and its razor-sharp claws unsheathed; she moved aside by pure instinct as a huntress, avoiding contact by a breath.

The leopard's abrupt appearance caused her hand, in defense, to release and harmlessly discharge the bow shot. It passed her by with enough momentum to rake Ragnar's shoulder, shredding him deeply with its claws. Having landed safely, the creature immediately turned to face them, growling and ready to spring. Groaning with pain, Ragnar staggered to his feet.

Sayiina saw the wound on Ragnar's back, blood spilling out quickly. "Ragnar," she screamed, "get behind me. The cat smells your blood now and wants to finish with a kill."

As the leopard slunk around them for a position to strike, she noticed a distinct limp. It favored its front left paw. A weakness. Her knives were now drawn, and she moved to circle the leopard, staying on its injured side. They were in an old ritual she knew well, a death dance.

Her eyes locked onto the leopard's, never faltering. Vice-like hands gripped the two finely honed knives, ready to strike like a viper with steeled arms. Muscular legs moved perfectly fluidly, constantly adjusting their position to match the cat's movement in this animalistic ritual. Keeping behind Sayiina for his part, Ragnar moved as one, blades at the ready. When the Amur leopard stopped circling, it sprung like a released coil straight for Sayiina's throat.

Unbeknownst to all, another pair of eyes watched closely, waiting for the right time to strike.

Suddenly, the air exploded in sound and violence as a great Amur tiger leaped from a concealed position nearby. In mid-air, it hit with violent rage, its formidable jaws biting deep and hard on the back of the leopard's neck. The tiger shook the leopard back and forth like a rag as the wounded cat's death screams pierced the air until it was rendered limp.

Still holding its prey in its mouth, the tiger faced Sayiina and Ragnar, almost daring them to take his natural enemy from him. Neither moved a muscle nor hardly breathed. They were astounded, having been witness to this primal ferocity. The great tiger clenched fast to the leopard's neck, turned, and bounded into the forest, leaving the two standing and staring, breathless.

Ragnar was the first to break their silence. "What just happened here, Sayiina?"

"I could give you a detailed account if you wanted one, but I think this was an old score settled between the two cats, and the tiger finished it.

"To this day, in my years as a huntress, I've never witnessed anything to compare. I thought we were going to die. First, the leopard attack. Then, the tiger's appearance. Our gods still watch over us, Ragnar."

"Aye, that is certain, lass, but I want to leave this place before they forsake us for staying too long." Lightly touching his shoulder, Ragnar winced in pain. "But first, I will need some help with my wound."

"Of course. I can dress your wounds until we can find someone who is a healer at our next stop."

So, there amongst the pines, Sayiina tended to his lacerations as best she could and quietly thought back to the blind woman in the lavender tent.

CHAPTER 13

Early the next morning, Ragnar and Sayiina climbed to the crest of a hill and sat down together. Their fingers first touched, then mingled with the green grass. Dew clung to its sides like teardrops might on a child's cheek. Unspeaking, they savored the moment. They breathed deeply, sensing the smell of wildflowers and woven meadowland passing by. Their broad sweeping view was a painted canvas of sunlight, with an array of colors gracing the land. Drifting white clouds filled a bright blue sky. The grassland rose to distant mountains, greeting the morning sky on the horizon. Far and away, a rainbow slowly manifested as a sign of God's pleasure watching over all. Looking down the valley, they could see where the Shilka and Argun rivers met to create the Amur River. This same water they had been sailing on since departing Khabarovsk.

Breaking their silence, Sayiina asked thoughtfully, "What was the word your people say when two rivers meet to create another? I'm trying to remember what you told me before."

"We call it a confluence." Then he turned to look at Sayiina.

She had thrown back her head in defiance of life's challenges, exposing her slightly curved neckline. Her long black hair fell over her shoulders like a dark waterfall might. Sayiina didn't immediately return his glance. He watched her, waiting for a response. Instead, she cast her gaze west to the valley before her.

"Con-flu-ence," she mused. "That is a big word to me. Do you know what the Yakutian people say to that?"

"No, I don't."

Now, turning to him, she spoke clearly. "When two waters, two souls, two minds meet to create something, anything at all, we say they are mating."

Her answer struck him as comical, knowing her sexual suggestion. He laughed, and she did, sharing the humor in it.

"Sayiina, resting here in this fort village has been good for us physically and emotionally. Not just for healing my shoulder, but also for us as a couple."

"I would agree, Ragnar, and I would also like to add spiritually renewing. Mind, body, and soul."

"Aye, lass, you're right. As I see things, we still have a way to go, although staying on the riverways seems the swiftest means to travel."

"I could find no land maps for us in town. All the hunters and trappers I spoke to told me we should follow the Shilka River. It joins with an even greater river the Mongols call the Onon. This, they say, will take us to our destination inside Mongolia. The great monk city of Ulaanbaatar."

"We'll find the way across this land together. No one could cross the land better than you, Sayiina, and I, the riverways. You never explained why it's called the Road of Bones."

"Stories my father told me are that Mongolia is a land littered with bones of the great tusk animal. The people who live there build great stone piles called *obos* on hilltops crowned with these animal bones. When a traveler becomes lost by storm or overcome by heat, these *obos* serve as a refuge. It is said there is, beneath the bones, a secret store of food for survival. These same locations also function as lookouts to the next nearest one. So, a person can follow them and survive."

"Your father was a wise man to pass this knowledge to you. We're traveling into the unknown, and all insight is good."

"How many days' travels to our destination do you foresee?" she asked.

"It's hard to say exactly. Without incident and with friendly winds in our sails, perhaps two weeks, maybe less. I want to reach Ulaanbaatar by early May. At that time, I think many caravans should be traveling the Silk Road west. We could offer protection services for safe passage."

Sayiina nodded reflectively and reached for his hand. He returned her touch.

"Ready when you are, Sayiina. *The Cat* only needs to be loaded with supplies."

"I'm ready."

"Good."

Ragnar stood, adjusting the new weapon he carried across his back.

"Here, let me help you with that," she said with a smile. "Are you expecting trouble on our voyage?"

"Not me, it's just in case. I never throw caution to the wind, lass. When I discovered this cutlass in the back of the blacksmith's shop, I immediately knew it was of good quality and workmanship. Being a sailor, it's more of my weapon of choice. I was never comfortable with a long sword. It's too cumbersome on the deck of a ship."

With that, they headed down to where their catamaran was tied and waited on the Shilka River.

"How is this possible?" Marko demanded to know from the carpenter, Artem. "I sail Major Stroganov's ship, the swiftest on this river, guided by his pilot. The two fugitives are paddling up this river in a canoe. I should have overtaken them and be awaiting their arrival here now."

Major Pavlov, more subdued than his Cossack visitor but no less desirous to know the truth, motioned Marko to sit and told him to control himself. He watched as his portly garrison carpenter, Artem Orlov, sat noticeably uncomfortable before him. The beads of sweat on Artem's forehead looked more like they were from panic than his usual jovial appearance. Perhaps, Pavlov surmised, a result of nervous apprehension upon being questioned.

Artem avoided Marko's glaring eyes, replying instead to Major Pavlov directly. "They travel on an unusual craft by design, Major. One I have not seen on any river or lake before, and it is very swift."

"Really? How unusual?" the major queried.

"Yes, how unusual?! Tell me more!" Marko echoed, violating military rank protocol.

"Shut your mouth, Cossack," Major Pavlov ordered. "I am in charge here, and I ask all the questions as well. Do you understand me? Now sit still and keep your lips shut," he commanded, pointing his finger at Marko.

"Yes, sir," Marko acknowledged, nodding slightly and hooding his hate-filled eyes so the major would not be aware.

"Again, carpenter, describe to me how unusual."

"The craft they sail is more like two slender canoes, separated from each other yet attached by poles. It has a fixed rudder for direction and a single lateen sail, allowing it to sail against the wind. The main mast is also completely collapsible in case of a storm or for concealment. Alone, a knowledgeable sailor could both navigate passage and man the sail as one. It's lightweight and fast, as I witnessed during their escape."

"And you didn't think this information was important enough to tell me?" The major's voice rose noticeably.

"They wanted to berth for only one night. I saw no harm in that, knowing the gendarmes would quickly find them out and question their intentions."

"Did they tell you where they're going?"

"The man said they were traveling upriver to the mouth of the Amur."

"You are aware of the rules of this fort, are you not a carpenter?" Major Pavlov pressed. "We live on the edge of a frontier. There is a Chinese army on the other side of this river. They would overwhelm our position if these crafts gave them an advantage. We are in a struggle for control of our country and our very lives.

"You're extremely fortunate that I need a carpenter in this fortress, or I'd banish you from it, master carpenter," Major Pavlov continued sharply. "Never put your interests before mine again, or you'll be sent to wander the Siberian wilderness alone."

At that, Artem quickly excused himself.

Marko fumed, his left hand tensed on his coiled whip, which cried out to him for release and judgment toward the carpenter.

Major Pavlov sat at his desk, silently considering the open letter Marko had delivered from Major Stroganov. With any means available,

Pavlov was to aid Marko Dragovich in pursuing and capturing two fugitives who had assaulted his guards. The major raised his head.

"Speak, Cossack."

"I can't believe you let him leave without penalty."

"Wants and needs, Cossack—something you have yet to learn. I know you desire to apprehend these fugitives beyond all cost. Your pride is before you, and it's obvious to me. Ask yourself, do you really need to? You could allow them to follow the river with no return. These two whom you pursue are uncommon folk. I see them as very resourceful and not afraid of the unknown land they're traveling on.

"If you make this personal, it may not go well for you. I will honor this letter of marque from Major Stroganov, which you bring before me, as much as possible. Now I ask, what do you want or need from me? Your choice."

Marko stood, looking at the man sitting before him. He didn't see him; instead, his gaze saw through him as if he weren't really there. *He's weak. First, he allows the carpenter to leave unpunished, then speaks to me in riddles of wants and needs. As if I don't know they're the same thing. He's a fool.*

Marko's disdain for Major Pavlov rose within, coupled with the natural conceit he always held for men lesser and weak.

"You're correct, Major, about a man's wants and needs. I want to capture these fugitives, and I need them to pay for their crime. For me, those two words are one and the same. A Cossack sees no difference. I intend to follow upriver to the last fortress at the mouth of the Amur. I'll need to resupply the ship for the journey."

"That'll be done. Is there anything else you need?"

"I need to get a message to the fort commander, alerting him of the two criminals headed his way on the river. I don't want them held; rather, I'd like him to gather as much information as to their intentions as he can. Also, tell him I carry a letter of marque from Major Strogonov."

"I can send a note by carrier pigeon, but there's no guarantee of success. Just a good chance."

"Good. I depart tomorrow if you would do this for me."

Major Pavlov could hear the open disrespect in the Cossack's voice. Both knew it was intentional, but he did not take the bait.

Instead, the major responded, "You'll have what you need by tomorrow. But listen to me now, Cossack. Trouble follows you; do not return here. You're an undisciplined and arrogant man with the rank of corporal. Something you have accomplished for no other reason but perhaps your size and strength of arms. In Russia, we say, 'A bad peace is better than a good quarrel.' You would do well to think about that," he said as he returned Marko's letter.

"See my quartermaster in the garrison and close the door behind you when you leave."

CHAPTER 14

Minutes moved as hours, and the hours flowed into days as Ragnar and Sayiina sailed on the Shilka with the same breath of wind that passed over its waters. Their travels had taken them along the length of the Amur, fed by this river. Side by side, they sailed its winding length, now south by southwest, through a land untouched by time. By the passage of tireless mountain streams was life fed into the Shilka. Its many tributaries carved the earth to gather as a single waterway, forming a mercurial line in its relentless pursuit of the eastern sea. Here, on their travels through the Eurasian steppe, life was good to them in May. It was a time of plenty, and the land provided for all God's creatures, great and small. Spring's bounty sustained new life and renewed hope each day.

These days, Sayiina was their provider and none her equal. Sitting elevated on a small hill, Ragnar was positioned to look behind and down to the river, where the tethered catamaran rested safely. Looking forward, there was a vast expanse of green grassland, sparsely mingled with wildflowers. A bright yellow sun hovered above. In the distance, hundreds of wild horses thundered across the plain, leaving a cloud of dust behind. They raced to quench their midday thirst from the banks of the river below.

He momentarily caught sight of Sayiina at the base of the hill, stealthily moving through waist-high grass. Her bow before her was half drawn, and she did not look his way. He marveled at her skills as a huntress, here in her natural element as a true predator. Compassion would hold her bow in check, but no more and no less was always her way for sustenance. Observing her every move as she graced the green field below caused him to reflect on how far they had traveled together and think forward to the long journey still before them.

Just as suddenly she was lost to his sight, he turned his gaze west. The unwinding ribbon that was the Shilka River disappeared into the horizon. He hoped they would soon reach and join the Mongolian river Onon, which would deliver them to the great Mongol city of Ulaanbaatar. Without notice, Ragnar was startled from his thoughts.

Sayiina dropped two large waterfowl and sat down beside him. She was smiling with confidence, just like a cat who had made a kill.

"Your approach, Sayiina, is as quiet as a bird on the wing. If I cannot see you before me, I might never know you're nearby," he said humorously.

"Good." Sayiina grinned. "This way, you won't take my presence for granted."

"Never." And he turned back to stare out at the great expanse.

Sayiina slipped her arm into his and rested her head on his shoulder. With her heart content, she followed his westward gaze. "The gods provide much in this land. We could stay longer if you wish," she continued hopefully.

"Nay, lass. I know how you feel about this place. I can see you are in your true native land. Your movements are grace and symmetry, and I could watch you hunt all day and never tire. But if we're found here when the first frost arrives, neither of us would be as content. As then, life would be all about survival. I'm not the homesteader type of man if that's what you seek. Only when we reach Norway, God willing, will I furl my sails. I don't belong here; I don't belong to this place."

Sayiina listened as Ragnar spoke. She felt remorseful, hearing his words and knowing he was not living in the moment as she was. His mind was elsewhere, traveling as far as his vision would take him from here. Her gaze turned away from the valley below. She looked at Ragnar. "Do you have any regrets in life?"

"Aye, a few come to mind, lass," he said, slightly taken aback by her questioning. "What would you like to hear from me? Do you want to see me pine for what I have lost in life? That's not a sailor's way, nor mine. But I've lived long enough to rue some past events. Aye."

"Tell me one, Ragnar," she encouraged and pressed her hand into his. "I know you're strong; this would not be an admission of weakness. Perhaps, by sharing your thoughts with me, I can help carry your burden." Her voice was not a dare, more the sound of encouragement, hoping he would open up freely about past events that may have changed his course in life.

Ragnar lowered his face to the earth in thought. "I have two regrets that I often think about." He nodded, searching for his next words, then lifted his eyes skyward and drew a deep breath.

"The first one is old, and I have carried it since I was a boy. It was when my father was slain by a pirate's musket ball in battle at sea. I was there and watched him fall. At that moment, I knew I was alone in a violent world. When I think back to that day, I believe that was when I closed the door to my heart. My childhood was over, and I have grieved his passing all these years. I loved him then, and still today, I wish I could have said goodbye.

"The second regret is more recent. Not two years ago, I took on an apprentice as a sail master. His name was Grigori Romanukski, and he was a good lad. He was a quick and able learner. I know I was a father figure to him, and I tried to guide his moral compass as my father did for me. But I've heard nothing from him since my injury and recovery. I used to walk down to the harbor whenever sailing ships came into port, asking his whereabouts. But no one could answer my questions. It's as if he disappeared from the seas entirely. He was about as much of a son as I've ever had. Now, I wonder if our currents will ever cross again. Sadly, I don't think so. I fear him dead. So, yes, Sayiina, like most seafaring men, I have some regrets."

"Those are heavy burdens you carry, Ragnar—the loss of a father, then an adopted son. But your gods smile on you. I have seen this a few times, and it is one of the many reasons I am with you. You are a good and brave man, more of a survivor in life."

"Aye, I've cheated a watery grave many times." Lowering his eyes, he asked, "Do you grieve Sayiina?"

"Just one. It is also very old but never forgotten." Just when Sayiina endeavored to speak, a gust of wind blew strands of her black hair about her face, partially concealing her from Ragnar's view. She sighed, leaning on his shoulder, softened her voice, and revealed, "I miss my mother to this day. I was perhaps only ten years of age when, on a long summer's day, I held her hand until she passed into the spirit world. The gods were cruel to me, as she was beautiful, and I was forced into an ugly truth with her passing. I had no one in the world except my father, Modun. He guided my path. He raised me and taught me all I needed to survive. It has been a lonely journey until I met you."

"It seems we're two orphans who both carry sadness in our hearts, Sayiina. Learning to accept the things in life that we cannot change makes us who we are today. But I'm also glad that our paths have met. I am sure this journey will test our resolve before it's done. Together, we are strong."

There was something gratifying about his words at times when they were together like this. She recalled Modun's own words of some men. "Still waters run deep." These were proving more true every day.

Ragnar slightly tightened his arm around her shoulder to reassure her of his commitment. Looking down at the two geese lying on the grass distracted him from his reflections. "You know, those two birds won't willingly cook themselves." He chuckled, standing to leave. He held out his hand to her.

She looked up and sighed. "You're probably right, and it's time for us to move on. I don't wish to break this moment."

She reached out, accepting with one hand while pushing away from the ground with the other. She stopped and looked downriver from where they had traveled. "Did you feel that, Ragnar?"

"What is it, lass? Is there something I should know?"

"I'm not sure, but I had a distinct forewarning from where we have traveled."

"What are you saying? Did you see something?"

"No, not that. I've always had a hunter's sense when being followed. You might call it a sailor's hunch, but for me, it's real. Something is coming our way."

"Hmmm . . . how far do you think?"

"I can't say. Tonight, in a week's time, I never know. I can never tell the 'when' of an event. I'm not a seer." Then she pulled herself upright.

Ragnar looked at the river below. "There can't be a living soul within a hundred miles of us on this steppe. This tells me, if your hunter's instinct is correct, any danger to us is at least three days' travel away, even on the most swift and tireless horse. Agreed?"

Sayiina didn't respond to Ragnar's query. Instead, she picked up the geese. "Let's eat, then go from here. I'll even cook today," she said with a smirk. "I don't like it here anymore."

"That's more to my nature, lass. You cook, and I'll make ready *The Cat*."

As they worked their way down the hill, Sayiina looked sullen. On the other hand, Ragnar was glad he didn't have to cook.

CHAPTER 15

With a lively westerly wind at their backs, Ragnar and Sayiina moved swiftly, south by southwest, along the Shilka River. Their passage marked two days of travel since Sayiina's ominous sense of danger behind them. Whether true or not, Ragnar was fully aware that both good and evil coexisted in the natural world. He had witnessed it firsthand, on both land and sea. Although not a seer, she had proven more than once her instincts held true. Over these past two days, her mood was noticeably distant. She was quiet, and so he let her be. Only occasionally would he glance her way, then return his sight to the river ahead.

His left hand touched the river water, letting his fingertips slip through and dance across its surface. There was a slight drop in temperature, and he called it to Sayiina's attention.

"What, Ragnar?" she shouted.

But his attention was quickly diverted to the water up ahead. The twin hulls of the catamaran banged against rolling waves. He stood, and although he didn't see any white water ahead, the sailing had become uneven and the water grayer. Still, with wind and water and trying to navigate, he heard Sayiina calling to him.

"What is it?" he cried out, not taking his focus from operating both rudder and sail.

"I hear a voice calling over the water."

"A voice? Are you sure it's not the wind you hear?"

"I'm sure. It sounds like someone in distress."

"From what direction does it hail?"

"I think it's coming from the fallen tree we just passed. The same one whose great branches sweep the river," she pointed to it urgently. "We need to turn around, Ragnar." Her voice sounded more like a plea.

"I can't turn *The Cat* around in these rough waters; she'll capsize for sure."

"Well, can you do something to help? Isn't this part of the law of the sea you've told me about?"

Her words struck a chord. He had always lived by the unwritten code of sailors to leave none to perish in the deep. She had rightly called him out, and although they were putting themselves in harm's way, he agreed.

"Okay, you collapse the sail and get back onto the outrigger quickly. I'll man and guide the rudder, and with a little luck, the current will hopefully pull us near the tree. When we get close to shore, grab the bow line and secure *The Cat*."

Ragnar redirected their backward drift closer to the fallen tree and shallow waters. Sayiina leaped from *The Cat*, running hard on the beach. She quickly secured the boat to a large rock nearby. He then quickly joined her as she dashed toward the fallen tree.

Ragnar could see someone or something snared in a fishnet. It looked all tangled up in the partially submerged branches. A woman's voice called for help, and then Ragnar distinguished a very disheveled woman hanging from the branches like a fish caught in a net. Somehow, she had entangled herself in both tree and net, with the river's powerful current pinning her there against her will.

"Ragnar, help me free her. She needs our help."

"You're right, lass, okay. But gently, in case any bones be broken."

They freed the soaked woman and briefly lay her on the beach. Even though the midday sun was warm, she was shivering uncontrollably.

"I think too long an exposure in the river water has caused her to chill deep, Sayiina. I'll build a fire to warm her, and she can wrap herself in my bear coat."

"She'll also need dry clothes and food," Sayiina added.

"Well, that's a problem. We don't have any extra clothing on board. But we can give her some of the food rations we carry. Tend to this woman while I go to higher ground to see where the rivers come together and study the waterway. In the meantime, get her out of those clothes and dry them near the fire. Find out what you can about her. Where she's from, her name, family nearby, anything at all would help."

"How long will you be gone?"

"The sun is still high, so maybe two hours. I must study the lay of the rivers ahead and our challenges tomorrow."

Ragnar set about gathering all the driftwood nearby to feed the enormous bonfire he had started. When he was done, he stood to leave and cast a look at Sayiina, who was comforting the ailing woman wrapped in his bear coat. The sight reminded him of her tale of regret. This woman could not be in any better care than with Sayiina, and so he departed.

Walking on the wooden pier, Marko listened to the creaking boards with each heavy step his boot heels made. The sound brought out images of things crushed under his heel. It was a good sound. If there were a single word that might describe his mood this morning, it would be "big." He was invigorated, knowing his size was intimidating to most, whether in simple persuasion or physical violence. His swagger was one of boastful arrogance, and he tossed his head back as he approached the two-masted riverboat he controlled.

His meeting with Colonel Philka Stoochnoff had gone surprisingly well, with few questions asked. Not that he would have replied honestly to the colonel's questioning if pressed. The colonel was a weak man to be exploited. Local soldiers for hire informed him that Colonel Stoochnoff had been given this command post, rank, and entitlement, all through family connections in Moscow. He hadn't earned them from trial in the field of combat. Even more, gossip suggested he hated Siberia and would do almost anything to return to Moscow. After securing full provisions for the ship's crew, the colonel and Marko's discussions turned to where the fugitive's final destination might be.

"Beyond this fort, there is only the open steppe," the colonel informed Marko. "Yes, many villages line the river, but nowhere of importance like here. Look at my maps over there on my desktop," he said, pointing to them. "There's nothing for hundreds of miles in all directions."

Marko leaned forward and carefully scrutinized the maps as Colonel Stoochnoff continued to speak.

"If winter catches them on the steppe, they will perish, as none can survive it. No, comrade, I think the ones you seek have turned back on this river to elude capture," he said with firm conviction, folding his arms behind him and waiting for a response.

But Marko ignored him, as he might be a subordinate. Instead, he pointed to a more distant location marked on one of the maps. "Where is this place?"

"That is the great Mongol city of Ulaanbaatar."

"What lies there?"

"Other than 10,000 monks, not very much." He scoffed. "They have no industry, and their commerce is small. People go there to pray and meditate. Although . . ." He paused, contemplating the map. "It *is* near the Silk Road. This travels east/west from Peking, China, to Constantinople, Turkey. Following that road would help them elude capture and return to Europe. Once there, as you know, they'll be nigh impossible to locate. Of course," he mocked with certainty, "they could not be that bold. There are too many dangers to overcome. Not to mention the cost." Colonel Stoochnoff spoke condescendingly as if he were a man who had endured real hardships in life.

Marko's eyes widened while one hand gripped hard the tabletop edge, and the other balled into a fist. A stark realization crossed his strained thoughts. A large vein beside his temple grew and pulsed noticeably. His head pounded as he was forced to listen to this so-called man standing before him. Colonel Stoochnoff was so full of himself and would not shut his mouth. His ignorance of what real men were capable of accomplishing was stupefying. Marko wanted to yell at him, but to do so would not help capture his hated enemies. So, he remained silent until the nonsensical talk ended.

Now, Marko saw their plan. Colonel Stoochnoff, pompous fool that he was, had shown him their actual destination. North would have them travel the frozen wasteland. South would take them to China, where they didn't know the language or culture, making travel more difficult. East would only find them hunted by Russian authorities. No, he knew they would travel west on the Silk Road. It's precisely what he would do, and now they were beyond his authority.

Marko straightened himself, face expressionless. His hooded eyes turned to stare coldly at Colonel Stoochnoff. "When did you say they were last seen in the fort?"

"Well, since your letter requested they not be held, my gendarmes lost sight of them here not two days ago. Perhaps they slipped past you on the river at night?"

Now, it was Colonel Stoochnoff's turn to rightly assess the Cossack enforcer, who stood arrogantly before him. He was an insolent man who thought he was superior to anyone else. No doubt a brute, with few uses beyond simple coercion, and easily replaced. Major Stroganov's letter suggested that his usefulness to Russia had expired, and given the right opportunity, his conceit would have the better of him. In a word, *stupid*. Stoochnoff would lure him into a trap.

"Is there something you want to share with me before we conclude here?" Colonel Stoochnoff's eyebrows rose above the top of his reading glasses as he stared unmoving at Marko. He then sat down and leaned back, relaxing in his chair, waiting to see if the other man would take the bait.

Marko could sense the colonel was leading him with this line of questioning. Where it was going, he didn't know, but he was hungry enough to bite.

"The fugitives are two days ahead of me and almost within my reach. You outrank the major and could order continued pursuit for me beyond the Amur region. These two criminals need to be punished," Marko said as his free hand lightly touched his *nagaika*.

"Punished? That is an unusual choice of words. My understanding is they are to be brought to justice and hanged. Am I not correct?"

Marko hated himself at this moment for exposing his true intentions for personal revenge, but he quickly recovered. He lowered his head, swallowed some bile, and coughed. "Yes, of course, you are correct, Colonel."

"Your words give me pause, comrade. You are insubordinate in asking for this, are you not?" The colonel's offhand tone was intentionally meant to demean Marko. "Then again, what would I receive in return?" he said loftily, as a princeling might address a peasant.

The room was suffocating; sweat formed on the back of Marko's neck, and his shoulders ached from stress. Head bowed, he answered dutifully, "Yes, sir, you are correct. It's an unusual request. I'm so close to capturing the criminals and, of course, bringing honor to the Russian frontier and justice for its subjects to see. If I had a horse and two men, I could easily hunt them down and return within a week. I am certain of this."

"Horses and men to aid you? You ask for too much, comrade. But I see your great determination to finish the task set upon you. This is obvious to me, and I respect this quality in men." Colonel Stoochnoff stood and turned to the wooden cabinet behind him, retrieving two glasses and a bottle of spirits. He placed them neatly on his desktop. "Look at me now, Cossack, as I speak."

Marko raised his head and, with glazed eyes, looked forward and listened.

"I have in this fort town a position for someone like you. Someone with your persuasive way among peasants. I can and will help you in your pursuit of the fleeing criminals you want so badly. Yes, I can see it is personal with you. But in return, I want two years of indentured service from you. Perhaps even at a higher rank, say . . . sergeant major? Unfortunately, I have no men available to assist you, but I can offer you three horses and supplies. I see it as a very generous offer on my part for your continued military service."

As Marko listened, his mind reeled at the cost of two more years of servitude, especially to this *mudak* of a colonel. It would feel like two years in prison. He could see both the bait and trap set before him. His left hand squeezed his coiled whip, and an ache of discomforting pain reminded him of his shame. He was so close to his intended prey, and he could smell the bait. Yet, the colonel's price of personal freedom weighed heavy. He realized that the colonel's voice had stopped, and he seemed to be waiting for an answer. Although mute, Marko had decided. He would accept the horses, pursue his enemies, kill them, and never return.

"So, do we have an agreement, Comrade Dragovich? Your time in return for 'honor and justice,' as you say."

"We do, Colonel. I would want to depart almost immediately."

"Very good. We will drink to your success." Colonel Stoochnoff cheerfully poured and offered a glass to Marko. "First, you must give these papers to your riverboat pilot, releasing you from Major Stroganov's service. Then return and see my quartermaster. I will make the arrangements for you ahead of time."

The two men drank, quickly saluted each other, and Marko left the room feeling smug. After the door had closed, Colonel Stoochnoff smiled and poured himself another drink. Things had gone exceptionally well with the foolish Cossack. Just as his ally, Major Vasilii Stroganov, had said in a second letter: "If pressed with few choices, Marko could be deceived." Stoochnoff had given the Cossack two choices: life in Russian service or death in the frontier. He chose death in the frontier by his own or his enemies' hand. Either way, removing a deserter's life for three horses was a fair trade.

For his part, Marko strode along the pier with false Cossack pride. Knowing his military bonds were unchained as a beast ran wild, he was relieved. Nothing and no one could stop him in his lust for revenge. For now, the ship's pilot, Vladimir, would be the first to learn a lesson in manners as Marko smacked a taut fist into his free hand.

CHAPTER 16

Wanting to reach higher ground and confirm his suspicions of where they were, Ragnar began his trek. From where he stood on the north bank of the Shilka River, the sandy shoreline gradually rose in elevation, so he started in that direction. The sun's position indicated noon, and he judged there was no real need to hurry. The sweat under his arms and down the back of his stained shirt proved that today would be hot.

It was ironic. He mused how he had partnered with Sayiina, whose knowledge of the land had few equals. He was a seafaring man who knew more of wind and water than the good earth. She was, in many ways, his opposite.

The lay of these open fields, although new to his eye, was not foreign. He slogged up dusty sand dunes above the river, arriving on a flat steppe with thick green grass everywhere. A dark line on the horizon revealed the forested foothills of an unnamed mountain range. Nearby, a large herd of antelope, startled at his sudden presence, quickly bounded away. Overhead, a pair of eagles circled low. He wasn't certain if they were sailing an updraft or hunting for their next meal. The pair represented survival in life as a beautiful struggle. The beauty was their silent motion in the sky, and the survival was for self-preservation. It was nature's endless way.

He felt the sun's heat on his back and removed his linen jersey. Just then, a gray fox darted across his path with no regard for him while pursuing a mouse. He could only laugh while watching the fox give chase, knowing the world around him was alive.

What was it Sayiina had said? *"Life is not bound to life,"* meaning it had no limits. He viewed Sayiina as a free spirit walking the earth. Good things came to the lives she touched, but many before had learned the hard way that she was not to be crossed.

His mind drifted to the Cossack slaver, Marko Dragovich, knowing bad things happen to evil men. That man had experienced her wrath when he assaulted her in the kabak and had paid a painful price for it. Karma!

Ragnar's course took him to the bluff's base, and he found he was now quite a distance from the river. He could no longer hear water flowing, and his sense of direction was momentarily gone. He was standing in a sea of green grass beneath an endless bright blue sky, and had it not been for the bluff, he would be lost. It was hushed, too quiet for his liking.

He felt out of place, then ducked at a sudden intrusion over his left shoulder. Out of nowhere, a large raven swooped silently and sailed right up to the top of the bluff, disappearing over its rim.

"That's my way," he declared aloud.

Upon reaching the crest, all doubts were removed. He could see the confluence where the Onon River became the Shilka River. They were only half a mile away, but the water, under closer attention, was turbulent. Once past this natural curve, the Onon turned hard south and out of sight. He needed to inform Sayiina of what lay ahead, and she might be pleased to know their passage was mostly unimpeded. Surely, that information would put a smile on her face.

So, he retraced his footsteps to both her and the reluctant fisher-woman. Upon his return, his abrupt appearance caught the women by surprise. The unknown woman was sunning herself on his great bear coat, divested of all clothing, and spread out on the sand as Sayiina retrieved her dried clothing.

Speechless, he could only stare at the woman's attractive form. It wasn't just every day he came across a compelling water nymph on a river shoreline. Today was a lucky day, and he smiled foolishly. But this moment passed quickly when his presence was discovered, followed by a shriek from the river nymph, who dashed for cover behind the fallen tree.

"Stop right there, Ragnar, and turn around. Don't you know it's not polite to stare?" Sayiina shouted while gathering up the clothes and passing them to the woman. Ragnar stopped and did as requested, waiting for the all-clear sign from Sayiina. He could barely hear the two women talking back and forth, but only three words stood clear. "All men oglers."

When everyone's dignity had recovered, Sayiina invited Ragnar to join them at the fire.

"What have you learned of her, Sayiina?" Ragnar asked.

"Her name is Zolzaya, and she speaks a form of our Russian language. She likes to be addressed as Zaya."

"Very well. Zaya it is, then. What else did you learn from her?"

"She seems to think her village is not far upriver, in the same way we travel. She also has a home near there."

Ragnar considered this new information a moment before sharing his own with her. He turned away from Sayiina to look at Zaya sitting quietly across the fire, listening to their discussion. He could tell by her demeanor it was her character not to interrupt but instead wait until spoken to directly. She seemed a thoughtful kind of woman.

"How did you come to be here, Zaya?" Ragnar asked.

"A poor decision on my part. That and bad luck. I was retrieving my fish net on shore when a long serpent unexpectedly swam into it, pulling me into the river. I held onto the net a short time but ultimately let go, as the serpent was taking me into deep waters, and there I would drown.

"I swam as far as I could until I spotted this fallen tree, and the river's current did the rest. I hit the tree hard but was exhausted and didn't care. While holding on to its branches as a lifeline, my drifting fish net found this tree and snared me to it. I wearied from trying to free myself when I saw your sail pass by. All I could do was cry out for help. It was my great fortune you heard my calls."

"It was Sayiina who first heard your cries of distress."

With that information, Zaya reached for Sayiina's hand, held it tight, and thanked her.

"Ragnar has good karma, Zaya. Perhaps your rescue is part of something more," Sayiina replied while holding Zaya's hand.

Zaya nodded as someone who understood life's changes and fate, then smiled at her.

"Sayiina, we're only a short distance from where the rivers meet. If we're close to Zaya's village, let's depart now; we can rest there overnight. Zaya can lie across the netting and hold on tight. There's a small area of rough water, but she'll be the extra ballast we need to stabilize our craft. What do you think, Zaya? We could be at your village in time for dinner."

"Maybe it's too soon for her, Ragnar?" Sayiina said.

Zaya stood up abruptly and started walking to the catamaran. Ragnar and Sayiina looked at each other, admiring her spirit for adventure, and followed.

"Okay, so where do you want me to sit my ballast on this boat?" Zaya turned and asked with a grin.

With that, the three set sail immediately, and Zaya was thrilled to be on the catamaran. She was astonished at the speed they were traveling.

"Where did you find this craft?" she asked Ragnar.

"It was a gift from a Russian friend downriver."

Zaya, very impressed, turned to Sayiina, asking, "Does your mate have a brother nearby?"

Sayiina laughed at her question, not in derision but knowing it was a genuine compliment. "I have met and know a lot of men but never one like Ragnar. He is an only child, born of the sea and wind, who sailed into my harbor."

Ragnar listened and occasionally looked at the two women conversing. He thought Zaya was a good fit as a traveling companion for Sayiina and himself, knowing firsthand that Sayiina did not make friends readily. Zaya's shoulder-length gray hair was streaked with black and lifted in the wind. It was in stark contrast to Sayiina's black hair. In his opinion, Zaya was more reserved, whereas Sayiina was brazen. If Sayiina was a raven, then Zaya was an owl.

Shortly, Zaya began to recognize and indicate her village landmarks. So, Ragnar steered their craft onto a sandy beach and dragged it ashore.

"Sayiina, why don't you and Zaya go ahead? I'll stay with *The Cat* and make ready here. I'll not drop the mast until your return and all is to your liking."

"Are you worried, Ragnar?"

"No, I just want to be sure we are staying here and for how long. Our last journey on water will soon be on us, and I don't like surprises."

With that, Ragnar watched as both women turned, walked away, and talked excitedly.

CHAPTER 17

Ragnar did not hear Sayiina's approach. His focus was solely on the condition of the catamaran's rigging. His inspection revealed how worn the netting between the twin hulls had become since the start of their journey. Some noticeable fraying in places concerned him, but more than that, they had no spare rope on board. He rubbed his thumb expertly along each rope line, feeling for weakness and paying close attention to the possibility of thinning.

"Well, are all things, as you say, shipshape?" Sayiina asked when approaching Ragnar from behind.

Caught off guard by her sudden appearance and the sound of her voice, Ragnar realized he had let his guard down. Instinctively, he spun around with his hand on the hilt of his dagger.

"Woman, you have got to stop prowling up on me like this," he chastised and put away his knife.

"Whoa, my man." Then she threw up both hands, with open palms facing forward. "I thought you sailor types could hear the wind whisper your name in a sea storm. Or is that just storytelling?"

Ragnar couldn't decide if she was mocking him or being her cheerful self, so he just frowned her way. "Sorry, I guess I'm tense. Our travels by water will be over soon. I want to be sure I haven't left any loose ends, lass. Ulaanbaatar will be a mark on our journey and perhaps our greatest challenge."

Sayiina watched as Ragnar continued inspecting every inch of the rope line by sight and touch. She thought he sounded stressed. "How do you mean, greatest challenge?"

"Ulaanbaatar, I am told, is a large city of 10,000 Buddhist monks. I do not practice their faith, and what's more, neither of us speaks their Mongol tongue. Ahh . . . I'm probably worrying too much." Then he shrugged.

Satisfied with his inspections, he looked at Sayiina and winked. "Are we staying the night? Can Zaya put us up?"

"We are, and she can. She lives in a yurt on the edge of her village, and right now, she is preparing a meal for us."

"Good, I'm as hungry as a bear. Help me lower the mast. We can then drag *The Cat* under some brush to conceal her for the night."

"Aye, Captain." Then she stood stiffly in his direction, giving a mocking salute for show.

Once satisfied their craft was sufficiently hidden, Ragnar and Sayiina walked toward Zaya's yurt. They kept along the village perimeter, not wanting to draw too much attention. Ragnar counted about forty circular abodes randomly placed. These yurts were all covered in heavy felt with stones on their rooftops. He assumed this was to prevent strong winds from blowing them away.

More impressive were the large corrals nearby, containing hundreds of sheep. Horses were tethered to standing poles outside of each yurt. Walking along, Ragnar felt the day waning like spring in this northern part of the world. A red sky blazed overhead, with the sun setting over the horizon. He turned to Sayiina and put his arm around her shoulder.

"You know that a red sky at night is a sailor's delight?"

With a light laugh, Sayiina replied. "Are you being romantic with me, or is this more a tall tale from the sea?"

"Both. To a mariner, it means a storm has passed us by, and tomorrow will be good sailing. You might say a sign of good luck. We will need all we can get."

"I agree." Comfortable in his arms, she pointed ahead to the smoke rising above the last yurt. "I think I can smell our next meal coming from over there." Sayiina lifted her head and breathed deeply, trying to detect any scent of the meal to come.

At that exact moment, Zaya appeared in the open doorway. "Welcome to my home. Honored guests, you are." Then she threw both arms open wide to give and receive hugs. "Come in, friends. It is tradition for guests to sit on the north side in a Mongolian home. I have prepared a mutton stew for us. It is called *khorkhog*. With added secret ingredients from my garden."

Ragnar and Sayiina looked at one another and stepped inside their new surroundings. The floor was covered in a soft felt, as were the walls. A few small, patterned rugs and animal skins decorated the floor. Simple pieces of furniture were placed for sensible use. Ragnar thought, for all intents, it was a very warm and comfortable dwelling.

Together, they sat with their legs crossed opposite a round metal pot. It was suspended by a chain over a compact fire and supported by a tripod. Smoke from the fire rose straight up and out through an opening in the ceiling.

"I hope you two are hungry," Zaya said as she stirred her stew pot. She then served their meals in wooden bowls.

Ragnar quickly ate zealously. "This is a delicious stew, Zaya." He licked his spoon with perfect satisfaction. "I have never had anything to compare."

"I'm pleased to hear this. It is a traditional Mongolian fare offered to guests, and this recipe has been in my family for generations. Being an herbalist by nature, I grow many of the spice ingredients in the gardens surrounding my home."

Ragnar and Sayiina listened as Zaya spoke of herself, her semi-nomadic people, and life on this vast steppe. She appeared quite different from the bedraggled woman they'd found snared in the fallen tree by the river. He guessed her to be sixty years old, but it was hard to discern. Her gray-and-black-streaked hair was parted in the middle, with multiple narrow braids falling to her shoulders. The light tan color of her skin sharply contrasted against that of darker Mongol people. Her ebon eyes were oval, casting a sleepy appearance. High cheekbones, a smallish nose that rested nicely above full lips. In all, a very attractive woman.

Ragnar interrupted her momentarily and asked politely, "Where do you come from, and where is your family? You don't appear to be entirely Mongolian."

Zaya stood, smiled respectfully, excused herself, and retreated behind a tall tapestry.

"Did I just offend our hostess, Sayiina? Perhaps I broke a custom as a guest."

"I don't think so. Wait for her return. I think there is still more that she wants to share with us, and I see her as a caring woman."

After a few moments, Zaya returned from the other side of the curtain. She had changed out of her domestic clothing, felt pants and vest, into more ceremonial attire. Her garment was a soft leather, knee-length dress adorned with multi-colored beads. In her left hand, she carried a small antlered deer skull on which a flaming candle rested. Her other hand held a long-stemmed bone pipe with a leather pouch. She wore a headdress of pure white fox skin, complete with the head attached. Eye sockets containing green gemstones rested on her forehead and sparkled in the candlelight. Ragnar noted she carried herself with assurance and effortless grace while crossing the room, then knelt before them. Her transformation was remarkable. She now looked like a wild pagan woman in her own right.

Pausing, she looked at both of her guests with a smile.

"My name, you know already, is Zolzaya. In Mongolia, it means fate, luck, and destiny. My father was Russian by heritage. He came to this land fleeing persecution of his government, so he told me." Zaya paused and filled her pipe with dried leaves from the pouch. "My mother was of Chinese and Mongolian descent and a shaman to the people of this village. I am an herbalist; it is my calling. She told me how she was so entranced when my father passed her way. One day, he stopped by, and she put a secret potion in his tea. This caused him to stop running and bound him to her." Zaya giggled at the thought.

"That's a sailor's tall tale, Zaya. I don't believe you," Ragnar was quick to say.

But Sayiina was intrigued. "Perhaps we could talk further when it's just the two of us," she said, winking at Zaya and then smiling at Ragnar.

"It is true. I alone know the secret ingredients. Unfortunately, all three of my previous husbands cannot testify on my behalf. Sadly, they have since passed away."

As she continued speaking, a long-haired, cream-colored cat with the bluest of eyes walked over to her and jumped on her lap. She lightly petted its head, creating an immediate purr.

"This is Kumeer! He keeps my house clear of mice and never talks back to me." Delicately, Zaya picked up a burning twig, touched it to the pipe bowl, and inhaled deeply. She passed it to Sayiina, who drew in the smoke and quickly licked her lips in recognition.

"What is it, Sayiina?" Ragnar asked before accepting the pipe.

"I think it tastes like mint. It has a distinct tang about it. Here, see for yourself."

Ragnar was pleasantly surprised at the result. He had, on occasion, smoked a pipe of tobacco after a meal. But he had never acquired a taste for it; it was too pungent for his palette.

"Tell me, what is your goal in Ulaanbaatar?" Zaya asked as she reached for their now-communal pipe.

"We seek to join a caravan traveling west along the Silk Road, ideally reaching Constantinople."

Zaya puffed on her long-stemmed pipe. Some of the drifting smoke she waved over her face and hair. She passed the pipe to Sayiina, looked at Ragnar, and said, "I know of the Silk Road, but not your destination. First, to start on this road, you must cross a great sand desert. Even together, I think traveling this way alone would be very dangerous. There is only one safe way, and this desert is haunted. It's filled with evil spirits day and night. Do either of you speak the Mongol tongue?"

"No. English, Russian, Norwegian, or Turkish sufficiently."

"That will be enough when you are on the Silk Road, but you must first find, then negotiate with a caravan leader to cross the desert."

"Aye. We want to hire ourselves as soldiers to the wealthy merchants who travel it."

"A good idea, but Ulaanbaatar is a city of 10,000 monks. When they are not in their temples praying to Buddha, they secretly trade in jewels of all kinds. This clandestine trade supports their city, for they produce nothing to sustain themselves. It is an open secret they keep hidden from foreigners. Even if you could speak their language, it is unlikely you would be welcome. To them, you are the unenlightened."

Stunned, both looked at each other. If true by Zaya's account, their journey was over. Her words carried crushing information.

With a worried look, Sayiina told Ragnar, "We can't turn back. We've come too far. I fear winter will catch us on the open steppe, where we'll perish."

"You're right, Sayiina. If Zaya is correct, it won't be easy for us in Ulaanbaatar. But we have few choices, lass."

Ragnar could see Zaya staring at them, unmoving as if to allow them time to understand the weight of their upcoming situation. She was calmly waiting for an expected question. Ragnar turned away from Zaya, then to Sayiina, and back to Zaya. With a tone of humility, he asked, "We are in need. Can you help us in Ulaanbaatar?"

A knowing smile creased her face after Ragnar spoke those words. "I've no objection to your request, as I speak their language. I see it as an opportunity for karma between us. What I do need to know is if you carry anything of value to trade with the monks for passage across the desert."

Ragnar turned back to face Sayiina, who had been quiet throughout their exchange. She appeared highly thankful, almost relieved, toward Zaya.

Reaching into a fold of his shirt, he presented a small gray stone, no larger than a robin's egg. Zaya reached for it and held it between her thumb and forefinger before her dancing candlelight. Instantly, a brilliant white light flashed. Her eyes widened, fully aware of its value. She spoke now as if in a trance.

"I know the true value of this stone, Northman. With this, you have just bought yourselves passage or anything you desire to cross the great Gobi Desert. I have been welcomed to the city of monks in the past to barter my medicinal herbs. I have also established contacts who I can approach to assist you on your journey to the Silk Road."

"Then you're the right woman for us at the right time."

Zaya secured her hand around the stone, slowly closed her eyes, and nodded. "The sooner we leave, the more opportunity for you to find a caravan."

"Let's sail tomorrow, Ragnar. I agree with Zaya. We'll make our fortunes in life and not wait."

"Aye, we can leave in the morning."

Ragnar rose, thanked his hostess, and went to a nearby bed. Sayiina joined him at his side and fell fast asleep, content in his arms.

Later that night, Sayiina was restless and couldn't find any comfort. She turned away from her mate, and in doing so, her fingers found and touched the earth between the felts. A feeling within immediately woke her survival instincts. She sat straight up in fear. Her sudden movement roused Ragnar.

"What troubles you, Sayiina?"

"I don't know. I felt a great evil pass over me."

"Maybe just a bad dream, Sayiina," he offered to comfort her uneasiness.

Sayiina turned to Ragnar and whispered, "My heart is not at ease here. I don't want to be here anymore." Then she lay back down.

Unbeknownst to both Ragnar and Sayiina, Marko Dragovich passed by their yurt on his way to Ulaanbaatar at her very moment of unrest.

CHAPTER 18

Early the next morning, Ragnar, Sayiina, and Zaya set out for Ulaanbaatar. According to Zaya, it was perhaps two full days' journey by sail. More concerning for Ragnar was they would be leaving the catamaran behind. River travel would soon be over, and he was more than a little apprehensive. He had purposefully chosen a land route to return home and now realized it would begin in the monk city. There would still be a lot of arrangements to be made once they arrived, but having Zaya on board was reassuring.

He was relaxed, sitting at the helm of their swift craft, expertly working both rudder and sail in unison. Sayiina and Zaya sat up front, talking idly. They sailed along the winding river through a slowly lifting fog, giving limited visibility. Damp air and a cooler morning made moisture cling to his face and bare arms.

"Keep a sharp eye about, ladies, as I can't get a clear view yet. Damn, morning fog is causing us to sail almost blind."

"Aye, aye, sir," Sayiina responded quickly, then she turned and winked at Zaya. "He likes to have his way in the mornings. Otherwise, like most men, they take spurned advances personally."

"I know. My third husband was exactly the same way. Once a day was never enough, always in a state of rut."

Both women looked at each other and broke out in laughter.

"What in the wind are you two talking about?" he demanded.

"Just woman talk, my man, about how we always seem to uncover big things in the mornings. What should we be looking for?"

"Trees, rocks, or a turn in our course. Anything I need to know for our safe passage."

He shook his head in disbelief at the women's cavalier attitude to the matter at hand. He knew Sayiina was strong-willed and didn't always take his orders from him seriously. With Zaya on board, she was even more distracted, having found a friend.

Eventually, the day's sun burned away the fog, making clear their way. In time, it occurred to him that the winding river was narrowing, and he maneuvered *The Cat* to stay in the river's middle. He called out to Zaya, "Does any of this terrain look familiar to you?"

"It's hard to say. If we could stop and go ashore, I might see a landmark. I know that before we reach our final destination, there is a small village where I rested."

He considered her suggestion and then agreed. A bird's-eye view would better help determine their location, so he turned to shore. Besides, everyone would benefit from stretching their legs.

Zaya wanted to lead the way as she knew what to look for but suddenly stopped. "The village has moved to new pastures."

"What do you mean, Zaya?" He peered about and rubbed his chin.

"Many people of Mongolia are nomadic. They follow the seasons in search of good grazing land for their livestock. It is common for whole villages to relocate, then return years later when the land has been replenished."

"Well, I'll be damned. Is anything recognizable?"

"Yes," she said, pointing west and indicating that Ulaanbaatar was a full day's journey on horseback. "But with swift travel along this river, we might arrive by noon tomorrow."

"Well, there's no time to waste," Sayiina stated and turned away but then stopped. Her gaze fell to rest on a small clump of earth not 10 feet away.

"What is it, Sayiina?" He followed her line of sight.

She walked over to a small divot of earth where her fingers traced out the shape of a horseshoe, and an icy shiver ran down her spine.

"We need to be more wary on our journey. Men and horses have passed this way as early as yesterday. I have a bad feeling about this place, Ragnar. Let's return to the boat immediately and sail with haste to our destination."

With pursed lips and furrowed brows, she turned briskly and returned to *The Cat*. Knowing her, Ragnar shrugged it off.

"She's strong-willed when her mind is set. I see no point in arguing when she's like this. Besides, unlike anyone I have ever met, she has a sense about her. It's almost a primal survival instinct. Aye, Ulaanbaatar can't come soon enough, Zaya and we will need your help navigating our way through its roads."

"Of course, you will have it. The sign Sayiina touched might be an omen, but for good or bad, I cannot say."

As she spoke, she tied her hair up in a more working fashion with a strip of leather, then followed Sayiina. Ragnar didn't talk while watching the two women walk away. Then, nodding, he quickly followed suit.

Later that night, Ragnar was restless, unable to sleep. The dark sky was starless and dull when he rose quietly, moving to the river's shoreline. The water passed before him as a ribbon of black velvet. He reached out his hand, hoping to draw inner peace from this troubling night. He was calmed for a moment and briefly found solace.

Drawing the cool night air in deeply, he could almost sense a palatable taste and was relieved. Wind and water were his bloodlines. Now, he would follow this course to its end. Hearing a slight sound behind him, he turned and looked at Sayiina, not an arm's length away.

"You're restless tonight, my man."

"Aye, lass."

Stepping closer, she put her arms around his waist. "Care to share your thoughts?"

"Tomorrow, we will come to the river's end, and we'll be strangers to everyone we encounter. At worst, no one will acknowledge us, as we are infidels. We must engage a caravan and then travel across half a continent to reach the Black Sea. My list of thoughts is both large and endless on this night."

He then looked into her eyes.

Sayiina placed her hand over his heart. "You worry too much. Yes, there is much for us to do. Let's take one day at a time. I feel Zaya will be successful in finding a caravan for us, and that is our first step. We will always have each other."

He whispered in return, not wanting to break the magic of their moment together. "Aye, lass, forever."

CHAPTER 19

"Stay close and do not be separated from me until we find my patron and a safe house," Zaya cautioned. "Remember, you are seen as infidels, and most will not welcome you. Look to me as your guide."

Ragnar, Sayiina, and Zaya moved through the crowded market, with many darting eyes following their steps openly and covertly. Whispered words in a foreign tongue followed in their wake. As Ragnar could see, the large populace were men whose heads and beards were shaved clean. All wore identical poor clothes under dull, gray-colored robes wrapped around and tied to their left shoulder. He surmised they were Lamaist monks, which Zaya had spoken about.

Littered amongst the teeming crowd were fierce-looking men. Their pointed helmets were adorned with long, thick strands of horse hair protruding from the top. Their body armor of thick brown leather plates was fitted over felt shirts. Many carried a long metal-tipped lance, and all wore a curved slicing saber on their hip. Strangely, there were no women nearby. Perhaps Ulaanbaatar was a male society, and the monks were forbidden to marry. Turning to Zaya to ask about his observation, he waited quietly while she finished speaking to a merchant.

"Have you ever been to a place like this, Ragnar?" Sayiina asked. "There are so many gathered together. It's like four walls closing in on me."

"Aye, lass. You and I are standing awash in a sea of bodies. Canton, China, is very similar to this crushing tide."

"Well, I don't like it. There's no obvious trail to follow. Give me an open steppe with a fresh wind in my hair any day. All here is a distraction, not to mention the pungent odor of dung everywhere. Leaving can't come soon enough. Where's Zaya?" Sayiina's discomfort was palpable, her voice filled with longing for the open steppe.

Ragnar turned to Zaya's last known position behind, then froze. The iron tip of a lance was mere inches from his chest, held by a grim, leather-clad soldier. His feet were braced, ready for a killing thrust. The tension in the air was thick, the threat of violence imminent, sending a chill down Ragnar's spine.

Sayiina moved instinctively and swiftly to Ragnar's side. Her hands gripped hard on the hilts of her two Yakutian knives.

"Keep your blades sheathed. Don't show any threat to these soldiers, Sayiina. We are greatly outnumbered. There are too many," he urged.

When two cold iron-tipped lances pressed sharply against Sayiina's back and neck, she stiffened.

"Scan for Zaya in the crowd. We need her help."

Within seconds, they were encircled by no less than ten stocky Mongol soldiers, each with a lowered lance directed menacingly toward them.

"I see her," she whispered through unmoving lips. "She is moving quickly to us on our right."

At an order, the circle of lances opened enough to allow a more prominent, muscular soldier of some bearing to advance. He had a flattened nose and puffy eyes that spoke of a recent brawl. His right hand clenched tightly in a balled fist as if to strike without warning. His left hand rested easily on the pommel of a large scimitar at his waist.

Unmoving, Ragnar determined that if this was their finest, he was pretty ugly. He strongly detected unwashed body odor, spice, and horse flesh approaching. Even without the man's order, the circle of lances closed behind him. He halted, not 3 feet distant, and commanded with a guttural Mongol tongue, "You two are to come with me now."

Watching silently, Zaya heard the order, aware they would not understand. She cried out desperately, pushing and clamoring to get closer to her companions, "Oh, great lord, oh, great lord, I am their guide through the city. They do not understand our Mongol ways. I only wish to lead them through it." She then threw herself prostrate, face down, as a slave in submission before him.

Flat-Nose partially turned his head in Zaya's direction. "Maybe they should not have arrived with no knowledge," he spat back angrily.

"They only want to find a caravan traveling west on the Silk Road."

"My orders are to bring them to the chief magistrate for questioning. Only he will authorize their safe passage through the city. Now leave before I decide to cut off your head for your impudence, woman."

Zaya stood to leave, bowing deeply to the soldier in charge. She chanced a quick glance toward Ragnar. He watched intently the verbal exchange between her and the brute standing before him. Bowing repeatedly, she threw Ragnar a look of hope by lifting her brows and eyes wide. He caught her meaning and acknowledged with a slight, almost imperceptible nod as she receded into the gathered crowd.

"Disarm both and bind the infidels' hands," Flat-Nose directed his lancers. "If they resist, subdue them. We take them to the jailhouse, where they will be questioned."

The soldiers began closing in on Sayiina. Not knowing their intent, she constantly shifted her shoulders and pivoted her weight in anticipation of an immediate attack. Standing back-to-back with Ragnar, attempting to conceal her nervousness, she whispered, "Ragnar, I have fight or flight burning in my blood. What will it be?"

"Neither, Sayiina. We cannot best all these soldiers and will not get very far trying to flee. Stand down, and we will find another way out. Remain calm; there is still hope for us. Trust me!"

"I will, but . . ." She stopped as more soldiers moved in closer.

Zaya watched as her companions' wrists were leather bound before them and led away at lance point. Still unnoticed and desperate for her friend's safety, she followed them stealthily and at a distance.

Instead of a magistrate's office, Ragnar and Sayiina were walked into a jailhouse. They were placed in thick, hardened bamboo cages. The bottoms of the cages were set in mortar for added strength. The front face of the cage opened outward as a hinged gate. As Ragnar could determine, their prison was 6 feet square and stacked two cages high. He tried peering down the length of the dark hall but struggled to count beyond three cages. His line of sight led to shadow, then obscurity. From the confines of his cell, he discerned very little.

Ragnar's nostrils flared to the acrid smell of old urine rising from the loose straw that lined his cage. His bound hands gripped a thick bamboo stalk hard, shaking and testing its strength. It didn't budge.

"Ragnar, are you there?" Sayiina said calmly.

"Aye, lass, still here," was his reassuring reply.

"Tell me, how did we stray into this hell?"

"Not strayed, but deceived. We're being held in this Mongol prison for unknown reasons and against our will."

"I wish to rid myself from this land and place, Ragnar." Her voice had no fear or quiver, only a strong determination. Sayiina, he knew, was not an animal that could be caged for long.

"With my last glance at Zaya, I am certain she conveyed a visage of hope."

"Good! The foul darkness in this detestable place conceals too much. What do you think the hour of the day is?"

"It's hard to measure, lass. We were led here late in the day. The sun should be down by now. More, where are our jailers?"

Ragnar turned abruptly, seeing the silhouette of a man slowly emerge from the dark hallway. He approached silently, then moved away to a dark corner. Lighting five black candles, he then placed each one on the five points of a red pentagram, possibly drawn in human blood. The candles flickered, exposing a portion of their prison room. Ragnar suspected the man was a Lamaist monk. He had a bald head and hairless face and wore a gray robe. He glided toward Ragnar and stopped to stare. His hands were behind his back, conveying the appearance he had no arms. Ashen skin, wide-set bulging eyes, a tiny nose with thin lips. His most distinctive feature was a strange symbol tattooed on a slightly sloping forehead. He did not speak, then moved to stand before Sayiina in the cage beside him.

Sayiina took one step back, not in fear but in a defensive posture.

"Ragnar, I recognize the dark symbol on his head. This is a black shaman, part of a large secret cult that even reaches Yakutia. He uses the garb of the Lamaist faith to hide his true self. His kind worships black demons and makes human sacrifices to sate his sadistic desires.

"Stay away," she warned. "Or I will kill you with my bare hands."

To Ragnar's surprise, with a neck-jerking motion, the monk raised his nose slightly to sniff the air. He then exposed a split tongue, wiggling it toward Sayiina, much like a snake sensing fear in a victim. Finding none, the monk pulled back his thin lips in a wide grimace, revealing that his front teeth had been filed to needle points.

"Away from me, demon. Go back to the dark realm you came from."

The strange, pale Lama hissed in response and faded into the shadows of the room.

"Steady, Sayiina. The creature is trying to provoke you. He is not the master. Fear is."

Ragnar's words to Sayiina were cut short when the front door of the jailhouse opened. Bright moonlight spilled into the room. Two stocky Mongol soldiers with lances and sabers walked in.

They were quickly followed by a huge, hooded soldier who had to stoop to gain entry. He closed the door but did not immediately reveal himself. He stood with his back to all in the dim yet lurid light of the room.

The cowled figure spoke in a cracked voice, saying, "I never really appreciated timing in life as much as at this moment. I am savoring it and your fate." He sneered before turning his red, hate-filled face toward Ragnar and Sayiina.

Ragnar was stunned and in shock. Sayiina was even more horrified, as if she had just witnessed a fiend from hell in the flesh.

"Marko Dragovich," Ragnar unerringly remarked.

"Yes . . . it's me. You seem surprised. You didn't think you could escape my reach, did you?" he asked. His noticeably strained voice croaked, then coughed, sounding exhausted.

"It seems your luck has truly sailed its course away from you. While my fortunes have been increased, northern dog," he said, purposefully growling out the last two words. "Get me *koumiss*," he ordered the two soldiers, who left immediately.

Ragnar ignored his insults. Instead, as a master painter, he scrutinized Marko as if he were a finished portrait. His gaunt face was burned red from the sun. Parched, cracked lips, paired with a raspy voice, indicated severe dehydration. Still, he was very dangerous, although he seemed to be missing the arrogant superiority usually associated with him. If there was a word to describe his countenance, it was fatigue.

"How did you know where to find us?" Ragnar asked.

"Do you think I'm stupid, Northman? North would have taken you into the frozen wasteland; South, you are in China, whose language has one hundred different dialects. East, and you would have had to run a gauntlet of both Russian and Chinese land and river patrols. You would never have reached the mouth of the Amur River without detection. No, your fugitive path would be west because it is exactly how I would travel to elude capture."

Ragnar said nothing. Marko walked stiffly toward Sayiina's cage and pressed two fingers to his cracked and swollen lips. He stopped, with only an arm's length between them, glaring with burning and hate-filled eyes. Marko seemed to shake angrily but did not take his eyes away from her.

"What I didn't expect was the swiftness of your rivercraft. You were always one step ahead."

Marko lightly touched, almost caressed, the coiled whip on his left hip.

"I only arrived here just this morning, with barely enough time ahead of you to set a trap for your capture. But I did, with my new Lama friend here. So easily corrupted. I see you have already met him. He doesn't speak much, but with coin and promises of more, he surprisingly speaks an older Siberian dialect. It is, of course, completely forbidden in his culture. Whatever that might be."

The white Lama hissed at Sayiina with this remark. The same two soldiers returned and placed four jugs of *koumiss* nearby. Ragnar clearly overheard Sayiina's defiant reply, "I dislike your little friend, Cossack, but I hate you even more."

Marko was infuriated by her arrogant words, and his face contorted. Blood broke free from his lips. He raged at Sayiina, screaming caustically, "You'll pay, Yakutian bitch. You've shamed me for the last time. The pain you inflicted on my hand is nothing compared to the shame I've had to bear. First before my men, then the people of the village. Somehow, you bested me with trickery or witchcraft." Then he added, with contempt, "And you—a woman!" He coughed and spat bile onto the dirt floor.

"And I could easily do it again," she mocked.

"Sayiina, don't taunt him."

Ragnar saw the hatred welling up again in Marko's face. He was a volatile man, easy to read. Worse still was the significant disadvantage they were at. Caged, weaponless, hands bound, and outnumbered before their enemy. He couldn't imagine a worse situation to be in.

Desperate to distract Marko's rage from Sayiina, Ragnar pressed his face to the bamboo cage. "Over here, Marko, I'm the one you want. Deal with me."

Marko turned, trying to regain control of his shaking. "You're right, of course," he replied hoarsely.

Unsteady, Marko reached for a bottle of *koumiss*, carefully put it to his parched lips, and deeply drank the strong white spirit.

"I am going to kill you," he said, peeking through bloodshot eyes and drinking more.

The Lama moved to Marko's side and whispered in his ear.

"But only last. First, I will break your mate's will to mine and give you every opportunity to witness it. Grab her arms and bring her to me," he ordered the soldiers. "If she resists, beat her!"

Ragnar could hear Sayiina's struggles. The thud-like sound of a fist to a gut resulted in no further sounds of resistance. The two soldiers half dragged a stumbling and bent over Sayiina from her cage. The wind had been knocked out of her, and she was trying to catch her breath.

"You'll pay for that, Cossack," Ragnar yelled in rage and charged the gate of his cage.

Marko laughed while drinking more of the *koumiss*. "From where I stand, I don't think so."

He pulled down a large metal hook attached to a thick rope overhead, then stopped when at shoulder height, then ordered Sayiina's bound wrists to be set into the hook. Satisfied, he immediately heaved, raising the hook and bringing her arms above her head. Then, just a little higher for discomfort, so she could only stand on her toes.

Sayiina let out a small groan. Ragnar's eyes darted between his struggling mate and the drinking Marko. He could clearly see Marko's intentions. His left hand frequently rubbed, almost soothed, his whip like a pet snake. Marko's eyes narrowed on Sayiina.

Violently shaking a bamboo pole with both hands, to no avail, Ragnar yelled, "You'll pay for this evil, Marko!"

Fully aware of her situation, Sayiina struggled to free herself but failed. Her head turned left and right to find her bearings.

Marko took a large drink and then set the bottle down. Swaggering slightly up to Sayiina, he licked his now bleeding and parched lips but did not look away. With contempt, he replied, "No, Northman, no. This is my arena, and you are my prisoners here.

"Now it is my turn, Yakutian witch. Now you will feel pain, then shame, just as I have." Stepping back, he ordered the soldiers, "Strip her to her waist."

Both proceeded quickly with a practiced lust, ripping and tearing her bodice and shirt until fully exposed for all to see. Sayiina's full breasts swayed as her hands were tethered to the hook. She struggled anxiously but found no way to free herself.

The white monk released a long hiss in gleeful anticipation of what would come next. Marko ordered the Mongol soldiers to leave, and to Ragnar they went reluctantly. Once again, Marko reached for the bottle of *koumiss*, this time draining it and watching it shatter when he tossed it against the wall.

He spoke aloud to no one. "In my homeland of Ukraine, this whip is called a *nagaika*, or flexible weapon," he slurred, then released the coil. "As young boys, we practice every day until its discipline is mastered."

He sent the whip cracking across the air, inches from Sayiina's neck.

"I'll kill you, you son of a brothel whore," Ragnar shouted angrily.

Better positioning himself, Marko laughed. "Try not to struggle too much, witch. It will cause your skin to sweat. I can tell you, my *nagaika* has been crying for the taste of your flesh every day since you impaled my hand on the bar. Wet skin only makes the lash taste sweet. Now you pay, bitch."

He released the whip with violent expertise, wrapping it as a coiled snake around Sayiina's neck, ending in a snap.

Sayiina screamed.

Marko's uncoiled whip revealed a pale, red circular welt around her neck. She was gasping for air as if a choking hand had removed itself from her throat.

"Sayiina, stay strong," Ragnar called out. "Don't let him break your will. I'm still here for you."

Marko reached for another bottle of *koumiss*, tipped it to his lips, and drank heavily.

"I will break her will, Northman, and she'll do anything I say to stop the pain. Everyone has a pain threshold, and I'll find hers. Then, when beaten down, I'll mount her as a stallion would a mare."

On hearing this, Ragnar raged like a confined animal, continually ramming his shoulders into the gate of his cage and throwing his whole body at it. His efforts produced nothing but self-inflicted pain. He might as well scream into a storm.

Again and again, he witnessed Marko's cruel deliverance. He did not proceed quickly. Each lash stroke was skillfully directed to the most tender of places. Her lower spine, underarms, and across her breasts. He was a pure sadist at work.

After what seemed an eternity, her screams became whimpers. Where they crisscrossed her back, the ugly red welts seeped blood. Finally, there was no sound in the room—only staggering boots on a dirt floor with a drunk Marko swaying in them. Saliva dripped in satisfaction from the corners of the white monk's mouth.

Ragnar heard Marko from a corner of the room.

"My arm wearies. I am satisfied with my work today. Help me drag her to the cage, monk, then leave. I will renew her punishment tomorrow."

Ragnar watched as they unhooked and dragged her torn and bleeding body, dropping her as a grain sack onto the rank-smelling floor. The monk turned and silently exited the torture chamber.

Marko crossed the room wearily and sat heavily on a wooden chair. The long, stressful journey across much of Siberia and into Mongolia had taken a physical toll on him. Consuming too much of the fermented liquid *koumiss* added to fatigue and cloudiness. Only raw, unfettered hatred for Sayiina kept his mind aware . . . until now.

His head nodded up and down, saying nothing. Finally, it drooped still. His mouth open and slack-jawed, Marko passed out in the chair.

Ragnar heard Sayiina moan. Her voice carried great pain with it when she said, "Ragnar, I cannot go on."

"Sayiina, stay alive. Do not let your soul leave. I can't live without you."

"I'm being torn apart, Ragnar. I hurt badly."

Helpless to aid Sayiina in escaping what was indeed to come tomorrow, Ragnar feared what a healthy, revived Marko Dragovich would do. It terrified him. Kneeling as if praying, his fingers wove tightly into each other, and he searched his own soul, seeing his mortality was near. With a bowed head in submission to his fate and all hope gone, he spoke to the only gods he knew: the sun, the wind, and the sea. The only life he had ever known until Sayiina. In the darkness of the room, his heart fell heavily in despair.

For unknown reasons, his thumb nervously rubbed the black stone ring gifted to him by Ayaana in Petropavlovsk. A tingling on the back of his neck snapped him out of his depression, and he stood.

Something had changed.

"Who's there?" he called out.

"You summoned me, mariner," came the softly spoken words from behind.

Ragnar spun on his heel to see a dark specter standing before him. His mind raced in fear. It looked like a reaper of souls. The figure's black cape and cowl concealed his features.

"What are you? How did you come by here?" Ragnar asked uneasily.

"What am I? A wisp of smoke, a shadow dancer in your world, perhaps a shapeshifter. What do you see?"

"Something like a man, but more. Not human. Do you have a name?"

The specter let out a heavy sigh. "I have been called many names. Tonight, call me Kane."

Ragnar stiffened on hearing the name and was confused. It was a common enough name. "You look to have a sinister aspect and to be feared. So be it if you are called to assist in ending my days. I only ask that you end Sayiina's life first, then mine. She has suffered enough from the hands of evil, and I am afraid she may be dying." A shudder ran down his spine at the thought.

"You are gifted, Northman. You possess something many shamans or mages greatly desire. With this object, I can be called to assist the owner when the moon is full and a soul is in great despair."

"I have nothing of value. All I have is a love for my partner in the cage next to me."

"Some might be willing to give up an eye for an eye, as you say. You carry a powerful ring on yourself. It is known as the Eye of the Raven. There are only two such stones in your realm, and you possess one of them."

"Take the ring." Ragnar held it before Kane.

"The ring means little to me. It can only be worn by someone of this worldly plane. What do you need?"

"Our cages are locked, and our hands are bound."

Kane raised his left hand as a wave through the air, releasing Ragnar's tied wrists, and the gates of the cage swung open without a sound.

Rubbing his tender wrists, Ragnar looked at Kane.

"There is an evil, cold-blooded heart beating in this room." Ragnar pointed to the slumbering Marko. "I wish to end it now."

The dark specter stared in that direction.

Ragnar re-armed himself with his weapons. From his belt, he withdrew one of his two sharp, long knives and positioned himself behind a slumped and sedated Marko. It would be grim work, but Ragnar saw it as the lesser of two evils. Either Marko died swift and clean by his hand now, or Sayiina would die a horrible death by torture in the morning. He would let his God be the judge of his actions tonight.

With that thought, Ragnar grabbed Marko's top knot and pulled back to expose his neck entirely. In the same motion, he slit his throat wide and deep. Marko briefly opened his eyes, astonished, only to hear Ragnar whisper, "You should never have followed us, bastard. Now you die with no dignity."

Ragnar released his hand, with Marko collapsing on the floor. Blood spurted profusely, pulsating from his neck.

He ran to Sayiina to comfort her, kneeling at her side. Her wounds were severe. She would need time and medicine to heal. He picked her up gently and carried her slumped form across the room to the front door. She groaned.

He paused before Kane and nodded, grateful for his aid. When Ragnar reached the threshold, he turned to say goodbye, but Kane was gone as mysteriously as when he'd arrived. Only his somber, hollow voice hung in the air. "Fair winds."

Zaya sat in a shadowy corner of a building across the street as Ragnar and Sayiina staggered into the moonlight with obvious difficulty. She had wrapped herself in a dark blanket and crouched as small as possible, as a beggar might, drawing little attention her way.

"Ragnar," she called out hoarsely.

He turned toward his name and watched as Zaya ran to them.

"This way, follow me," she said, helping to support Sayiina.

"I have horses and secured a safe house. How badly is she hurt?"

"Bad. She'll need time to rest and medicine to heal."

"I have powerful medicine for her. But you need to know the last caravan leaving on the Silk Road West departs at midnight in three days. There is still much to arrange before then and no time to waste."

CHAPTER 20

With great care, Zaya applied a poultice to the wounds across Sayiina's back. Ragnar's presence in the room was her reassurance that Sayiina would survive her terrible ordeal. She would need him in the days to follow.

With genuine concern, Ragnar asked, "How is she, Zaya?"

Without looking up, Zaya continued to apply the remedy gently. For three days, she had cared for and redressed Sayiina's bandages, using both ointments to ease her pain and crushed herbs to form a healing salve.

"Physically, she is improving every day. She is young, and her life force is strong."

Zaya stood slowly and motioned Ragnar aside. She spoke in a whisper. "I am more concerned for her mental well-being, as she has not yet spoken. I am afraid the scars in her mind and across her soul are far worse. She will require more time before she is whole."

"How long?"

"I do not know. Only she has that answer."

"Well, we leave tonight. Can she ride?"

"She can. I have also prepared additional medicines for your long journey home. She will need all of them. Remember, the heat of the midday sun will be the worst of it."

"You've been a good friend and a steady hand in our time of need. I would wish you fair winds and a calm sea wherever your travels take you."

"You saved me in a desperate time. I am glad to have assisted you in yours. But I will not say goodbye, not yet. At midnight, I will bring your horses to you. Everything you must have to survive the desert has been prepared. It is a Turkish-led caravan, and that's good, as you all want the same destination. One last thing, Ragnar." She retrieved a small black silk veil from the sleeve of her shirt. "She may be required to wear this mask when near Turkish men. Their Muslim faith requires all women to do this." Then she handed the veil over to Ragnar. "It is called a hijab."

"I don't know how to pay you for all you have done, Zaya."

"Not to worry about fees, Ragnar." She winked. "I took one of three shards of the robin's egg as my payment when I had it broken. The monks took one, and your caravan owner has received the third." Then she held open her hand as proof. The small shard was shaped like a crescent moon. The inside curve was crusted with brilliant diamonds, and the outside was perfectly smooth.

"I like your choice, Zaya. I hope it's charmed like you," he said with a thoughtful smile.

Politely, Zaya returned his smile. "I think I will make a pendant of it, then infuse a spell to ward off evil spirits and perhaps attract a fourth husband."

Ragnar chuckled. "I hope you didn't share your mother's secret tea recipe with Sayiina."

"No need to worry about that, Ragnar. She doesn't need it. I see good karma between both of you."

"Well, good fortunes to you and your future husband. I will expect you here at midnight then?"

Zaya nodded, then quietly exited the safe house into the night.

With a heavy heart, Ragnar sat down beside Sayiina. She lay on a cot on her side, facing away from him. Her breathing was easy and relaxed, and her eyes were closed. Reaching out, he held her warm hand, wishing away her pain. But the reality was, he couldn't.

"Sayiina, I know you can hear me. Zaya tells me that your body is healing. I'm truly sorry for what happened to you in the jailhouse. Marko will no longer haunt our footsteps. I ended his hateful life while he slept. It was a murderous deed, but I had no choice. I took his life away so you would live, and I have no regrets. You'll never be able to forget Marko's savage cruelty toward you, and nor will I.

"In a few hours, the last Turkish caravan departs from here. Zaya has made all the arrangements for us. We can make our own good memories together if we sail our course. You don't have to speak. I understand you'll need more time to heal both body and soul fully. Only nod, so I see you understand my words, and we travel as one together."

Sayiina opened her eyes and blankly stared at the felt wall before her, then nodded. With her indication, Ragnar lay down, waiting for midnight.

From his glass hukkah, Tarkan Ozturk casually drew hashish smoke into his lungs. Exhaling, he watched the smoke drift upwards, only to redraw it into his nostrils. He occasionally allowed himself a true self-indulgence before his caravan's departure, and only once had all necessary arrangements been made. Tonight was one of those nights. All had been made ready by his caravan master, Hasad Karga.

His thoughts drifted to when he was a boy, living in his father's house in Constantinople. Uncle Okan, a very successful traveling merchant, often stayed with them. He would sit quietly, listening to every word of his travels to distant lands. Tarkan, a rapt listener, was always fascinated by tales of savage desert people whose sorcery could turn day into night. Or rivers filled with jeweled stones, just for the taking.

Before long, his uncle's wild stories had convinced him of his destiny. After every visit, he would ask his father if he could travel with his uncle. But his answer at all times was no. His father wanted him to follow in his footsteps as a minor government official in the tax collection department. Like opening an old wound, Tarkan's repeated attempts only angered his father more.

In his sixteenth year, his father and uncle called him to a meeting, offering to give him a different perspective of life in a caravan. Uncle Okan talked of the real hardships men and beasts endured. The lack of water when crossing the desert. A cruel, relentless sun. Murderous bandits and being stalked by lions and wolves. All this and the stench of sweating camels and pack mules, day upon day for months.

When Uncle Okan had finished speaking, both waited for his response. The world seemed a lot more grim. At this time, Tarkan didn't fully realize his father was testing his resolve to make the incredible journey.

His father broke the heavy silence invading the room. "Do you still want to travel after hearing of the hardships and dangers, Tarkan?"

Something in his father's tone of voice suggested this time, he had a choice. Shocked and sitting upright, Tarkan's eyes widened and looked at both men, who sat motionless, expressionless, and waiting.

"It's a simple yes or no answer, Tarkan."

"Yes," he blurted out, grinning ear to ear.

His father turned to Okan reluctantly. "It's done then, brother. Your tall tales have won over my son. But only one journey, Tarkan," his father warned. "It will take two years of your life to complete the road to China and back. Allah willing, you will survive all the dangers. I will pray for your safety and safe return every day."

That had been almost twenty years ago, and many caravan journeys since. His uncle had taken him under his wing and shared all his trade knowledge. Tarkan learned much by his side. First, the essential trade languages of Russian, Iranian, and Mandarin, then many people's different arts and cultures. However, the true value of trade was how to read both body language and eyes.

The camel herders taught him equally as long as they had extra willing hands to help them. After his first trek to China, he was well-versed in mercantile trade and never looked back. Now, he was the caravan owner, once again waiting to depart that night for Ulaanbaatar.

He regarded the jewel-studded stone in the palm of his hand. It was a shard and sickle-shaped as a moon. Its back was perfectly smooth and gray. The inside crescent was crusted with diamonds. It was a stunning piece of jewelry worth a small fortune. He had accepted it as payment for the safe passage of two pilgrims to his home city of Constantinople. As a rule, he did not accept pilgrims this way. Merchants and mercenaries only, as he found pilgrims too needy. His was a smaller, swifter camel train with twenty-five merchants, their loaded beasts, and twenty-five of the best Tajik mercenary's money would buy for protection. The late request made him reluctant, but their form of payment was very compelling. They must be very wealthy to purchase a place in his caravan in this manner. So he agreed to their offer and now awaited their arrival.

A sudden rap on the door of his yurt turned his attention. The familiar voice of his caravan master, Hasad, requested entry.

"Come." As Hasad entered, Tarkan knew immediately that something concerned him. "What worries you, friend? Is everything made ready for our departure?"

"It is. We can depart any time, but . . ."

"Just say it!" Tarkan demanded and crossed his arms.

Hasad stiffened, unaccustomed to the owner's harsh voice. He deferred by lowering his gaze and placed both hands behind his back. "Are these two late pilgrims necessary? I fear they will hold us back."

"Did you purchase the horses for them?"

"The best of the Mongol breed available, Tarkan, as you requested. A large mule also, to carry the food and supplies they will need for their journey."

"Then Allah will determine whether they survive the journey, not us. I also insisted they introduce themselves before we depart, and they should be here now. Wait with me and judge them for yourself."

Two raps on his door, a pause, and two more from his Tajik bodyguard outside signaled his pilgrim guests had arrived. The door opened, allowing them to enter. Shrewdly, Tarkan watched their every approaching step.

He was surprised to see one of the pilgrims was a woman who correctly wore a hijab to conceal her features. She was tall and square-shouldered, with muscular thighs, unfettered black hair, and bright coal eyes. She carried herself as a lioness might, from the Barbary Coast, North Africa.

The man was as tall as him, but here their similarities ended. A distinct feature was his white hair and green eyes. Broad shoulders tapered down to a narrow waist. A barrel chest and big knotted hands, swinging freely in a brazen swagger.

Both had penetrating gazes as if evaluating everything, including himself. Both stopped before him. They were not simple pilgrims as he had anticipated. No, these two foreigners moved as predators might and were not to be underestimated.

"*Selam*, in the Turkish language, or *privet*, in the Russian tongue?"

Ragnar responded, "*Privet*."

"My name is Tarkan. I am the owner of this caravan. Welcome. I'm told everything has been made ready for you. Horses, food, and provisions are necessary for our journey's first part."

"We have everything we need. My name is Ragnar, and my mate is Sayiina."

They all shook hands.

"Your jeweled offering for provisions and safe passage is generous. As we travel the Silk Road, you will want for nothing."

With a sweep of his hand, Tarkan introduced Hasad. "This is my caravan master, Hasad Karga. He will lead the way."

Hasad nodded politely.

"Might I ask how you came into this jewel's possession?" Tarkan asked.

"We discovered it by chance in a Yakutian cave along our way."

"Really! A simple cave?" Tarkan lowered his head and raised his brows, peering directly at Ragnar. "Are you trying to trick a fellow traveler? Are you telling me that the caves of Yakutia are littered with gems for the taking?"

"No, I don't tell stories to strangers. And no, the caverns are mostly dark and damp. It was a once-in-a-lifetime opportunity, or call it a sailor's hunch."

Tarkan held his glare to Ragnar and reflected on his words. "I'm a traveler in life and have heard of this Yakutia land but never seen it. Perhaps one day I will pass by a cave filled with diamonds." He then threw back his head and laughed aloud, revealing a less severe persona to his guests.

"Your mate is wise to wear the hajib among Muslim men, who would otherwise openly insult her. But I appreciate you are infidels, so the same rules do not apply to you. In my tent, the hijab is not necessary."

With his hand, he indicated Sayiina should remove it. It surprised him when she removed her hijab but also pleased him. He felt an instant attraction to her, even beyond her feline beauty. The vertical scar on her cheek confirmed his initial thoughts that her bearing was as a woman warrior.

"I know you are not simple pilgrims. Too much confidence exudes from both of you. I see it in both your eyes and your gait. Why you would need my protection is uncertain to me. It seems I would need protection from you. You both strike me as soldiers of fortune. Am I wrong?"

"Our answer is simple, Tarkan. We don't know the way to Constantinople. Not the deserts, mountain passes, nor the many languages of the people who live along the Silk Road. We need a guide."

"And Hasad will provide this. He is the best. We leave in one hour and move west to Karakorum, then across the desert of the Altai Mountains."

"I was told we would travel south and over the Gobi Desert, no?"

"That is a ruse. I never give out exact information to those who may do me harm. We travel light and swift."

He watched as Ragnar and Sayiina nodded in agreement. They then turned to leave.

"Oh, one last question for Sayiina, if possible." He used a silky voice. "Where do you come from? Who are your people? I have never encountered anyone as exotic as you. I have traveled to many lands filled with beautiful women."

The obvious compliment did not go unnoticed by Ragnar, who quickly announced, "She is spoken for."

"Yes, of course she is. It is my simple way of expressing approval of the finer things in life, friend." Then, as a lure, Tarkan smiled in her direction.

Sayiina instinctively sensed the tension in Ragnar, and it was growing rapidly. A quick glance at him confirmed her suspicions. He stood perfectly still, slightly tightening his lips and eyes and glaring at Tarkan. She stepped forward and spoke proudly for the first time in days. "I am Yakutian. They are my people. My mother was Turkish, my father Yakutian."

"That is very interesting." Tarkan pulled on his chin whiskers for a moment. "Hmm, that is of real interest to me. Your Turkish bloodline would answer to your height, and your Yakutian heritage gives you your original skin color and appearance. Do you like to hunt?"

"I am a hunter, tracker by profession. It is an instinct flowing in my blood."

"Excellent. Do you like to hunt with falcons?"

"I have never hunted that way. I have yet to learn it."

Tarkan continued. "Well, I just happen to have two of my favorite peregrine falcons with me. They are from the same nest and hunt as a pair. Perhaps you would like to join me on a hunt with them? It can be very exhilarating."

"Perhaps," she replied evenly. "If the time is right."

Tarkan smiled, delighted at her positive response.

Turning away, she walked out with Ragnar at her side into a cool, dark night.

"Do you think he's handsome?" she asked in a light, quizzical way.

"How would I know? I don't see him that way." Sayiina slipped her arm into Ragnar's. "I'm glad you have found your voice. I was becoming worried for your mental health."

"I want more time for healing. But when I saw your anger building, I knew it was my time to speak out. What are your thoughts on our caravan owner?"

"I don't like him," he said with contempt. "Way too charming, and he thinks a lot of himself."

"Tonight, why don't you tell me a fine sea tale with a happy ending? How about the story of the bastard you killed after he hurt me? And how did you escape from your cage?"

"Ah, just an old sailor's trick, lass."

"Hmm." Sayiina looked at Ragnar suspiciously while walking toward their horses.

Tarkan watched them walk away into the night. "I think she would make an excellent fourth wife for me, Hasad, or maybe a consort. What do you think?"

"The white-haired infidel has jealousy in him and is very protective of her."

"I would agree. But more than one pilgrim has been swallowed by the desert, never to be seen again."

CHAPTER 21

The city of Karakorum was a shadow of its former greatness, a city in slow decay located in the center of Mongolia. The luster of this once-thriving city had long since disappeared. Dilapidated buildings, given up and abandoned by their owners, were left unused and unrepaired. Roads and cobblestone walkways were now weed-infested and unusable because of shifting geological movements under the earth. Surprisingly, a few temples of worship were littered throughout the inner part of the city, having survived either by chance or better design.

After the exodus of the great Kublai Kahn and his people, only 1,000 monks remained, along with 200 female slaves. These women were used to do the monks' bidding and assist in their perversions. These were not true monks of any good faith. These men were sorcerers, practicing the pure evil of the dark arts deep within their temples. They could not relocate with the great Kahn, as their power was drawn from the same ground they had been infusing with dark spells and human sacrifices. They would have to leave their powers behind and be forced to start anew to go elsewhere. In the end, they chose to stay. Over time, only three of the most powerful sorcerers remained.

In the desert, Ragnar and Sayiina led their horses to drink at a bubbling artesian well. Their caravan leader, Hasad, informed them they would rest there for the night, which suited them both just fine. Ragnar stood still, placed his hands on his hips, and arched his back until he heard a small crack.

"This desert has to be the worst of our journey. I can't imagine a grimmer land to cross over. No birds, wildlife, or vegetation to be seen."

"What are you saying? Are you missing the old salty days at sea? Too late to turn back now."

"Well, you're right about not turning back. Life's too short; besides, we are traveling over a sea, don't you think? It's just not what you see, but a sea of sand. It's good that our caravan master knows precisely the way to each watering hole. I wouldn't want to be cast adrift in these dunes. A person might go mad before dying of thirst out here."

Before Sayiina could reply, a Tajik mercenary approached Ragnar for his attention. He nodded, spoke briefly in a broken Russian dialect Ragnar could scarcely understand, and departed. Sayiina watched the brief exchange while loosening the straps under her saddle flap.

"What did he want?" she quietly asked after he walked away in the direction of nearby soldiers. "I don't trust any of those Tajik mercenaries. Something about them tells me they have low morals. A woman's instincts can read men pretty clearly."

"Seems our host, once we've set up camp and settled ourselves, has invited us to speak with him tonight. He is also sending someone over to brush down our horses for us. I said okay."

"That's generous of him. Do you trust him?"

"I trust few people. For me, trust has to be earned, not just awarded on someone's word. No, I trust you, me, and maybe our horses, lass, in this caravan. Certainly not the far-too-charming Tarkan Ozturk."

With a wry smile, Sayiina said, "I detect a little jealousy in your voice, Ragnar. Could I be wrong?"

"Our Turkish host keeps pushing his boundaries with me, especially when it comes to you. All his flirting tells me he thinks a lot of himself when around women. Since you are the only woman in the caravan, he must feel compelled to share all his wisdom and wit with you. Doing this, he shows me no respect."

"His stories bore me, Ragnar. He is a boy compared to you." She slipped her arm around his waist to reassure him.

"Am I jealous? Probably, but I won't show it. We still need him to lead the way across the desert. I could compass our way west anytime, but I might never find the next watering hole. No, I won't say anything yet. He has all the advantages over us. But before we part ways, I'll privately share some carefully chosen words with him."

He then loosened his horse's saddle straps. "Let's unload the mule and build up our tent for the night, Sayiina, preferably upwind from any camels. I find these two-humped Bactrian beasts stink after a day of travel."

"Fine by me. I couldn't agree with you more. I'll lead the way."

Later, in the early part of the evening, a young soldier came to their fire. Sayiina was the first to observe his approach and stood to acknowledge him. But he shunned her, choosing instead to speak directly to Ragnar. After a brief exchange, Ragnar indicated by hand that his horse was the sire and hers the mare. The soldier made his way to the two tethered horses.

Sayiina spun angrily and faced Ragnar. "What's with these people here? That soldier wouldn't acknowledge my presence or look my way."

"I saw it all, lass. It's their Muslim religion that holds them back. In their world, women are not considered equal. There are exceptions, of course. Some women are more prized than others. But generally, a man must speak to a man when given a choice. It makes me wonder if he would ignore you when in dire need. Forget him, Sayiina. It seems our host is expecting us. Let's see what he's about tonight."

As they walked to Tarkan Ozturk's tent, Sayiina looked over her shoulder to watch the soldier brushing down Ragnar's horse.

"Welcome to my tent, Sayiina and Ragnar. Relax and be my guests this evening. Please sit on these pillows and be comfortable. I have provided figs and some mild wine for our enjoyment. Our faith does not allow us to partake in strong drinks, so we bring the wine to a slight boil. This changes its consistency enough to indulge in its benefits."

Ragnar noted with suspicion Tarkan's almost joyous reception. Still, he thanked him for the night's invitation.

"I have also invited our caravan master, Hasad, to sit with us if you have a question I cannot answer."

Ragnar turned to Hasad and gave a slight nod. The caravan master looked a lot more serious than his usual self tonight. Sitting stiffly on cushions, he seemed less friendly than any other day. Hasad was staring unblinkingly with what sailors called dead man's eyes.

Tarkan, who was in great spirits, clapped twice, and a servant arrived carrying two bowls of figs, a large vessel filled with white wine, and four wooden drinking cups. As the servant poured the wine, Tarkan continued. "You might consider this lifestyle somewhat excessive, and you would be right to think so, but I like to indulge myself at times." He then sampled the wine.

"Indulging figs and wine in the middle of the desert is an astonishing act I will never forget. But crossing a desert, I don't want to repeat." Ragnar then sat down and reached over to choose a dark fig.

"And what are your thoughts this evening, Sayiina?" Tarkan asked.

"I would like to be away from this desert and hunting on an open steppe," she said, ignoring the figs and wine before her.

"Direct and always to the subject at hand is Sayiina. It is a strong trait I am beginning to appreciate more. I like it, as most women in Turkish culture, because of my stature and wealth, are meek and submissive to me."

With a contemptuous but knowing smile towards Tarkan, Sayiina replied, "Yakutian men and women are born equal, live equal, and die as equals. I do not think I would fit very well in yours, Tarkan."

"But this is one of the reasons I accepted your request to join my caravan. Yes, your payment was handsome, but more important to me is learning about new cultures. I am a traveler and want to engage with other people to hear their religious views and ideas. I am certain there is much we can learn from each other, Sayiina."

Tarkan then reached for a plump fig, held it before his eyes for inspection, and ate it greedily while leering at Sayiina.

His lecherous gaze did not go unnoticed by Ragnar, who challenged his integrity by saying, "Well, then, Tarkan, perhaps you could tell us where we are and how long it will take to get to our next destination."

Tarkan was slightly agitated, having to break his desirous thoughts of Sayiina. He turned to answer Ragnar's questions in a more business-like manner.

"Of course. You will be pleased to know that in three days, we will be in the area of Karakorum. It is in the steppe land of the Altai Mountains. Once a great city, but now in ruin. Sadly, only a few temples remain standing today. We will rest there for one day and one night before crossing the steppe and being away from this parched land. The Altai Mountains are the range we will cross.

"I want to stress this: do not let your vigilance down. Strange things can occur in a desert to the unwary. They can be haunted or cursed for the unlucky, being in the wrong place at the wrong time. Wouldn't you agree, Hasad?"

All eyes turned to the caravan master, awaiting his reply. He looked up from his wine cup at the question. He had been quiet, preferring to listen rather than engage Tarkan's guests, to speak only when asked, and now was the time. So, with little emotion, he answered.

"I would agree, Tarkan. Desert travel is not for everyone. It is perilous. I have seen people swallowed whole in a sandstorm, never to be seen again. Worse still, a dust devil coming out of nowhere, able to strip the flesh of a man clean to his bone. Very unfortunate." He shrugged. "That is Allah's will."

Hasad sipped from his cup.

"Well, that's an interesting story," Sayiina directed to Hasad. "A dust devil I have never seen before. How does someone defend against this creature?"

"It is not a physical creature but more a curse on you. No one can defeat wind and sand in a desert. The only chance of survival is to run from it and quickly."

"And you say it is Allah's will?" Ragnar queried. "It sounds to me more like terrible luck to be caught in the eye of a tempest."

"Exactly," Tarkan chimed in. "But soon, we will be traveling the open steppe. It will be very different there. Perhaps, when there, I can show you how to hunt with falcons, Sayiina."

"That is very generous of you," she replied, genuinely interested.

Tarkan had caught her attention from the tone of her voice. Pleased, he continued to entice her. "It is a unique form of hunting."

"I think I would like that. Ask me again when we are crossing the Steppe."

Ragnar didn't like the direction of the conversation. So, he stood to leave, as did Sayiina.

"You're leaving already? I am surprised."

"Aye, it's been a long day. Thank you again." Just before turning to leave, Ragnar yawned. At this, Tarkan and Hasad froze, shocked at his gesture.

"What's the matter? I'm tired, is all."

"In our Turkish culture, by yawning in a host's house, you just invited the devil into it."

"Really! Now that is interesting, Tarkan. You just taught me something of your culture. If the devil is on his way, I would like to say goodnight before he arrives." Then, smiling, Ragnar turned and sauntered away with Sayiina on his arm.

"Did you have to ridicule his culture with your last comment?" she asked.

"Nope. I just felt like it."

Tarkan asked Hasad quietly, "Did you send the courier ahead?"

"Yes, Tarkan, our best man on a swift camel, as requested."

"Good. I am sure they will accept my request for their nefarious arts. The handsome payment in jewels and gold would be hard to resist, and it shows my respect. Besides, their pride is in their practice. They care for nothing else. One soul lost to the desert is like a single grain of sand. It is meaningless to their kind. But she is worth the price and risk, Hasad.

"I am completely fascinated with this Yakutian woman. She has the heart of a warrior princess. I will make her the newest addition to my harem by fair or foul means. The sorcerers will help me accomplish this unpleasant business. She will be mine once her white-haired paramour is removed, leaving me the only one to comfort her. He will soon be forgotten."

"As you wish, Tarkan, but might I suggest you use caution in what you say to them? Only Allah can foretell the future, but these two know when something isn't right. The woman has an uncommon instinct for survival."

"Yes, yes," he replied dismissively to his caravan master. "I have also heard the talk of our Tajik mercenaries at night around their fires. They see this in her as well. She is confident and bold amongst them, almost an equal."

Three hooded, black-robed sorcerers stood silently encircling a large, milky-white porcelain cauldron. It was suspended waist-high by a chain over a recessed stone fire pit in the floor. Encircling the vessel were motifs of black-horned demons in exquisite detail, arranged as if chasing each other endlessly around the bowl. Between each running figure was a blood-red runestone of archaic design, whose meaning was lost in antiquity.

The room was cast in shadows with various flickering gray hues from burning torches fixed to the surrounding stone walls. When standing perfectly still, they would have been difficult to perceive in this grim setting, like dust blown in the wind.

The men had no identifying features among them, save one. All had long, black fingernails shaped and filed as razor-sharp talons. They were not necromancers or shamans. They were occultists who practiced the dark and arcane arts. Through their black witchcraft, they sought to control the supernatural, even demons from hell. For a princely sum, they were available for hire. Their services were not for the faint.

Three days prior, a rider had approached their temple. He was a simple messenger, of course, but a highly trusted one to carry a rogue request for their unique talents. They had known this before his arrival; they just didn't know precisely what he would be asking. When they accepted his pouch, containing precious stones like rubies, lapis lazuli, and gold dust as payment, the dark arts were put into practice.

One of the sorcerers proceeded to retrieve a medium-sized cotton sack, deceptively marked as grain seeds. With harmful intent, the other two moved to secure wood and flame and began building a fire beneath the cauldron. The starved fire burned with hunger when the first sorcerer slowly poured the contents of the sack into the ceremonial cauldron. Only it wasn't seeds of grain he released, but desert sand. The sand heated quickly, becoming white hot when another sorcerer tossed a tuft of horse hair into the pot. It sizzled instantly, then evaporated in a puff of smoke. At this sign, all three, in unison, rotated their hands palms up in a circular motion.

Chanting, they released an ancient incantation sounding throughout the room. This beckoned black-horned demons forth from the cauldron. The words were unknown to men of this world, and few would even dare to repeat them aloud. To do so would summon great evil. Only the cauldron, magically infused with dark spells, could hold the demons in place as they were drawn to its power. With more heat, the blood runes pulsed, and motifs on the cauldron moved in a circle, which the demons followed, first as a flurry, then as a blur. Right away, a swirling dust devil rose before them, suspended above the cauldron, but the horse hair's location would determine its projected place in the outside world. Their chanting increased.

Ragnar could see the direction in which Hasad was leading their caravan. It was through a large grouping of sand hills ahead. It made sense because to travel around them would add hours to this day's trek. The sun was at its zenith, and Ragnar's sweat-stained shirt clung to his back like a wet rag. To make things worse, Hasad had requested two things from Sayiina and him before their early morning departure.

First, he'd asked Ragnar to ride at the rear of the caravan with the other Tajik mercenaries for support. In the past, when approaching Karakoram, bandits—what Hasad termed "desert rats"—had attacked them, usually from the rear. Of course, Ragnar agreed, but being at the back of the convoy with a headwind, he would be on the receiving end of kicked-up dirt, dust, and, worst of all, the pungent odor of sweating Bactrian camels. It could make the hair in a man's nose curl in disgust, and today was just that day.

His second request had been for Sayiina to ride alongside the caravan at various locations and have her Yakutian longbow readily available.

Many of the merchants liked having her nearby, and they considered her a personal bodyguard. She spoke their Turkish language, and more importantly, her confidence among them was uncommon in their male-dominated world.

Ragnar watched Sayiina throw her head back at one exchange and laugh heartily. He liked what he saw, and she was proving her right as an equal.

Sayiina held her horse back until Ragnar moved up alongside her. He could see she was in her element.

"How are you, my man?" she asked flirtatiously.

"Awful. But I see you're in a good mood. You're getting along well with the merchants."

"I am."

"What was said that caused you to laugh so?"

"The merchant wanted to know if all the women in my country were like me. I told him, to his regret, no. He then asked me if I had an available sister I would introduce him to. That made me laugh because it's exactly the same question Zolzaya asked about you."

Grinning, he said, "He doesn't know what he's asking for, Sayiina."

"Well, I'm finding these Turkish men very flattering toward me."

"Enjoy it. Hopefully, soon, we'll have this sea of sand behind us."

At that point, Sayiina moved ahead, more to the middle of the caravan. They were entering the dunes.

Ragnar pulled his bandana back over his mouth and nose and wiped the sweat from his forehead with his palm, knowing it would be a long, hot day. He observed the dunes were big. Twenty to thirty feet high and no straight line to follow. A person could so easily get lost in them. He couldn't see the front of the camel train as it snaked its way within this labyrinth of sand as a single-file camel train. An increasing hot wind caressed the tips of the sand hills. It blew loose sand gracefully in the form of long, whipping tails.

Eerily, the air around him stilled. He looked at the soldiers, but none seemed to notice any change. There was an audible murmur about when a violent dust devil suddenly appeared directly overhead and fell upon him. With enough time and sensibility, Ragnar shielded his eyes with his arm. His horse neighed continually. It bucked, turning left and right, but could not escape the whirlwind and the cutting sand within. It stung like a thousand prickling needles.

The other mounted soldiers, horrified by what was happening, quickly distanced themselves, not wanting to be sucked into the vortex. They called out loudly for the caravan to halt. All at once, Ragnar's horse recklessly bolted away in a desperate attempt to flee the dust devil, to no avail.

Unnaturally, the whirlwind took on a will of its own, pursuing the fleeing horse across the sand. Ragnar's tunic was shredded to his waist by the constant sandblasting wind. Slowly, blood flowed across his torso.

Worse still, running blind, his horse was bleeding everywhere. It stumbled, and Ragnar instinctively threw himself away from the fallen steed. He staggered back a few feet and was horror-struck as the dust devil, with increasing velocity, circled over the horse. At first, the horse screamed uncontrollably, shaking as his skin was being shredded from him. Then all went quiet except for the sound of sand and wind tearing into flesh until only its skeleton remained.

As if satisfied with its accomplishment, and no more was required, the dust devil was lost in the wind.

CHAPTER 22

Sayiina could barely discern the call of men for attention behind her. Knowing Ragnar was there, she looked back, quickly pivoted her horse, and raced to the source: a group of mounted Tajik soldiers gathered at the rear of the caravan, talking excitedly with each other. There was no sign of Ragnar among them.

"Where is my partner? Where is he?" This time, she lifted her voice in a more accusatory tone.

A giant, brutish-looking mercenary, who resented her tone of voice, looked her in the eyes and raised his hand, pointing north. "The wind took him!"

"What? What the hell does that mean?" she charged.

The mercenary's eyes widened, outraged that a woman would dare question him this way. He stood up in his stirrups and reached for his sword handle.

Quickly, Sayiina nocked an arrow in her bow, also standing tall. Both adversaries did not flinch. Their eyes locked on each other, waiting to see who would make the first strike.

Just then, Hasad arrived to assess the situation at hand and demanded that both antagonists stop. "What's going on here?" He directed his question to the Tajik.

"The infidel woman was insolent to me, and I was about to teach her a lesson."

"She is a guest of Tarkan Ozturk, and you and your men will not harm her. Understood?"

The Tajik said nothing but spat over his horse's shoulder. He released his hand from his sword and reluctantly sat down.

Sayiina gave the Tajik a contemptuous smile and lowered her bow.

"Where is her companion?" Hasad demanded. "I assigned him to your rear guard."

"A dust devil descended on the infidel. His horse bolted north across the sands to escape Allah's judgment."

Sayiina spoke out firmly. "I'm going to search for him."

"Let me inform Tarkan of the situation. Only he can stop the caravan, not I or anyone else."

"That's your business; mine is to find my mate."

"Wait. The desert has no mercy. You will be lost in the sand and die of thirst. Just wait. I am certain Tarkan will gather a group of men to aid you when he learns what has happened."

Sayiina shook her head. "I'll go now. If you want to help, assemble a group to follow, but I leave now. I can't track him at night, and tomorrow will be too late."

At that, she nudged her horse in the direction the soldier had shown. With a grim but determined face, she pulled up her neck scarf to shield her nose and mouth from wind-blown dust and sand.

Hasad saw her determination, and that she would not be swayed, so he shouted from behind, "The caravan will halt on the river outside the city 5 miles west of here."

Sayiina acknowledged Hasad's words with a raised and clenched fist, then rode into the dunes and from his view.

Witnessing his horse's flesh stripped to the bone by the dust devil shocked Ragnar to his core. He had been but a hair's breadth away from suffering the same fate if he hadn't cleared himself from his falling horse.

"What now?"

His shredded goatskin water bag lay useless in the sand. He could wait until night and try to find his way out, but the sun's heat on his skin reminded him he didn't have time or coverage to wait. His shirt, now threads from the ordeal with the dust devil, and with only a few hours of daylight remaining, time would dictate what he had to do. He wouldn't survive very long without water, and just sitting and waiting for a possible rescue served no purpose. He would only become weak and dehydrated.

Ragnar decided to risk retracing his horse's steps to where it had bolted from the caravan, then trek straight west until he found the river of Karakorum.

Sayiina knew it would take all of her skills as a huntress to find Ragnar. Unlike a forest, the desert gives up none of its secrets. They're buried in the sand. All tracks are filled quickly, disguised from sight. Any scent in the air is suppressed by overbearing heat. The dunes absorb every sound.

This time would be different. She would now hunt as the wolf. A she-wolf, only aware of the direction in which her prey had fled. A frightened, bleeding horse, desperate to escape the chaos and, ultimately, death. Pure intuition alone would guide her through these pillars of sand. Under these conditions, many creatures would unknowingly, or by their own survival instincts, take the path of least resistance. She would do the same to follow her prey and hopefully rescue her northern man.

How she traveled would make no sense to someone watching her from above. She needed to keep moving, doubtful the fleeing horse would travel far. When a dune imposed itself as a wall, she would turn left or right, whichever presented the quickest escape. Sometimes, there was only one choice; others, she relied on her pure gut feeling until, ultimately, she found herself standing before the skeletal remains of a horse.

It was partially buried in drifting sand. Its bleached white bones suggested it had been there a while, but the saddle told the truth. Sayiina recognized it was Ragnar's. Not seeing any human remains, she experienced a temporary sense of relief immediately followed by a question she voiced aloud: "Where is he?"

Sayiina knelt on one knee and pressed her palm onto the warm sand. She allowed her breathing to slow, clear, and calmly focus her mind to be even more conscious of the world around her. An inner voice might reveal itself to her and her question at times like this. Her father, Modin, called it her "gift." She liked to think of it as another sense.

After a moment, she stood, aware Ragnar was trying to retrace his horse's wild flight. She knew the way back, but he would not. Nor would he survive long without water.

Sayiina mounted her horse and quickly set out in his direction.

The heat of the sun in the latter part of the afternoon was oppressive. The temperature of the air surrounding Ragnar had been steadily rising. Sweat ran from every pore in his body. It was nature's way of protecting him from overheating. His essential body fluids were leaving him faster than he liked. To make matters worse, he was not replacing them. Every step caused droplets to fall and silently disappear into the sand. His hair was wet and stringy from profuse perspiration. Dust tenaciously clung to his bare skin, unwilling to let go. He thirsted, and his throat was dry. His grim ordeal was beginning, but to stop moving would be the end. His head pounded, his breathing heavy.

"Damn, could it get any worse?" He cursed and wiped the stinging sweat from his eyes.

When his vision cleared, he stopped. Shocked, he stared at Sayiina standing in his way. "Is it you? Or are you an illusion conjured by the evil spirits who inhabit this desert?"

"It's me, Ragnar. I told you once before I would follow you to the end of the world. I think we have arrived here together. You look like you need help. I've brought water."

Sayiina retrieved a goatskin bag looped to her saddle and handed it to him. "Just drink slowly. We must conserve; we aren't out of the desert yet."

Ragnar sipped the water in relief, then asked, "How did you know where to find me?"

"The hard part was finding your horse, and once I did, I used a little Yakutian magic." She then smiled, and Ragnar just shook his head, unbelieving. "We must keep moving, Ragnar, while the sun is still up. Why don't you ride and rest a while?"

"Lass, you are my lifeline in this ocean of sand. I don't think I would have survived much longer."

Sayiina knew his words were true but remained quiet, taking the horse's reins to lead the way out.

Later, walking alongside, she looked up to Ragnar and spoke. "You have very good karma, Ragnar."

"I think you're my karma, lass. You will have to tell me how you do Yakutian magic."

"I will when you tell me how a little Norwegian magic freed us from our cells in Ulaanbaatar."

At that, Ragnar touched the ring on his finger. "I will, lass. It's a long story, but I'm drained right now. How much farther to the caravan encampment?" he asked, wanting to change her line of questioning.

"Probably another hour."

"Good, I think I need a bath in the river."

"Trust me, we both do."

CHAPTER 23

Tarkan read the script from Hasad's note, causing his hands to tremble slightly. It was an older Turkish dialect, but he understood its meaning clearly. It read, "Your request we have fulfilled. Speak to no one of our arrangement unless you wish for a similar fate."

Tarkan noted that the red-colored lettering looked like blood to emphasize the point of the business dealing. Also, it appeared to have been scribed over dried and stretched human skin. He shuddered at the thought of his flesh being stripped from his bones, alive. Allah could not give a worse death to anyone. He tossed the message into his campfire and watched it sizzle, then burn to ash.

"Did you witness the tempest, Hasad?"

"I did not, but many did in the rear guard, where I assigned the infidel. They were shocked when describing the descending violence on both horse and rider.

"I am told there was no escaping its fury. The horse suddenly bolted from the caravan straight into the desert in panic. Having lost his steed's lead, the infidel needed both hands to grip his saddle for support. The effort was futile, as the infidel may have been cursed.

"The men were stunned as it became more apparent the dust devil was increasing its intensity and following above them over the sand. I feel he is a lost soul this very night. Quite unfortunate."

"So, it is done, Hasad."

"I hope you are right, Tarkan. We will know for certain if the woman returns alone. I told her the location of our encampment."

"Alert me as soon as you have word. She will need comforting and perhaps a warm bed tonight, which I am able to provide for her. Let's speak privately in my tent, beyond inquisitive ears."

"As you wish."

Tarkan sat on a considerable silk pillow and indicated that Hasad should do the same. He then offered him a cup of tea. Tarkan was most at home in a tent while traveling the Silk Road, subject to no one but himself.

The only possible exception being at a caravanserai. These littered the road as a trail of breadcrumbs for weary travelers. All the local men would remove themselves from their homes for three days at these rest stops, leaving behind their wives, daughters, and sisters. Each man's home became a den of iniquity for a brief time. When the men of the caravan arrived, they would negotiate on an agreed price and enjoy all the creature comforts these women had to offer. Many families took great pride in the wealth they would accumulate.

Pensively, looking up from his teacup, Tarkan spoke. "Allah has been good to us this day, Hasad. Would you not agree?"

"So far, I agree, Tarkan, but caution . . ."

Hasad stopped speaking when a guard outside called out his name for attention.

"They are here, Hasad," the guard said excitedly.

"They?"

"The two infidels."

Hasad and Tarkan immediately stood, turning away from the tent entrance to gape at each other in disbelief.

"Is it possible, Tarkan?" Hasad whispered in his ear.

"Not possible. No one has ever escaped the sorcerers' black hands." Tarkan was very puzzled by this thought. "Give them entrance!" he called to the guard.

Ragnar and Sayiina entered together, halting before the two slacked-mouthed and mute Turkish men. Ragnar locked his gaze on Tarkan. "You look a little pale, Tarkan. Is everything all right?"

Tarkan couldn't find the words to reply immediately. He just stared, not believing his eyes and ears. "You're alive?" he stuttered, looking very confused.

"Ragnar has good karma, Tarkan," Sayiina said.

Hearing her voice brought Tarkan back to attention. Although the night was cool, he touched a bead of sweat from his temple and spoke as a good deceiver would, returning Ragnar's steady gaze.

"No one, to my knowledge, has ever survived a dust devil. You would be the first. Tell me, how did you escape from such a dangerous situation?"

"Just by chance. My horse and I were blinded by the sand when the steed bolted, running wildly. He must have broken an ankle and fell, neighing loudly in pain. His fall threw me forward onto the sand, and lying there, I watched the dust devil tear the flesh clean off of his bones. The beast died in agony. Only some Yakutian magic saved me from wandering aimlessly in the desert."

"That is good fortune indeed." Then Tarkan looked at Sayiina. "Is there anything you can't find?" he asked her, this time wiping sweat from his brow.

Sayiina detected a subtle but distinct nervous tone in Tarkan's voice. She suspected he was hiding something, but what? "In my country, we say "nothing is lost in life that cannot be found. Even death," she said, narrowing her eyes in his direction.

Tarkan noticeably stiffened at Sayiina's unexpected reply. Was there an underlying threat meant to induce fear in him?

Not waiting for a response, Ragnar asked. "I have a question for you, Tarkan, or even Hasad. Have you ever heard a spoken word or mystic tale of the sounds created by dust devils while at work or play in the desert?"

Sayiina noticed Hasad slowly inch his sword hand toward his blade at this question.

"Huh? What do you mean?" Tarkan asked as even more perspiration accumulated on his brow.

"When in the eye of the tempest, I distinctly heard chanting overhead, in a language I had never heard before, and I am familiar with many. The tone was dark."

"Dust devils do not have a voice. But the dunes have been known to give voice to those lost in the desert, only to lead them farther astray. Perhaps that is what you heard."

"Perhaps, but I'm not convinced. The world is full of strange occurrences, many by design. This was different as if an evil intent were at play. I could almost feel it."

Tarkan was eager to change the subject and purposely did so. "Well, you survived the desert, Allah be praised."

Still doubtful, Ragnar paused momentarily and looked at Sayiina with a raised brow. "Do you have anything else to say here?"

Sayiina shook her head, not letting her gaze stray from Hasad. "What is our next destination?"

"With three days' travel, we arrive in Hami."

Tarkan interjected. "Hami is a caravanserai on the Silk Road. There we will stay one day and one night to rest, replenish our supplies, and sate ourselves fully."

"I will need another horse, Tarkan," Ragnar spoke up.

"And I will make the arrangements for you, of course."

"That's all then, Tarkan. We'll take our leave."

Tarkan raised his right hand to touch his lip and forehead before replying. "As you wish. Allah be praised for your safe return," he said, nodding with hooded eyes.

Once outside Tarkan's tent and walking to their own, Ragnar turned to Sayiina. "Did he seem nervous or not himself to you tonight?"

"Not nervous, Ragnar. I saw a man trying to control his own fear. What that is, I don't know. Your mention of voices in the tempest caused Hasad to move his hand to his sword's hilt. Both are hiding something, and I wouldn't trust either."

"Aye, lass, good advice. Let's turn in early. I'm exhausted from the last couple of days' trials."

"Aye, aye, matey!" she said, and both laughed together as Ragnar put his reassuring arm around her shoulder.

Meanwhile, Hasad witnessed a petulant Tarkan in a tantrum inside the tent. He paced back and forth, both hands clenched into fists, and a low growl emitted from his throat.

"He still lives, Hasad! Tell me, how is this possible? No one survives the dark ones' sorcery, and yet he stands in this camp. The attempt on his life cost me a small fortune in jewels.

"Then he is found wandering the desert with no water, returning here safe. Unbelievable fortune. Arrgh! I pray to Allah faithfully every day, do I not?"

At this point, Tarkan threw his arms into the air in frustration. "Tell me, why would Allah deny me this woman, Hasad?"

Hasad responded cautiously. "Perhaps, Tarkan, Allah has plans for her other than yours."

Tarkan snapped with intolerance toward Hasad. "Your meaning by that?"

"With respect, perhaps she is not the one for you. Allah may have another woman in mind for your harem. Who can say?"

Tarkan turned his gaze toward the tent entrance, not wanting to accept Hasad's opinion too quickly. "The Silk Road is long. I still have time to convince her otherwise," he said, narrowing his gaze outward.

CHAPTER 24

Three days of travel across the eastern grasslands of the Altai Mountains brought Ragnar, Sayiina, and the caravan to the mountain pass they were seeking. Two more days' travel through this pass would bring them to the village of Hami. Although it was a time of plenty, both began noticing seasonal changes on their journey. Shorter days and cooler nights brought morning dew, clinging to blades of grass as a summer teardrop might before the fall. Everywhere on this steppe, wildlife abounded.

Every day, Sayiina took Ragnar on foraging excursions for fresh game. She never failed to provide for their daily meals. This caught the attention of two young Tajik soldiers, who asked if they could join the hunt. Sayiina agreed for the next day.

No sooner had they set out when she spotted a more significant new trail. At her lead, they stealthily followed their prey and soon discovered it was an argali, a large mountain sheep native to the area. She directed them to wait on the trail and be ready to shoot to kill, then left quickly and circled to get ahead of the beast.

In just a few moments, a giant horned, frightened male argali charged directly toward the men with its head down. It burst out of the tall grass so suddenly that the two soldiers had no time to aim their muskets properly. They both discharged their shots simultaneously at the charging animal. It died, falling forward and skidding to a halt at their feet. Both claimed the kill shot, but their argument was never concluded as Sayiina bounded out of the grass toward them.

"Well done. Let's gut it right away so we can feast on this tonight. There's enough meat on this sheep for the whole caravan."

"Are you going to share with us how you turned around a 300-pound sheep and sent it back in full flight?" Ragnar asked, a little annoyed. "You know I don't carry a gun with me."

Sayiina laughed, not mockingly, but more like she wasn't giving away more of her secrets. "Perhaps if you join me next time, I'll show you how."

"Fair game, lass."

Late in the afternoon, many merchants and soldiers slowly gravitated toward each other and around the now almost-cooked sheep. A spit had skewered its length, and over a fire, two men were turning it slowly to roast. Ragnar lifted his nose, knowing the aroma permeated the air.

"Just drawing in the scent makes me hungry, Sayiina. I think it's ready to eat. Let's go see the cooks," he added with enthusiasm.

"Look at everyone here. All this comradery reminds me of my sailing days gone by. We would drop anchor on a distant shore. A hunting party was assigned immediately to secure food, and many times, a wild pig would be caught, then roasted over a beach fire." A fleeting memory of the Romanukski brothers at such a time came to mind. He whispered softly, for none to hear, "Those were good days now long gone."

Ragnar could hear his and Sayiina's names being hailed. It was Tarkan calling, and they watched his approach with Hasad behind. Tarkan greeted them both equally and then immediately directed his line of questioning to Sayiina. "Is there no animal you fear?"

"It's not about fearing the animal. For me, it's all about what your adversary fears more."

"Really! The two Tajik claim you chased it from the open grass straight toward them. What kind of fear would a 300-pound male argali have from anyone? Even a great huntress such as yourself."

"Well, maybe it wasn't afraid of me personally, but the Yakutian spell I invoked upon it." She gazed unwaveringly at Tarkan.

"Ha. Huntress, tracker, and now spellcaster. I've never met a woman of your kind."

Ragnar watched Tarkan closely. He could see everything was a flirting game with him. But he knew this flattery toward Sayiina would fail. She did not judge people by their appearance but instead if they were kindred spirits.

Tarkan thought himself a handsome man, one all women desired. His vanity would not allow him to see Sayiina's attitude to him as distant. He could not compete on her level; if he persisted, he would learn the hard way. Before they parted ways, Ragnar would have a few choice words for Tarkan.

Hasad then stepped forward to speak. Ragnar and Sayiina both turned to him.

"Some of the Tajik soldiers are openly talking of your prowess as good fortune to our caravan. We will travel the mountain pass for the next two days and two nights. It is very treacherous and dangerous. The road is narrow, and it follows a steep incline alongside a gorge.

"At one point, we must all travel in a single file, including our hired soldiers. We are very vulnerable when in this position. There are known bandits who would be waiting for us.

"The Tajik have asked me to ask you if you would take the lead with me tomorrow. Much like a forward scout. The men greatly regard your skills, and I would consider it a privilege to join you."

Hasad, then in respect, not submission, nodded to her.

"I won't be separated from my partner again, Hasad, but I will accept your invitation if you agree Ragnar rides with me. If I can be of any help, I will."

"Allah's will be done."

"I will need a rifle, Hasad," Ragnar interjected.

"I will provide, and the men will be pleased to hear this."

"Good then," Tarkan spoke up. "All is arranged as it should be. Let's eat."

Ragnar could see everyone in the caravan ate their fill. Many merchants and soldiers alike came by to speak to Sayiina, giving thanks to both her and Allah. It was all but a festive occasion, celebrated to forget the dangers coming in the days ahead.

After dinner, there were games of chance, arm wrestling, and, of course, storytelling. It was good to see people coming together in friendship. He almost felt at home with these people in a strange land but quickly brushed those thoughts away, knowing he and Sayiina were more than halfway home to Norway. There would be no turning back.

Later, they made their way back to their tent, and Sayiina remarked casually, "You know, your words earlier today, when you said you don't carry a gun, just aren't true."

"What do you mean?"

"Well, you don't have a rifle, of course; it's more like a large pistol." She gave a comely wink. "The next few days will be challenging for us. Perhaps we should make sure your pistol is in good working order tonight, my man."

Ragnar caught the inference and laughed heartily while putting his arm around her shoulder. He pulled her close to him. "You know you're shameless, lass."

"With you, absolutely," she said, smiling his way.

Ragnar and Sayiina rose before dawn the next day. They wanted Hasad to fully brief them on what to expect and be aware of. Just ahead, they could see Hasad readying himself outside his tent.

Before engaging him, they secured their mule with a nearby merchant, who asked, "Will you be leading our caravan today?"

"Aye," replied Ragnar.

"Allah is good. I prayed last night that you would do this for the better of our caravan, and here you are."

"The next few days will be challenging, and this mule is yours if we fall."

Surprised at Ragnar's generosity, the merchant's eyes opened wide. "Blessings be upon you."

Ragnar turned to Sayiina. "If we don't survive, only a few in this caravan might." He then nudged his horse toward Hasad and dismounted.

"What do we need to know, Hasad?" Ragnar asked directly.

Sayiina's question immediately followed this: "And what exactly are we looking for?"

"The attacking bandits are known. I have been fortunate to escape their grasp twice before. Allah watches over me, and I pray to him, especially when I travel this way.

"What you need to know about this land is that they are a different breed of men. No one seems to know what their origins are. If you see one, you will understand my words."

"What do you mean by that? Are they not human, or what?"

"They are men. They look Tartar, but unlike Tartar, they are heavily bearded in appearance. I believe Tartar soldiers long ago took female slaves of another race to produce their kind. Still, today, they make slaves of any they can capture. They are the worst kind, committing many depredations on those who cannot arrange for their ransoms.

"More important to know is they have learned the art of deception. Some might call it magic, but I don't believe it. Like a motionless deer standing in the forest, if you do not know what to look for, you will never see it until it is right before your eyes. They are practised masters of disguise, nearly invisible in any environment they choose. They even color their rifles the same way."

"So, they are cowards and thieves," Sayiina replied contemptuously.

"Where is our weakest position, Hasad?" Ragnar asked.

"A person can easily mark the other side where the gorge comes together at its middle. It's not more than 50 feet wide at its most narrow."

"Tell us more, Hasad, and the lay of the land," Sayiina said.

"The gorge is shaped like a crescent. On our left, we follow along a stone-faced wall. Our right side is a sheer cliff to the bottom of the chasm. To fall is certain death. The other side is forested with many places for concealment."

Ragnar was silent all the while Hasad spoke. They would potentially be walking into a deadly trap.

"So how do we defend ourselves if we are fired upon? Are we just moving targets?"

"The bandits will allow those first in the caravan to pass by. They usually target the merchants at the rear. The caravan will not turn back to rescue them. To do so, the bandits would block the forward exit at the top of the crescent, where we travel on a more equal footing."

"Then it's not a fair fight," stated Sayiina.

"Each merchant is assigned a Tajik soldier. The merchants drew straws last night for their position in today's caravan train."

"Has no one ever thought to take the fight to them?" Ragnar was unconvinced that their fate was already determined.

Ragnar's question caused Hasad to squirm. "It's not possible, and they hold all the advantages."

"There is one they do not hold, Hasad. They will not expect the unexpected or an attack on their position."

Sayiina's curiosity came alive. "What do you have in mind, Ragnar?"

"When at sea and fighting ship to ship, to board the enemy's vessel, we would use grapnel hooks with tow lines to fasten onto their decks. Then, we'd cross the distance with lanyards.

"I'm just thinking aloud, but Sayiina, with her bow, could send a grapnel into the trees on the other side. With some luck, it would catch, and we would tie off our end to a camel's saddle. Using lanyards will speed us across the chasm; from there, we get behind their position to ambush them. They would not be expecting us."

"That would give us the vantage ground," Sayiina replied.

"I like your idea, but two against many seems risky." Hasad sounded skeptical.

"Give me two of your best soldiers, and we'll make a difference. There's no risk to you, and no one in the caravan needs to die this day. If successful, we'll send their village a message never to return."

Ragnar sensed the last point of his message appealed to Hasad as a nasty grimace crossed over his face.

"No more than two."

"Good. Sayiina and I, along with the soldiers, will take the lead to the start of the gorge and look for a good place to cross over."

"I will inform Tarkan of your plan. He will need to know, as your safe passage is his concern. I will request the two young soldiers you went hunting with. I think they are the adventurous type you seek."

While waiting for the soldiers to arrive, Ragnar and Sayiina fastened three small meat hooks to an arrow, forming a crude working grapnel. He also cut four 5-foot lanyards, knotted on both ends to prevent sweaty palms from slipping off.

"Have you done this before, Ragnar?" she asked nervously while inspecting the integrity of the grapnel.

"Aye, lass, many times. Not over a chasm, of course, but over shark-infested waters. You look hesitant, but don't worry; this will work. When the time comes, I'll go first and demonstrate how it's done."

"At times," Sayiina said, "strangers have told me I'm fearless, but I have fear. I fear losing you on the journey we travel. Also, the unknown can create fear, such as our diabolical encounter with the leopard and tiger. I've never attempted this, what you have done many times. This action will be a first for me. It'll be a leap with fear into the unknown."

Surprised to hear her bold words admitting her weakness, Ragnar stopped what he was doing and held one of her hands with one hand. "Our days together have only begun. I feel this way because I live each day, each moment, and every breath for us. I would never put you in harm's way. You mean too much to me."

Sayiina squeezed his hand tightly. "Thank you. Now explain to me how this is done."

Ragnar looked over her shoulder. "Aha, our volunteers, Salar and Hamasa, have arrived, Sayiina."

She turned to watch them approach. They owned an easy gait, almost alike.

"I'm curious," Ragnar asked, "but are you two brothers?"

"We are," replied Salar.

"Good. I knew two brothers long ago like you, and both were strong, daring, and courageous. I'll take your being here as a good omen. Did Hasad inform you of what we are attempting?"

"All he said was, 'The infidels need some assistance,' so we volunteered," Salar said with a grin.

"I was just about to explain to Sayiina what my plan is, so I'll share it with you now as well."

After closely listening to Ragnar and understanding the mission goals, the brothers looked first at the grapnel, then the lanyards, and finally at each other. Salar declared, "An ambush behind ambushers. It's bold, and I like it a lot. If successful, we will be made famous, brother."

Hamasa replied excitedly, "Not just famous, but legendary."

They both turned to Ragnar and, in unison, asked, "When do we leave?"

Ragnar approved of the location Sayiina had chosen to release the grapnel across the chasm. It was forested, and the grapnel would find a hold with any luck. More importantly, it was at a slight decline in elevation to their position, making the use of lanyards their best choice for crossing.

Sayiina released the tethered grapnel from her great bow when all was prepared. It sailed over the ravine and disappeared into the trees.

At this point, Ragnar slowly pulled back on the rope, and it caught almost immediately. Now, he tested its strength with the two brothers, all pulling hard to see if it would release itself under the strain. When it held, he was satisfied and tied it to a camel's saddle horn. He turned to Sayiina.

"Nice. Well placed on your first attempt. I'll go first, then Sayiina, then Salar and Hamasa. Just watch me and do the same. Remember, don't look down. Eyes straight ahead. The descent will be over in seconds. Once we all gather in the forest, Sayiina takes the lead. This is her domain."

Ragnar began by placing his lanyard over the tethered rope line spanning the chasm. He gripped hard with both hands on either end of the lanyard, then pushed himself away, sliding downwards from their position. Halfway along, he lifted his legs horizontally and disappeared into the forest. Landing and spinning, he watched Sayiina cross the divide, legs raised waist high. He knew it was an illusion, but she seemed to sit on air with the earth moving below. Then he braced himself to catch her and slow her forward motion. She was panting heavily, with sweat covering her brow. She appeared stressed.

One of the brothers had pushed away.

"Stand aside and gather yourself, Sayiina. Salar is crossing, and he'll need my assistance."

Hamasa arrived last, thrilled at his crossing, but Ragnar cautioned him to silence. "We don't know their position. Wait and say no more."

Having regained her composure, Sayiina began sharing her strategy. "I can't tell you how many bandits there will be, but I can tell you where their position is known. According to Hasad, they always attack at the narrowest point of the chasm: this midpoint may be 300 yards ahead of our current position.

"These villains cannot become invisible, as the rumors tell. What they do practice is the art of deception. They disguise their clothes, skin, and weapons to suit their immediate environment. So, like the deer in the forest, they can remain perfectly still and avoid detection by other predators.

"Today, we make a difference. These cowards will position themselves at the edge of the treeline for a clear shot at the caravan. Not at the leaders, of course, but the rear merchants and camels. When they do this, they'll expose their locations to us.

"We're looking for something like a deformed tree trunk. Perhaps a large bolder with a stick pointing out from it, suggesting a rifle barrel. Focus on these irregularities and mark your targets. Our greatest advantage is surprise, but we must get close to them without their knowledge. Everyone must remove their boots now."

"What!" all three men exclaimed as one.

"The boots we all wear are clearly heard on a forest floor. The snap of a single twig might draw unwanted attention to us."

Knowing her to be right, they agreed and quickly removed them.

"Leave them here. We'll retrieve them later. Also, from here forward, no speaking. Hand signals only."

They all nodded in agreement and observed her steps in silence. Sayiina moved cautiously with cat-like grace. Each step was measured between obstacles the forest put before her. Stones, leaves, fallen branches—anything, if disturbed, would bring the bandits' attention to their position. She crouched, advancing to their goal, and the men followed her example.

Sayiina successfully carved a path through the woods to the middle of the crescent, then stopped and dropped to one knee. Everyone did the same. She had led and positioned everyone 100 feet behind the treeline and motioned all eyes to the forest edge with a sweeping hand, then remained perfectly still, like the excellent hunter she was.

There were still a few minutes before the caravan would arrive, and they would be ready. The silence was eerie. Nothing moved, as if time did not belong here. Ragnar looked at a tuft of yellow grass that seemed out of place on the brown earth. A slight breeze passed over it, and the blades of the grass did not bend to it. He saw the outline of a combatant lying prone, with his rifle at the ready, as an apparition came to life. With a hand gesture, he indicated the location until everyone acknowledged him.

Sayiina looked up at a tree branch, too thick for its position on the trunk. The silhouette of a man sitting on the branch, with his back resting against the tree, came into view.

Salar pointed to a flat rock with a round, head-sized stone resting on its surface.

Slowly but surely, the forest came alive and revealed its secrets to the four stalkers. Ragnar counted ten ambushers in all. It was a small muster, considering the near-approaching caravan greatly outnumbered them. Their successes over time made them overconfident. To the caravans, they were invisible, and they had never been retaliated against. They had become soft, and now the hunters became the hunted.

At Sayiina's command, hell was unleashed on the bandits. Her first arrow downed the bandit hiding above them. As one, Ragnar and the two brothers fired upon three more, leaving them lifeless. The ambushers all turned to look behind their position. They were shocked and in disbelief, knowing they were compromised.

Confused, they didn't see where their assailants were until Sayiina and Ragnar stood and rushed two more bandits to their right. The brothers ran to their left, engaging two more. With everyone exposed, Rangar could see a bandit sighting his rifle on Sayiina, who was rushing toward this enemy.

Simultaneously notching her arrow, she suddenly halted to draw back the bow. At this precise moment, she made a feint that would have impressed an illusionist. The bandit, with murderous intent, had discharged his weapon only to miss his mark. He turned to flee, but Sayiina took her shot, piercing through his right thigh. Screaming, he fell and clutched his leg.

More gunfire came from the direction of the brothers. Ragnar wheeled to the sound, only to see a shaft sticking out from the chest of a would-be assailant behind him. Sayiina's arrow had found its mark.

"Are you alright?"

"Aye, lass."

"Good, there's no more here on this end. Let's go help the brothers."

Running to their aid, Ragnar picked up a fallen rifle and then arrived beside Sayiina undetected. She motioned for him to aim but not yet fire. They watched a scene play itself out.

Two bandits stood over Salar and Hamasa, who were kneeling with hands over their heads, execution style. The bandits were screaming at the brothers, their backs turned to Ragnar and Sayiina. Each bandit held a rifle to the back of Salar and Hamasa's head. They demanded to know who they were and how they had been found out. To their courage, Ragnar witnessed the brothers look at each other for strength, refusing to answer. When the questioning stopped, one bandit aimed his rifle, positioned for the kill shot.

Sayiina released her arrow, impaling deep between his shoulder blades, killing him instantly. The impact caused him to fall awkwardly between Salar and Hamasa. The second bandit stood very still, then let go of his weapon.

Ragnar and Sayiina approached the remaining bandit and bound his wrists behind him. When Salar and Hamasa stood, they were visibly shaking, a result of the near-death they had faced.

Ragnar patted both their shoulders for reassurance. "Your lives are yours again, and your courage is immense. I don't think your Tajikistan countrymen will be able to match you when they learn of this. Why not call out to them now as they are traveling the narrow part of the gorge? Tell them we are all safe, and we bring prisoners for questioning."

Elated with their freedom, both brothers ran outside the treeline and told the caravan of their success. They raised their rifles in a victory salute, and the Tajik soldiers on the other side acknowledged in kind.

"I presume you shot that bandit in the leg on purpose, Sayiina?"

"We needed prisoners. He was the first to flee, which makes him a coward. His kind talk when threatened."

"Okay, we take this one here and the wounded one to Hasad for questioning. Lead the way. But first, I want my boots."

CHAPTER 25

After recovering their boots, Ragnar, Sayiina, and the two Tajik brothers walked out to meet with the caravan at the far end of the gorge. Stumbling behind Salar and Hamasa were their two Tartar prisoners. Their ankles were hobbled to prevent them from running, and their wrists were bound and tethered before them, one to each of the brothers' saddle horns. They struggled to keep the pace set, especially the one with the wounded leg. Ragnar had removed the arrow and battle-dressed it to slow the bleeding, only to be continually cursed by the ungrateful wretch.

"You know, Sayiina, he keeps saying what he and his people will do to me and my family if he gets free. Perhaps he'll shut up if I tell him you're my only family."

"Stupid man, I don't think he'll survive much longer. Not if the Tajik mercenaries have their way. For me, there is no doubt that he has taken many Tajik lives over their years of traveling this road. They'll want a special punishment."

"Ahoy." Ragnar raised his right hand, greeting Tarkan, Hasad, and several heavily armed mercenaries.

"You have accomplished the unthinkable," Tarkan said. "You prevented certain death to both merchants and mercenaries alike. Allah be praised. I have never traveled this portion of the road without barbarous attacks from bandits. You must tell me how you managed this." He had a note of admiration in his voice for Ragnar.

"Hasad informed me of your plan, but I doubted its success. Much too dangerous," Tarkan replied.

"My role was small, Tarkan. I managed to get everyone across the chasm safely, but Sayiina took the lead after that. She was the first and the last to strike down your enemies."

"But how did you even see them? They are masters of disguise."

"Their greatest strength is also their greatest weakness," Sayiina responded confidently. "It was Hasad who told us where they would ambush from. We only needed to get close to their position, undetected, and wait for them to reveal themselves to us. They had grown soft over the years, with easy spoils and no retaliation from passing caravans. It was almost too easy.

"There is a natural order to all things in a forest. Look for the unnatural, and soon, your enemies will give themselves out. It was the two brothers who faced death and walked away. They are incredibly brave, but I will let them tell their own story."

Hasad spoke up now. "It's good you have all survived. It seems to me Allah favors the faithful and infidels alike." Now, in a more serious tone, he said, "There will be time for storytelling later. I want to keep the caravan moving this day. The fate of the prisoners will be determined tomorrow after their interrogation tonight. But for now, we travel west to Hami and caravanserai."

"You are welcome to rejoin the caravan in any order you choose," Tarkan said. "But I would consider it an honor if you both would ride with me. I wish to hear your version of this victory, and please do not leave out any details."

Ragnar turned to Sayiina about her preference. She didn't reply verbally but merely shrugged, indicating it was his decision.

"Okay, Tarkan, we'll join you shortly at the front of the caravan and tell you a tale you will not soon forget. A story of two soldiers, a sailor, and Yakutian magic."

He looked to Sayiina and gave her a wink. Sayiina laughed heartily.

"I am looking forward to 'this story,' especially the Yakutian magic parts," Sayiina said.

Later in the night, everyone in the caravan gathered around a large bonfire. Ragnar and Sayiina stood alongside merchants and soldiers alike. The fire crackled as if signaling a festive mood was in the making. When speaking to the merchants, he could see they were particularly animated tonight, and why not? Not one merchant had lost their lives or any merchandise. There would be large profits for everyone due to a brave few. Tajik soldiers frequently engaged Ragnar and Sayiina with thanks and more than a few asked to be part of any future excursions. They wanted to prove themselves, just as the brothers had.

"I don't think we'll have a shortage of volunteers, Ragnar. Some of these soldiers are now ready to take the fight to our enemies."

"Aye, lass. I can see the eagerness in their eyes."

Amid all the boisterous reveling, a small delegation of Tajik mercenaries, commanded by their leader, Sorbon Sherzod, broke through the people. Everyone quieted at the grand entrance, led by this large, brutish soldier. Sayiina recognized the leader as the same one she had confronted in the desert.

The men marched straight for Ragnar and Sayiina, who were speaking with Hasad, then stopped. Considering everyone was in good cheer, these men looked sullen as grim reapers. Their leader spoke clearly for all to hear.

"You all know who I am. I lead the Tajikistan mercenaries who protect you. Now, hear my words and bear witness. We follow Islam, and these two before me are non-believers of the true faith, Allah!"

From the corner of his eye, Ragnar spied Sayiina, who stiffened unnoticed by anyone but himself.

The Tajik continued, "We convened a special council for two hours to hear the words of our brothers, Salar and Hamasa. They told us of their exploits and how you saved them from certain death. You showed them how to see the unseen. How you taught them a way of silent stealth. They say your bow has no equal. And last, they were shown how to sail across the skies. You have killed our enemies, four against ten. You do us great honor by bringing us prisoners.

"I ask myself, why does Allah protect you so? We Tajik soldiers are the best of the best."

Ragnar could see the Tajik leader struggling with his words. He did not understand the world around him, and he almost questioned his faith at this moment. "Tonight, our council has decided that perhaps Allah wished us to meet an infidel who is our equal. One cannot know the future, but we have counseled on your presence here."

Surprised to learn only now of a secret meeting in his caravan, Tarkan said, with authority, "The two infidels are here as my guests. Counsel to me first."

"As you wish." Then he bowed to Tarkan with respect. "We Tajiks have determined to invite the two infidels into our sacred brotherhood as honorary members."

At this point, Salar and Hamasa stepped out from behind the delegation, each holding an armband of the Tajikistan mercenary brotherhood.

Tarkan was stunned, speechless, knowing that this was their highest bestowed honor. He was shocked to his core seeing Sayiina and Ragnar accepting the armbands.

At this moment, he came to realize he was not their equal. The Tajik would now not aid him in his planning to remove Ragnar, thus having Sayiina to himself. The Tajik did not turn on their own.

As the two brothers placed armbands on a smiling Ragnar and Sayiina, Sherzod continued speaking. "Anywhere you travel, with one of us or in our country, you will have shelter and safety. Your enemies are now ours, and your friends are welcome among us. Allah!" he cried out, and as one, all the soldiers resounded "Allah" three times.

Sorbon Sherzod reached out with both arms, embraced Ragnar and Sayiina, and stepped back for other soldiers to do the same.

"The red, white, and green horizontal stripes. What do the colors on the armbands mean?" a curious Sayiina asked.

"The red represents the blood of our people. The white is the snow on top of our mountains. The green is for the valleys of our land," he answered proudly.

Sayiina regarded her old antagonist keenly. He was a natural leader of hard men. Their strength and arms are upheld by honor. A true bond of brothers. Sayiina lowered her dark brows and raised her eyes to him, saying, "Are you willing to trust an infidel woman?"

"You have already earned it."

"Then I will wear my Tajik colors with great pride." She reached for the leader's forearm as he did hers and welcomed their newly formed friendship.

The following day, Ragnar witnessed Tarkan, Hasad, and a group of mercenaries standing and arguing over the two prisoners. They sat tethered to stakes in the ground. It seemed the Tajik wanted to cut off their heads. Tarkan was claiming ownership, and he wanted to sell them as slaves. "There is no profit in killing them," he insisted.

"But killing them would honor our dead brothers, who were slain by their villainous hands."

Hasad backed away from the argument and, noticing Ragnar, hailed him. "This argument could go on all day, and I need this caravan moving. What would you say to this?"

"I don't see an easy solution, Hasad. Both sides are far apart. Tarkan wants money and the Tajik blood. I would bet Tarkan would be willing to give up his coin for a few years' safe passage. I think a message should be sent back to these Tartars' village. Something more obvious," Ragnar suggested.

"Their ways are not secret anymore. More will die if they continue to ambush travelers on this road. I would send them back in disgrace to explain themselves to their leaders. Perhaps removing an ear from the prisoners would satisfy the Tajik's blood lust.

"I don't know, Hasad. That would be my best advice."

"A good solution, and it might be acceptable to all. I will propose this, and we will soon know Allah's will." Hasad then turned to rejoin Tarkan and the Tajik.

"What did Hasad want?" Sayiina asked.

"Not much, just some friendly advice."

"Did he take it?"

"I think he's waiting on Allah's will to be done. We'll know soon."

Behind them, all three men were yelling and talking over each other. It seemed they were coming to a conclusion, and abruptly, the men went silent. The Tajik leader moved to speak before the bound prisoners. Ragnar couldn't make out the words, but when he stopped talking, he withdrew a knife from his waistband and cut an ear from each prisoner's head.

"I think they have concluded their negotiations, Sayiina."

When the prisoners' bonds were cut, they were given rags, which they pressed to the side of their heads to stem the flow of blood. Ragnar watched the two stumble to their feet in their eagerness to get away. They were then driven away from the caravan at sword point.

Sayiina came up alongside Ragnar as the two former prisoners fled. "They're fortunate to be alive."

"Karma."

For the next two days, Hasad pushed everyone hard as they were behind schedule. From dawn to dusk, the caravan train continued moving west. Water stops only, forcing everyone to eat upright in their saddles. Finally, near dusk of the second day, saddle sore and weary, the caravan arrived at the village of Hami, which was more than a thousand years old.

Hami was nestled in a beautiful plain surrounded by mountains. Long shadows cast by a setting sun indicated the beginning to the end of another day. As different as Hami was, so were its customs. Many established towns and villages held secrets, both large and small.

Sometimes, people buried them deep to forget. Others, like Hami, hid them in plain sight.

The sight of Hami was a welcome relief for Ragnar, Sayiina, and everyone else on the caravan train. This would be their first stop, or caravanserai, as they passed through the Tian Shan Mountains along the Silk Road.

As they neared, the village became more defined. A large two-story building with an open ceiling served as the central hostelry, much like a hub in a wheel. The main floor was for dining; the upper level consisted of rented rooms as sleeping quarters. Merchants' shops encircled the inn completely, where travelers and shopkeepers could buy, sell, or trade their goods. Replenishing was a necessity for both men and beasts who were traveling onward. Behind the shops were the homes of all the villagers. Each had a large garden.

The land was fertile and provided for the people of Hami, who were noted for their fine melons and good wine. It all seemed idyllic to a stranger passing by, and why not?

Once inside the hub of the village, they dismounted and secured their horses and mule in an empty stall. Ragnar arched his back, looking at Sayiina.

"Let's go see what the rooms for rent offer. I am saddle sore and want a soft bed tonight and the next."

"We still have things to do, Ragnar. The horses need feed, water, and to be brushed down."

"Okay, I'll look after them. Why don't you choose a room to your liking and secure it for us? I trust your better judgment to our needs in a bedroom." Then he gave her a promising wink.

Sayiina walked away and laughed, thinking, *Men. Just as Zaya said, "Always in rut."*

Ragnar watched her leave as she climbed the stairs to the rooms above, then returned to look after their horses.

A few minutes later, an angry Sayiina stood frustrated before him. "We're not staying here, Ragnar. There is nothing in the rooms except a wooden floor and mice, nothing else. It's as if they don't want to accommodate weary travelers in the upstairs rooms."

"Really? Where is everyone sleeping then for two nights? Let's ask around. I see a couple of familiar merchants eating at a table over there in the corner. The horses are feeding, and they can be brushed down tomorrow. Let's find out."

They approached the two men, who rose, welcoming them to their table. "Do you wish to dine with us? I will order more. The lamb kabob is the best anywhere. Please sit with us."

"Thank you, but we'll be eating later tonight. We thought we'd ask you for information."

"Please, what do you need to know?"

"Why are the upstairs sleeping rooms empty of beds and other amenities?"

"Ah, a simple enough question for the uninformed. Hami is a unique village on the road we travel. All citizens can profit from its commerce with the many caravans passing through. Sleeping arrangements are made with the matrons of every home in the village. The upper rooms are purposefully left bare to discourage visitors. But I can assure you," he beamed, brazen-faced, "the villagers' rooms are the most generous you will find anywhere. Everything is negotiable. A rich man's paradise, some would say."

"Thank you, I understand now."

The merchant bowed slightly and placed his right hand on his forehead. "Salaam."

Ragnar knew this meant peace and returned the motion in kind. "Now we know. Should we get a room?"

"Yes, but somehow, we are the last to know about this. I hope there are rooms still available."

Once outside the inner hub and past the markets, they randomly walked past villagers' homes. Some were quiet, while others were decidedly raucous.

"We might be too late to find any suitable room, Ragnar."

"Aye, lass, let's press on a bit farther. The sun's not yet down. Look over there. That house beside the willow tree. Is that a woman there?"

As they approached the home, a mature woman came into view. She was standing outside her front door, smoking a pipe and watching them. Her black-and-white-streaked hair was lifted and pinned atop her head. She didn't stand at attention but instead lazily tilted her neckline. To Ragnar, this suggested a *"come hither young man and see what I have to offer"* look. She had a sultry appeal with the look of an attractive woman who had seen and done much over her years. She beckoned them with her hand to approach.

"I have good beds here for rent and nice daughters."

"I missed that last part, Sayiina. What was it?" Ragnar asked.

"I didn't hear it either. Let's take the room and turn in for the night."

"Aye, agreed."

CHAPTER 26

Upon entering, Ragnar and Sayiina stopped and stood still, allowing their eyes to adjust to the candlelit hallway. The matron introduced herself as Ying Ying, bowed respectfully with a welcoming smile, then pulled aside a bamboo curtain. She motioned them to enter the adjoining room.

The spacious room immediately impressed Ragnar, who nodded at the level of comfort and amenities the room contained. The central area was dominated by a four-poster bed with many soft furs and rich silk pillows strewn over it. A draping silk veil opaquely concealed a bath in one corner for privacy. Beneath an exterior window stood an ebony table and two chairs. The matching legs of both tables and chairs were carved as distinctive lion paws. A blue and white porcelain teapot with two cups rested delicately on the surface. On every wall hung Turkish tapestries with motif designs.

"We'll take it." Sayiina snapped.

"It's a bit opulent, don't you think, Sayiina?"

"It is, but you only live once, my man. I want to indulge myself. Can you also arrange a bottle of wine for us, Ying Ying? Oh, by the way, I am Sayiina, and this is my mate, Ragnar. We will stay two nights but do not wish to be disturbed tonight."

"Very well. I will inform my daughters of your decision. They will wait for you when you rise tomorrow. I will bring wine to you immediately. How do you wish to pay for the services?" she queried.

"We have silver coin. Is that acceptable?"

Ragnar loosened his purse strings and bounced the bag in his hand so she could hear the jingle.

"Silver is good, one coin each night and one more for two bottles of the best Hami wine. Anything additional can be negotiated tomorrow."

"Aye, right then."

Ragnar placed the silver coins onto Ying Ying's open palm, who quickly secreted them into a fold of her dress. Turning, she departed from their presence without a sound.

Sayiina sat on the bed to test its firmness, running her hands over the softness of the furs. "These furs are fabulous, Ragnar. The dark ones are sable, and here is a blue fox." Her eyes absorbed their suppleness with what her hands could not see, and she was enthralled.

A soft clatter from the bamboo curtain announced the arrival of their wine. A tall, handsome woman carried it to their table and set it down. More astonishing was the sheer pale-blue silk dress that flowed over her lithe form. She wore it like a flowing breeze over supple leaves on a tree. All of her was laid bare in opalescent motion. Turning to leave, her firm, round buttocks were revealed for Ragnar to admire.

"It's not polite to stare, Ragnar," Sayiina brought to his attention.

"Aye, it is rude." Still, he did not look away from her mesmerizing figure.

The young woman stopped before the curtain and pivoted to stare back at Ragnar, asking seductively, "Is there anything else you would like?"

At those words, Sayiina stood, pointed sharply to the exit, and yelled, "Out! What is with everyone here?"

"I think she's just being hospitable, Sayiina, although her gown was very . . . interesting."

"You were not just looking at her gown," she said in a softer tone. "I don't hold you wrong in looking. She is very attractive. But when she suggested something more, she crossed a line."

"Slow down, lass. This woman's behavior is not much different from Tarkan's advances toward you. Tell me differently."

"I can't. I see the roles are reversed now, and I don't like it. Something is going on here in Hami, and no one is speaking of it."

"What do you mean, Sayiina? What do you think is going on?"

"I don't know." She squinted and pursed her lips tight. "I don't know. It's like an . . . an . . ." She struggled inwardly to find the words.

Her jaw tightened as her perception strained to see the truth, but she was disrupted when Ragnar asked, "Would a little wine help to relax your thoughts?"

"Might as well. I am at a loss for words."

"Really? I look at you as the strong, silent type. What makes you think something is different in the wind, lass?"

Ragnar filled two cups with wine and handed one to Sayiina. She accepted the cup of amber liquid, raised it to her lips, sipped lightly, then gazed into her cup.

"Tell me, Ragnar, is there a name for something invisible, but everyone is aware of it?"

"Well, my first thought would be God."

"True, but something a little more tangible, yet not necessarily solid to touch."

"Is this a riddle, lass?" he asked, engagingly staring at her over the rim of his cup.

"No, just a question."

"What about a 'secret' then? Does that word qualify?"

"Yes, it does." She stared back, unblinking. "And how do you hide a secret?"

Ragnar poured more wine for them. He looked out the window, contemplating her questions. "If the secret were so large and impossible to hide and it was everywhere when behaving like nowhere, it could hide in plain sight. That is my best and last answer."

"That's it, Ragnar!" Sayiina exclaimed loudly. "That's exactly how I am feeling. I don't know what the secret is, but I intend to find out."

"So, how will you find out if no one speaks of it?"

"I'm not sure. I could begin by asking the Tajik soldiers. They may give a hint or a lead to follow."

"Aye, it would be a good beginning, just not tonight, lass. Let's enjoy our time shared with this wine and maybe make more memories."

"Aye, tell me a story of Norway and its people. If it's going to be my new home, I would like to hear more of it and learn its customs. What gods do they pray to?"

"Odin is the name of an older pagan god. He was the god of war and magic. On each of his shoulders sat a raven, who informed him of all the ways of men. Nowadays, I am told the people belong to the Lutheran faith, a Christian people."

Ragnar sipped his wine, enjoying its taste of fresh melon. Outside, the sky was dark; it was eventide.

Across the table, Sayiina watched him. It was her way during these thoughtful moments. "Do you believe in the old gods?"

Ragnar drew a deep breath, held it for a moment, then slowly released it with a faint sound into the air.

"I've been in many wars and seen the worst of men. I believe in magic or, what some would say, the unexplainable. I also believe there is life after death. In what form, I don't know. But how we live our lives, for good or evil, is how God will judge our souls in the end."

"You're talking karma, Ragnar." She reached out gently to touch his hand. "I, too, believe the same as you, and I think I like your pagan god. Strong men are best."

"Aye, but his ravens gave him real power, for they provided him with knowledge."

Sayiina remained silent at his insight. It spoke of wisdom and truth to her.

"Let's end this day, Sayiina; that bed is like a siren calling me to sleep." Then, he emptied his cup of wine with a gulp.

They stood together. She moved in closer to kiss his cheek. "Aye, aye, captain of my heart, we sail together."

The following day, Ragnar and Sayiina woke to the subtle sound of the bamboo curtain parting. They both sat up as Ying Ying entered their chamber, followed by three young, attractive women. Each wore a distinctive, sheer pink, green, and blue frock. This left nothing to the imagination of their physical beauty. They stopped beside each other at the foot of the bed, each with a shy smile on display.

"These are my daughters. They are beautiful and youthful, are they not? Each one is available, or all three for a negotiated rate."

Ragnar and Sayiina turned to look at each other, speechless, then stared back at Ying Ying.

"Are you selling your daughters to us?" Sayiina sputtered in disbelief.

"They are not for sale; they are more for rent or hire if you prefer."

"Is this a joke?" Ragnar asked.

"Not a joke." Ying Ying politely responded. "In Hami, it is a custom; this is caravanserai."

Sayiina interjected angrily, "No, this is prostitution!"

Ying Ying was taken aback by Sayiina's furious rebuke and moved her fingertips to cover her lips. Her eyes widened now, and she fully understood her guests. "You two don't know of our tradition in Hami, do you?"

"What tradition is this?" Ragnar queried. "Is this tradition an open secret?"

"It is. I am sorry. I only assumed you knew what transpired here during your stay with us or any of the village houses."

"So, please enlighten us," Sayiina insisted. "Hold nothing back."

Ying Ying told her daughters to leave the room and listen beyond the curtain.

Ragnar could see this woman had pride and dignity by standing before them with no shame.

"We are not prostitutes. It is not our way. This is how we earn an income."

Sayiina raised herself a little higher on the bed. "Where are your men? Do they not care enough that you offer yourselves to strangers?"

"Our men are fully aware and encourage us to earn as much as possible entertaining strangers. When word of an approaching caravan is near, they depart from our village and will not return to their homes if travelers still occupy them."

"I've sailed all across the world and have never found this custom anywhere. Can your men not provide for you?"

"Here in Hami, the land provides in great abundance. Our men only desire every manner of pleasure. They do not toil the earth as other men do. It gives them a special gratification to allow weary travelers access to their homes and any female as if they were their wives. For a price, of course, as this is our custom," she explained in a proud yet quietly submissive voice.

"Well, this is not for us, Ying Ying," Sayiina asserted. "No one touches my man without my approval, and I say no!"

"But my husband will shame my daughters and me for being lazy and not earning money for the good of our family. He will lose face in our community."

"I don't care about lazy men," Sayiina spat back in contempt.

"Wait, Sayiina. Wait. Slow your anger here," Ragnar said. "Perhaps we can find a mutual understanding to navigate during our stay."

"What? Are you really going to negotiate with a woman in charge of a whorehouse? Don't include me in anything you two agree on," she said, showing actual irritation toward Ragnar.

Ragnar ignored Sayiina's words, rose naked from the bed, and walked casually to a large pitcher of water nearby, pouring some into a cup. All the while, he felt the eyes of both females staring at his naked form.

"Wants and needs, Ying Ying. Do you know the difference between those two words?"

A slight grin crossed her lips at the question. In her profession, it was only a matter of how much. "Of course."

"Good." Unashamed, he turned to face her directly, allowing her a moment to gaze at the make of his masculinity. Then he continued assuredly. "You have a need, and I have wants. You need to earn coin to save face, and I am prepared to pay you and your three daughters handsomely if you take care of my wants."

"Yesss . . ." Her carnal mind raced anxiously in anticipation of what his desires were. Her loins heated as always, and her face flushed in lust.

Ragnar turned his head to look at Sayiina. Her hands gripped the furs with clenched fists. Her jaw was set, and her eyes were like slits. She was furious with him, so he sent her a wink.

"My wants, Ying Ying, are simple. I want a hot bath and a haircut. As well, all my clothes cleaned and dried for tomorrow's departure. They smell horrible. After I bathe, I want a full massage. Oh, and bring good fresh food and tea for now. That is everything."

"What?" Ying Ying exclaimed in disbelief. She could feel the heat in her subside like a riptide. Her face expressed servile disappointment.

"Wait, wait, Ragnar," Sayiina chimed in. "I've changed my mind and would like to be a part of your negotiations. I like your way of thinking."

"Aye, lass, welcome aboard. Well, Ying Ying, can you accommodate us?"

She bowed with dignity, replying, "Yes, but the fee just doubled."

"Fine, we will begin with a hot bath and bathe together."

"Yes." Sayiina, now excited, moved to Ragnar's side. Also, completely naked, she walked over to kiss his neck.

"You've made me very happy, my sailor man. Few men could resist the company of four attractive, nubile women together in one bed."

Ragnar smiled at that. "The decision wasn't all that difficult, although the thought was entertaining. Having one angry woman in my bed for a lifetime would be more challenging than four docile women for one night's pleasure."

He then lowered his hand to cup her firm buttock. Sayiina did not move away from his touch, instead replying in kind by clutching his backside hard.

"So, what do you want to do before our bath is drawn?" she asked immodestly, leading Ragnar to the fur-lined bed.

Following her, Ragnar replied, "Well, we could talk about the first thing that pops up."

"Take me sailing, Ragnar," she said as she laughed at the thought.

CHAPTER 27

After a day's trek into the Pamir Mountains, Ragnar, Sayiina, and a few Tajik soldiers sat around a fire. Caravan tradition required each individual to tell a story. Shadows and red flickering light illuminated each person's face, like glowing orbs suspended above the flames.

Ragnar noticed the two brothers, Salar and Hamasa. They were listening eagerly to an elder's tale told in the twilight. A lull entered their group, and all talking ceased. Everyone stared toward the dancing flames, reflecting perhaps on their past or future days to come.

Sayiina moved closer to the fire, unable to warm herself this evening. She rubbed her hands and arms vigorously. "Is it me, or does this fire not give out heat?" she challenged anyone in the group to answer.

An elder Tajik knowingly replied, "Your observations are good. Fire does not burn well here. It is the highest point of our journey. Some believe Allah is offended, as it is an impure light made by men so close to his realm."

Sayiina stared across the fire at the elder who'd responded. She remained quiet. She did not believe fire would not give heat because it offended the gods. While continuing to rub her arms, she returned her gaze to the flickering flames.

Salar spoke out next, with a challenge to Ragnar. "Give us one adventure while sailing the oceans, Ragnar. You must have one or two worthy of telling us."

Ragnar heard the challenge in Salar's tone of voice. It would be difficult to deny the young soldier's request. The other men who gathered nodded in approval, with hand gestures for him to begin.

Sayiina, sitting beside Ragnar, sat up and chimed in with a purposefully sugared tongue. "Yes, Ragnar, why not tell us of your miraculous escape from the notorious sea pirate, Cheng I Sao? I'm sure everyone would like to hear that tall tale."

She raised an eyebrow at him, then smiled.

Ragnar glared back at her, sitting smugly beside him. They both knew telling that story might put him in poor favor with these men, who would never run away from a fight or a woman.

"Something daring with a fight to the death," said Salar.

Ragnar liked the young soldier. He was reminded of himself as a youth, adventurous and eager to challenge the world around him. "Aye, would you want the truth or maybe a child's bedtime story?" he asked Salar, knowing he would choose truth.

"I am no child, and I know the truth from a lie." He then laughed, as did some others.

"Truth then," Ragnar declared.

"This is a story of courage, a death dance against arcane sorcery and survival. I will tell you this story as true because I was there and can prove my words. Sayiina was with me and would say if I am lying to you or not. She fears no man's wrath, not even my own."

With this promise, not just a few of the soldiers leaned forward so as not to miss a word.

Sayiina, now put on the spot as vindicator, seriously wondered what he would reveal to these Tajik men. She stopped staring into the fire and faced Ragnar. He winked her way and began.

Slowly, he told of their encounter with the leopard and the tiger on the Amur River, leaving out no details.

During the telling, the men occasionally looked to Sayiina for a rebuttal, but there was none. She nodded yes to the ancient stone altar and how she sensed malevolency in the air. They were suddenly surrounded by an unnatural and fast-moving cloud when the leopard appeared before them. Ragnar spoke of their dance of death on the plateau, resulting in his back being viciously mauled by the leopard. Then, the explosive appearance of the tiger and the outcome of the leopard's violent death.

When Ragnar had finished, no one spoke. The crackle of burning wood was the only sound among them. The soldiers looked at each other in disbelief.

"How is this possible?"

"Do you have proof of this?" one elder soldier asked Ragnar.

Ragnar then stood and removed his jersey. His raked back revealed to all four striped, raised scars and a fifth dew claw mark. There was no doubt among the Tajik. All were stunned.

"A fantastic tale, Ragnar. A worthy life," Salar exclaimed excitedly.

When pointing to the scars, one soldier spoke aloud what all were thinking. "You two infidels live unnatural lives. Your story seems impossible, yet the scars on your back speak truth."

"Aye, seeing is believing. Truth is not always what it seems."

"I've seen you survive a dust devil. Also, you helped defeat our enemy against great chance, and now you've shown me proof of defeating great sorcery and surviving. I think Allah has saved your life for something more."

With Ragnar's story told, many of the soldiers left. Salar and Hamasa held back a moment to speak privately to Ragnar.

"Your story was excellent," Salar said. "Our faith does not allow us to believe in sorcery. It is forbidden. My brother and I also think your eyes can deceive and tell you a truth as one thing. We have been to such a place near Samarkand, an upcoming city destination. Would you like to go see something that defies understanding?"

Ragnar turned to Sayiina, looking at her with raised brows. "Are you interested in going?"

"Am I putting myself at unnecessary risk, Salar?"

"There is no risk. Hamasa and myself have been there once before when passing through Samarkand."

"Aye then. If it's on the road, we travel."

"Wonderful," both brothers replied together, nodding and grinning.

"But first, we will be in Tajikistan country, our home. 'May the evil eye and misfortunes be far.'"

Ragnar and Sayiina watched the brothers leave the fire. When the night's dark concealed their forms, Sayiina asked, "Are you certain the story of the leopard and tiger was a good choice? Their religion tells them we are godless infidels already condemned. Now even more, as the 'evil eye and misfortunes' follow in our steps on this journey together." She mimicked them.

"Aye, lass, you may be right in their opinion of us. But I sure wasn't going to share the sea tale of Cheng I Sao. There is a sea chest full of shame in that telling tale. No, some things are better if unspoken."

"Well, this fire is of no use to us. I've been cold all night. Why don't you take me into our tent and warm me up for a while?" A smiling Sayiina threw her arm around Ragnar's waist, quickly coaxing him toward the tent.

"I don't know, lass. Are you sure?" Ragnar feigned wariness. "Allah might not approve of us being so near his heavenly realm."

"I don't think he cares much about us; we're condemned infidels. Besides, he can watch us if he wants to."

Both chuckled at her last remark and eagerly entered their tent.

CHAPTER 28

Just as they had finished loading their gear onto an ass, Ragnar watched the brothers' approach on horseback. It was early morning, and the caravan wouldn't be ready to depart for another hour. So, as previously arranged, he and Sayiina agreed to go off the Silk Road with Salar and Hamasa on a brief excursion outside of the city of Samarkand. The brothers had promised there was something very unusual, even unexplainable, to see. Salar and Hamasa had earned their trust enough to follow their lead and were curious to learn what the brothers had discovered.

After reining his mount to a halt, Hamasa asked, "Are you ready to depart, Ragnar and Sayiina?"

"We are, but Sayiina and I would like to know how far off course we'll travel."

"Maybe twenty minutes, not much more."

"Good. I don't want to stray too far from the caravan. You lead, and we'll follow."

With those words, Ragnar and Sayiina rode closely behind the brothers. A short ride west from Samarkand brought all to a halt before a small, narrow ravine. It was sparsely treed, but a thick underbrush would not allow their horses clear passage.

"What were you two doing to find yourself at this place? It seems to be in the middle of nowhere, with just a few trees growing beside a grassy knoll," Ragnar asked.

"Hunting rabbits," Hamasa replied with a beaming smile. "We refer to this place as 'the rabbit hole' by name."

"And what is so special here, besides it containing rabbits?"

"It was hard to believe when you told the tale of the leopard and the tiger. You also proved it to be a true-life experience, witnessed by the scars across your back. Hamasa and I also agree with your thinking. Not everything in life is as it seems.

"What we found here we have not shared with anyone, especially with the followers of our Islamic faith. It might be considered blasphemy to bring a truth to light. But you are non-believers, good people passing through this land. So we decided to share this wonder with you."

Ragnar looked at Sayiina for her thoughts, but she merely shrugged. Turning back to the brothers, he asked, "What now?"

"Now we dismount and tie off the horses. We'll be following a faint trail leading to an almost hidden entrance into the side of this mound. We will guide you. Then you, too, will see the unexplainable in life."

"Are you saying there is a door, Salar?" Sayiina asked.

"No, I'm saying a window!"

Accompanying the brothers for a short distance, they soon abruptly stopped. They stood before many long, exposed, tentacled roots from a tree above. The brothers pulled aside the dangling roots like a curtain, revealing an arched-shaped stained-glass window of archaic design.

Inquisitively, Ragnar and Sayiina peered forward at the sight.

"What lies beyond, Salar?" Ragnar asked.

"A circular stone stairwell taking us to the base of a marble column."

"Are you uneasy, Sayiina?"

"No, not at all," was her calm reply.

"Aye. Then how do we enter?"

Salar let go of the tree roots he was holding, then aided Hamasa in moving the curtain he held further aside.

"The mortar used to secure this window frame in place has broken down over the ages. It is completely removable by hand. Take your knife and use it to pry the window free. Together, we can lift it away and gain entry."

The window was narrow and modest in size. Ragnar guessed six feet tall by three feet wide. Its position on the knoll faced east. When it was extracted, the bright morning sun sent a shaft of light to illuminate the area inside and below.

"Stay close to the wall. We will descend along flat stone steps, each set into a curved wall. I believe it's safe, as Hamasa and I had no difficulty going down or up when last here. I will go first, then you, Ragnar, followed by Sayiina and Hamasa. Agreed?"

"Aye. Lead our way."

Once inside, Ragnar adjusted his vision to the dim. A shaft of sunlight pierced through the dark, striking a white marble column that stood alone in a cavernous room. The effect was illuminating, and their visibility went from pitch black to a light gray haze. Although it was dull in color, Ragnar could easily see the stone's stairwell and spiral route before him. The height was great, so they all proceeded with caution.

Ragnar was reminded of the crow's nest or lookout perch atop the highest mast of a three-masted sailing ship.

No one spoke. Better to concentrate on sure footing, for to fall would cause grievous harm or even death. When everyone stepped away from the last stone, all sighed in relief. The column, approximately 50 feet before them, was in the center of a large hall.

With its high domed ceiling, Ragnar surmised it was not unlike the inside of a cathedral. He stood on an inch of fine dust. When disturbed, it lifted upwards effortlessly, floating around him. The tiled floor revealed a pattern of runes, strange in design. The reflected sunlight caused the dust to appear in varied colors of red, gold, green, and blue, much like the twinkling of starlight. For a moment, they stood inside a world of wonder.

Ragnar felt Salar's hand on his arm. He was indicating they approach the column. Ragnar nodded in agreement and moved toward it cautiously. He also cast a glance at Sayiina's graceful movement beside him. The closer he got to the column, the more it seemed to glow and take on a pulsating light of its own—more like a living thing.

Salar stopped a few feet away and pointed straight up to the ceiling.

Ragnar could see the column was a keystone. It alone supported the entire ceiling. He watched Salar lower his hand slowly, tracing the length of the column, then stop. Kneeling on one knee, he indicated that all should do likewise and look at the pedestal.

For Ragnar, here the light shone brightest. Perhaps the sunlight was more intensely focused, or the dust more profuse. Either was a mute reason when the visual reality briefly staggered his mind.

Kneeling closely beside him, Sayiina let out a gasp as she, too, was shocked by the revelation. There was no base stone to support the column. A space separated the tile floor from the marble column about three hands high.

"Unbelievable," Ragnar uttered. He slowly shook his head in disbelief.

The two brothers were staring at him and Sayiina, awaiting a response.

Sayiina rose gradually, and in doing so, her hand touched the tiled floor. In that instant, an image of an old man appeared in her mind in perfect clarity. She heard his voice say, "From this place, leave in peace, child of God."

"Ragnar, we need to leave this place."

"Why? Are we in danger?"

"Now, please!" Sayiina almost pleaded. "I sense no danger but feel we are witness to a living miracle. It is unnatural . . ." Sayiina struggled to find the words, then she finally expelled, "We are standing on sacred ground. The energy beneath the column is a gift from almighty God. I have no other words for this."

"Aye, lass."

Ragnar backed away first, walking slowly and trying not to disturb anything.

"I also think we are intruding on a spiritual force. Back up the stairwell and out!" Ragnar led the way and exited out of the window above.

They were surprised when met and surrounded by five large armed men, all dressed in black but for a red Maltese cross worn over their left breast. Beneath their sleeveless tunics, all wore chain mail. Four men were pointing loaded crossbows at them, fingers on the triggers.

The fifth man held the tip of his sword on Ragnar's chest. He spoke directly to Ragnar calmly, "We are Knights Templar. Tell me, stranger, why should I not kill all of you for desecrating our most holy of temples?"

"We only stumbled upon it by chance. We were out hunting rabbits for fare," Ragnar replied equally, knowing the last part was a lie.

"Not good enough, foreigner," was his reply, and he cocked his right elbow up for a killing thrust of his sword.

"Stop!" Sayiina yelled. "I had a vision in the temple, and the man who spoke to me said, 'Leave in peace, child of God.' Would you break his promise to me?"

"No." He glared at Sayiina. "We are the protectors of this sacred temple. Describe your vision to me and speak his words."

In the most minute detail she could remember, Sayiina painted a portrait of the vision that came to her. When she finished her telling, the black-robed leader nodded and lowered his sword away from Ragnar. Reaching into his tunic, he brought forth an image of a man etched in silver and showed it to Sayiina.

"Was this the man in your vision?"

Shocked at the similarity, she replied, "It is the same."

"Then you are blessed. The man you described to me and who spoke to you is Saint John the Baptist. He is our patron saint. He performed the miracle you witnessed in the temple centuries ago, now lost in memory."

"Who are you?" Ragnar asked.

"Christian warriors living in an Islamic time and place. Our faith is persecuted, so we remain in the shadows, protecting what is our own. If the Imams of Islam rediscovered this location, they would want to destroy it as being profane. We will honor the words spoken in your vision. Leave in peace, speak to no one of this place, and never return. The penalty would be death."

"We will not be passing this way again. Fair winds," Ragnar said to the protectors as he rode away.

In response, the leader made the sign of the cross over his heart, saying, "May the Christ King in heaven protect you."

Sayiina turned in her saddle for a final look, but the men had disappeared.

They returned to the caravan base camp in silence. Their encounter with the living miracle and then the protectors caused everyone to pause for thought.

"There are always forces in life at work that we will never truly understand," Salar said.

"Aye, you're right, Salar. Sayiina and I will not likely pass this way again. But not you or Hamasa. My best advice is to never go there again. I don't think the protectors will be so forgiving a second time. There is an old saying in my country that is still true today. 'Do not awaken sleeping wolves. Just pass them by.'"

"Good to know. Hamasa and I will leave you now, but we were pleased to share our unbelievable story with you two."

Hamasa nodded in agreement.

"I think there is more to this miracle story. Only after seeing for myself would I ever have believed it true," Sayiina said.

"Aye, that's true, lass. We can speak more of it on the road."

CHAPTER 29

The land claimed by the Tajikistani people was rich and varied. Snow-capped mountains reaching breathtaking heights surrounded Ragnar and Sayiina everywhere. Having crossed over the Pamir Mountains, their caravan route led them through lush valleys. The vegetation was so nutritious that horses and beasts of burden might gain weight due to grazing. Rivulets and streams of the purest fresh, cold water followed alongside their steps, like ribbons of silver flashing in the sunlight.

"A beautiful land, Sayiina."

She remained silent.

"You've been quiet this morning. Is everything all right?"

"I'm fine if that's what you're asking. I've been thinking a lot of Yakutia today, that's all. Perhaps I'm beginning to realize it's gone from me forever, and I'm missing it."

"You're fortunate you can feel this way, Sayiina. Cherish your memories and hold them dear to your heart. If you do this, a part of Yakutia will always be with you."

"Do you do the same, Ragnar?"

"Yes. There are fragments of my childhood I still hold on to. I'll never let go of them. Most of my life has been spent at sea, never really having a permanent home. I look forward to making many memories with you and our new life in Norway."

"Thanks, Ragnar, you can always lift my spirit."

With Hasad hailing them, they both turned his way. He rode to their position from the lead, then pulled up alongside them. "There's been a change in our schedule for today. We are well ahead of our calendar, so Tarkan has decided we will stop and rest in the large village of Dushanbe for two nights.

"Dushanbe has an excellent market where you can purchase seasonal fruit, fabric, leather, and even weapons. Some of the Tajik's best artisans gather here every Monday to buy and sell their products. So, knowing tomorrow is Monday, Tarkan would like to see what is available.

"Enjoy your rest." He then rode back to the front of the caravan.

"You know, Sayiina, this is just what you need. A large bazaar is a distraction from your present state of mind. It might be exciting."

"Aye, Ragnar," was her unenthusiastic reply. "We'll see."

The sun had reached its zenith when the caravan finished establishing itself on the outskirts of the village alongside the Varzob River. Some of the merchants and soldiers trekked into the market. The one rule was no beasts of burden were allowed entry for sanitary reasons.

Once inside, Ragnar noted it was both busy and noisy. A melting pot with many people of different cultures engaging with each other. The primary language spoken was Farsi, but he also heard a lot of Russian.

"Ragnar. Over here," Sayiina called out. She was standing beside a merchant's table of weapons. "These knives and swords are remarkably light. The edge is so keen. I've not seen anything like them before. This seller also says they are resistant to pit. What do you think?"

"They are very fine, and the coloring is more silver than gray. Where are they made?" he asked the merchant.

"They are Iranian-made. Only the best craftsmen in the world forged these. There is no secret of steel their ovens have not uncovered."

Ragnar nodded in appreciation while lifting a long, curved saber in his hands. It was twice the length of the cutlass he carried on his back, yet lighter to wield.

"You hold an Iranian 'shamshir,' stranger. Deadly in the right hand."

"And what of arrowheads?" Sayiina asked.

"Ah." With a knowing look, the merchant nodded, thinking she might be an archer.

He reached under his table, retrieving a rolled piece of leather, then laid it open for view. He revealed six of the most exquisitely crafted arrowheads Ragnar had ever seen. They were made of the same silver-colored steel as his swords. The tip was perfect, and the tang was long. The overall shape was of an elongated heart, with sawed tooth edges from tip to midpoint. From midpoint to barb, a razor-sharp edge. Deadly in the hands of an expert. Ragnar watched Sayiina hold one up by the tang for closer inspection.

"It's so light, Ragnar," she marveled. Rolling it in her fingertips, she just stared at its beauty. "How much for one?" Sayiina enquired politely.

Ragnar could tell Sayiina was captivated by its beauty. She did not turn away when the merchant replied, "100 rubles."

"That is a lot of money for one arrowhead," Ragnar interjected.

"They are of the finest craftsmanship in the entire world. There are no two alike anywhere," he insisted and was unmoving with his price.

"Do you take silver?"

"Da," was his friendly reply.

The smile Sayiina conveyed Ragnar's way was a come-hither look.

Ragnar knew he was done for. He shook his head in defeat to her. "I will offer you two silver coins for one arrowhead."

"Three," the merchant countered, lifting his thick, bushy eyebrows.

"Five pieces of eight for two arrowheads, final offer," Ragnar bartered back and crossed his arms.

The merchant paused, weighing Ragnar's offer. He slowly squeezed his chin with his thumb and forefinger. It was a fair offer but not a great offer. Still, he would make a modest profit. He looked down, then up at Ragnar.

"Allah has decided we should do business together this day. Da! Choose any two from the six before you."

As Ragnar handed the silver over, he said, "Go ahead, Sayiina, you choose."

She leaned forward for a closer look, then discretely selected two.

"Excellent choices. You have an eye for quality."

As he wrapped the arrowheads in leather, the merchant asked, "Where are you from, may I ask?"

"Yakutia," Sayiina answered quietly. "I am Yakutian and shall always be. Thank you for reminding me."

"Judging by your decision today, your people must be of high quality."

Sayiina smiled at the merchant. She then turned, placed her arm in Ragnar's, and entered the market.

"Nice choices, Sayiina, but before you can use them, let's buy some real food for a change. I am tired of tea and dried biscuits for breakfast, and I'm hungry now!"

"Lead the way," she said with a spring in her step.

Even in the busy market, people would occasionally stare their way. So, it was no surprise to hear the brothers hail as they approached through the crowd.

"Welcome to Dushanbe, friends. This is our home. We were born and raised not far from here in a cotton field, so we are told." Salar was enthusiastically speaking, and Hamasa nodded in support.

"We have a dinner invitation for both of you tonight at our father's house. He says he would like to welcome far travelers in need of rest. It is good karma, and Hamasa and I would consider this an honor." He beamed.

Ragnar turned to see Sayiina already assenting with a slight bow to them.

"It seems the decision has been made, then."

"Excellent!" Hamasa said. "Our mother makes the best *osh* in the village, perhaps in all the land. You will have no regrets about your choice. Travel west on the same Silk Road we've traveled for one-half mile. On your right, in a cotton field, is a light-gray, flat-roofed house made of wood and clay. You will find us and our father's hospitality there."

The brothers then smiled and went on their way.

"Yours was a quick decision for us, Sayiina."

"Aye, it was matey." She laughed at her reply. "Free food, no cooking, and good company. What more could a woman want?"

"Oh, I don't know. How about a bath and some fresh clothes? Help me find a new jersey for tonight, and how about a silk blouse for you?"

"That's generous of you."

"It is, but I feel a wind of change coming about for us, lass. I like the lay of this land."

It was late in the afternoon when Ragnar and Sayiina arrived at Salar and Hamasa's family home. Three raps on the door and a smiling Salar greeted them in Tajikistan dress with a skull cap and traditional robe. He placed his left hand over his heart and bowed slightly.

"Sayiina and Ragnar, welcome to my father's house. Come in." He gestured with a sweeping arm.

"Everyone is waiting." Then he quietly whispered, "Also, everyone is hungry, and you are the guests of honor. Please follow me."

Salar led them into a large central room. When they entered, everyone stood to greet them. Salar made the introductions, saving the last for the brothers' parents and their hosts, Farrukh and Yasaman Aslonova.

Ragnar was the first to speak. "Thank you for welcoming us into your home."

"My sons could hardly stop talking about you two. I had to see for myself what kind of people you are," Farrukh replied. "But also, a noisy raven was sitting on the roof of my house this morning. A traditional sign that guests are coming. So here you are. Please be seated."

With that, everyone sat on the cushioned floor except for Yasaman. She quietly stepped into an adjacent room, only to return quickly with two other women, all carrying bowls of hot food.

"This is *Osh*," Farrukh said. "A traditional Tajikistan food. It has onion, carrots, and lamb on a bed of rice. My wife is the best at making *osh*. She uses a secret, old family recipe when preparing the meat. It is highly pleasing to the senses."

Ragnar and Sayiina sampled the dish, and their palates were instantly sated. They looked at each other, then at Yasaman, surprised at how really good it was.

"This is an excellent dish," Ragnar declared.

"And so simple a meal. I've never tasted anything like it," Sayiina followed up.

Sayiina noticed Yasaman blush, but Hamasa had everyone's attention just then, repeating, "Have I not always said our mother makes the best *osh* anywhere?"

Other invited guests in the room agreed with nods and grunts between mouthfuls of food.

Farrukh spoke proudly for everyone to hear. "I have a beautiful wife who prepares good food. Two strong sons, land, and friends."

"You are truly blessed, Farrukh," Ragnar commented.

"Allah has given me much, but I cannot grow a beard. Allah forbids me this until I have grandchildren." This remark he directed at Salar.

"Father, not now," he objected. "With respect, we have guests. They do not know our faith or customs. Please."

Yasaman touched her husband's hand as an unspoken signal to quiet or change the conversation.

Farrukh continued, "I have heard word, Hamasa, there will be a *buzkashi* event tomorrow. Perhaps you could find someone to partner with."

Hamasa loved the sport of *buzkashi*. He had participated many times but had never won victory.

"I choose Salar," was his quick response.

"Sorry, brother. Tomorrow, I have other responsibilities with family business to attend to."

Surprised at Salar's response, he looked around the full room of family and friends looking for a potential riding partner.

"Hamasa, what is *buzkashi*?" Ragnar queried.

"It is the best horseback riding competition ever."

"So, what are the rules?"

"A rider must pick up a headless, footless goat from one end of a field, then carry it to the other end and drop it into a hole in the ground. The hole is named The Circle of Justice."

"That doesn't seem very challenging, Hamasa. It sounds like a children's game of tag on horseback."

At this remark, all the men in the room openly laughed. Ragnar felt foolish not understanding the game's rules. "What? What don't I know?"

Farrukh raised his hand for his guests to quiet, then spoke. "You are correct, my friend. The goal is simple enough. But the holder of the goat must now face every other rider trying to stop him from accomplishing this task. Including pulling the goat out of his hand. The fight for possession can be very challenging when surrounded by many seasoned riders."

"I see. How many riders participate?"

"There is no limit. Sometimes 20, other times 200. The greater the number, the greater the difficulty of success. There is a reward for the winning rider or team, but in our culture, prestige is more important than money."

"Ragnar, why not team up with me?" Hamasa challenged. "You have the best karma of anyone I know, and I can provide you with a smart, seasoned horse for the competition."

"I see you are keen to compete, Hamasa, but I am not the better rider. You should be asking Sayiina. She is fiercely competitive and knows how to handle a horse more than me."

Sayiina shot Ragnar a glance and raised her brows in question. Staring at Hamasa, she waited for his challenge.

Hamasa hesitated a moment, surprised at Ragnar's remark.

"Women don't play *buzkashi*. Only men."

"Well, if you say there are no formal rules other than to throw a headless, footless goat into a pit, why can't a woman do this as well?"

"It would be a first time, but why not? Sayiina, would you like to—"

"I accept your invitation, Hamasa," she intervened. "There is a first for everything."

Everyone in the room cheered their approval, even the shyest women attending.

Yasaman called out to Sayiina, sitting opposite her, and immediately had her attention. "My sons have shared some stories with us of your prowess. Why not tell us about yourself and your people's culture? I would like to hear of the strong women of your land and family."

Sayiina, knowing what Yasaman was asking of her, knew it would be difficult. It wasn't her way to share her life or past with others. She had only shared this with Ragnar. But she was comfortable among these people. They were hospitable, humble to a fault, and respectful to her.

So, for a little while, she spoke openly of her life for all to hear. A story of courage, compassion, strength, and even regret. She tried to paint an honest image of herself and Yakutia. The room was silent as she wove her story of truth and humanity in her world. Finally, she went quiet, her story now over.

"My child," Yasaman said, "your story was beautiful. Thank you for sharing it with us. The Tajikistan people are not much different from your own. Always keep your memories close. Your past will always be a part of you."

"Thank you. I feel welcome here."

Tea was being served, and as per custom, the host drank first, showing it was safe to drink. Once proven, Ragnar looked around the room, and a quiet fell upon him. He heard Sayiina's voice beside him, talking to Hamasa regarding the next day's event. Their hosts and all the guests were engaging each other more like a family gathering. Just for a moment, all concerns and all his troubles fell away, like a single leaf falls from a tree. He was at peace.

The next morning, Ragnar and Sayiina rode to meet with Hamasa at his father's house. Once there, Farrukh explained to both that only stallions were allowed on the field. Sayiina dismounted and asked Ragnar if he would look after her mare.

"Of course. You know Hamasa made the right choice by asking you to be a teammate."

"Aye." She smiled back. "We discussed some strategies last night, and I don't like to lose. If we have our way, the players are in for a surprise or two."

Hamasa rode out from behind his home to greet them. He rode an average-sized but very spirited chestnut stud. The other horse he was leading was a massive black stallion, maybe even greater than 17 hands high, broad across his chest, shoulders, and withers.

"That is a king-sized horse!" Sayiina exclaimed. "I've never seen a breed this large."

"His name is Alexander. He is easily controlled in the right hands. Also, very familiar with *buzkashi*. Here, take his reins, Sayiina, and say hello."

As she patted Alexander's neck and rubbed his shoulder, she whispered into his ear. With Sayiina's foot in the stirrup, he snorted and shook his neck as she straddled the saddle.

"He's big and strong, Sayiina, but not fast. Our rivals, as much as they try, will not be able to throw you off balance. But know they will try!"

The saddle was smaller than what she was used to. The stirrups were raised so her knees could also control the steed's direction. Sitting comfortably with reins in hand, she looked at Hamasa. "You lead the way. Why not share the rules of *buzkashi* again with Ragnar?"

Hamasa explained while riding to the field. "The rules of the game are simple, Ragnar. The name *buzkashi* means 'goat in the hole.' The goat is headless, and its hooves are removed so as not to injure horse or rider. It can weigh 50 to 90 pounds."

"That's inconvenient for the goat," Ragnar replied sarcastically.

"At the opposite end of the field, there is a hole in the ground, twice the size of the goat. In the center of the field lies the goat. The purpose of each contestant is to pick up the goat, then drop it into the hole."

"Sounds simple enough."

"Yes, but you'll find it's not. The moment you get a grip on the goat, you will be attacked from every angle except a direct charge to your horse's ribs. This is not permitted.

"It will be a swarming of men and horses attempting to take the goat away from you at every turn. It can be very frustrating when unable to break free. Your arm will grow weary while defending your possession of the goat from many.

"It is a relentless attack. Many players form teams to have the option of passing the goat forward. The new goat holder might break free and carry it downfield to the hole."

"Today will be the first time I see this sport, Hamasa. I wish you success, but I suspect you and Sayiina will make a difference on the field. I look forward to watching it."

"Good. It is a sport of horsemanship, strength of arm, and prestige. A king's game," he said proudly.

Sayiina heard Hamasa's last remark and threw him a dark look over her shoulder. Seeing this, he quickly added, "And a queen's game as well."

Ragnar laughed, as did Hamasa. Both men saw her character come alive.

She held her voice, ignoring their laughter. Focusing instead on the game ahead.

Now, at the field, Ragnar looked for a vantage point. Once found, he could easily watch the game unfold. There were maybe forty contestants on one end of the field. Approximately 100 yards down the pitch was a circular hole in the ground. Mid-field, the headless goat lay flat.

Sayiina and Hamasa were surrounded by other contestants, sitting on their restless steeds, waiting for an official hand signal to begin. On one end were forty stallions, bunched together tightly, all uneasy, neighing and snorting. Some bucked, others raised a foreleg.

Hamasa had positioned himself on the front line, with Sayiina behind him. Some of the other riders were pointing her way, laughing mockingly. Ragnar thought these men were fortunate she could not speak or understand the Farsi language. More than one man had been subjected to her boot to their arse.

Just then, an official ran out to the middle of the field and stood beside the goat. He raised his hand and just as quickly lowered it, signaling the start. With this, all horses and riders exploded toward center field to snatch up the goat.

Ragnar noticed Hamasa's steed was fast, but two others were ahead of him. The leaders nearing the goat reined in their horses, fighting for position to retrieve the carcass. This proved very difficult, as riders were not allowed to dismount when snatching it up. Leaning over their saddles was the only way. Also, the momentum of the stampede behind them kept pushing them away from their desired object. It quickly became a brutal circle of struggling horse flesh and screaming riders.

One rider dropped from sight and then reappeared, holding up the goat and declaring ownership. The game was on! He turned his steed toward the hole with one hand on the reins and the other gripping the goat, then urged him forward just when the goat was jerked from his hand. He cursed the other rider to no avail. Everyone was swarming the new goat holder, and still, he managed to move downfield.

In the relentless confusion, with Sayiina right behind him, Hamasa was maneuvering closer to the rider currently holding the goat. The unruly scrum kept moving, crawling toward the hole, and now Hamasa was close to the goat. He leaned over his saddle, reaching desperately with his left arm fully extended, and snatched the prized leg of the goat. He set his heels hard into the stirrups, then pulled back with all his weight and strength. Hamasa succeeded in wrenching the goat from his opponent's grasp. Yelling over his shoulder, he called out, "Now, Sayiina, now!"

Sayiina heard his call and charged forward, clearing a path to break up the scrum for Hamasa, who was right behind her. Other riders were stunned but saw their strategy. The big black stallion was being used as a blocker for any opposition to Hamasa's chestnut, now racing wildly over an open field to the hole in the ground. Everyone in pursuit was trying to snatch the goat from Hamasa. But his strategy was to change his carrying hand from right to left and back again. This forced the pursuers to go around Hamasa or face being blocked by Sayiina.

Ten yards away from their goal, Hamasa cried out to Sayiina, "My arm grows weary. I can't hold it any longer. Take it from me."

"No, Hamasa, do not give up; we'll carry it together!"

She stopped blocking and dropped alongside Hamasa, grabbing the other leg of the goat. Riding together, they released the goat carcass directly over and into the hole in the ground.

Wildly, Hamasa pumped his fist into the air in jubilation. Sayiina threw both hands high. Exuberant in their victory, Hamasa and Sayiina cried out as one, "*Buzkashi*," while receiving congratulations from many contestants on the field.

When the accolades were done, Hamasa spoke out eagerly. "My first victory, Sayiina. We ride again?"

"No, not again, Hamasa. I proved my point with this victory. I think I'll sit back with Ragnar as a spectator for a while."

After she spoke, she saw some disappointment cross his face. "Your performance on the field was outstanding, Hamasa."

She then reached out, and they shook hands as friends.

"I will never forget this day and accept your words favorably." He then turned and rode back to the starting point, joining the other riders for another game.

"Well played, Sayiina," Ragnar said as she neared.

"Thanks, but I won't repeat it. I made a difference today, and that's all I care about." She dismounted and immediately regretted the move, grabbing her right thigh in pain.

"What's the matter?" Ragnar asked with concern.

"Just bruised and beaten a bit, that's all."

"Will you be able to ride tomorrow? Or should I secure a cart for you on our journey?" Ragnar was intentionally feigning sarcasm and smiled her way.

Glaring his way, she said, "Don't feel sorry for me. Feel sorry for all the goats around here. They need it more."

"Aye, lass, you're right on point there. Let's make our way back to the caravan camp. You can rest up there."

Sayiina agreed, and Ragnar watched as she favored her thigh while walking beside him. She never complained. To take her mind off her condition, he asked, "So, tell me how you feel knowing you bested thirty-eight men at their favored sport?"

He then smiled, waited, and listened.

CHAPTER 30

The next morning, the caravan was making ready to depart Dushanbe just as Ragnar and Sayiina finished loading their supplies.

"Good timing on our part, Sayiina; we can now wait and get in line at our turn."

An argument up ahead caught Ragnar's attention. It seemed Tarkan, encircled by merchants, disagreed with all of them, and no one was conceding. Ragnar walked over to a Tajik soldier standing nearby. "What's the argument about?"

"It seems the caravan owner, Tarkan Ozturk, does not want to stop in Tehran. Yet all the merchants are demanding this of him. Tehran is a very populated city with tens of thousands of people. All these camels and asses carry heavy loads of goods for sale. They argue that Tehran is an excellent place to do business."

The soldier shrugged. "It makes sense from a merchant's reasoning, plus a couple days' rest would be good for everyone. As long as this quarrel continues, we won't be moving," the soldier said.

Ragnar returned, explaining to Sayiina what he had learned from the soldier. "It doesn't make sense to me. Why not stop and set up a market? The buyers are in Tehran, the sellers are here, and some needed rest for man and beast could be had."

"There's more to this, Ragnar, and I think we'll soon find out."

"Aye, lass, I agree."

When every merchant had had their words heard, the scene quieted. The issue had not been resolved, nor had any amicable solution been found. Unhappy, the angry merchants broke away, complaining to each other. The caravan started moving west, and Ragnar and Sayiina fell in line with everyone else.

A half-mile travel down the road brought them to the brothers' family home. Ragnar saw Salar and Hamasa embrace their parents and then depart. Farrukh and Yasaman stood on the side of the road, beckoning them over.

"We should say goodbye, Ragnar. They're good people."

"I agree, Sayiina. Let's."

Dismounting, they walked over to them, and as they approached, both Aslonova parents placed their left hand over their heart and bowed slightly. Smiling, Ragnar and Sayiina replied in kind.

"Thank you for your hospitality and warm welcome," Sayiina started.

"It is I who should thank you," Farrukh replied. "Winning *buzkashi* yesterday with my son Hamasa brings honor to my house, and for this, I say thank you."

He then retrieved a stringed pouch containing coins from his tunic and gave it to Sayiina. "This is your share of the winners' purse."

"I can't take money from you," she blurted.

"Why not? You have earned it. Besides, every rider in the match bet against you." Farrukh laughed. "Very foolish of them to bet against a great rider and a smart horse."

"Take it, child," Yasaman pressed. "For a woman to best so many men at their own game is worth ten times the amount you will receive here. The women of Dushanbe will be talking of it for years."

"Well, thank you. I appreciate it," she said, accepting the pouch.

"Fair winds, Farrukh and Yasaman," Ragnar said sincerely. "Our sails may not pass this way again, but if they do, we will drop anchor and say hello."

With that, Ragnar and Sayiina mounted their horses and waved goodbye.

"May the evil eye and misfortunes be far," the Aslonovas replied as one.

The days passed, moving the caravan westward and bringing them closer to Tehran. Tarkan continued to quarrel with the merchants without end. They all wanted to do business in Tehran. With only two days' travel remaining from the great city, Ragnar noticed the tone of the men's voices was changing. They were turning more volatile toward Tarkan, who was also more adamant in his position. Ragnar turned to Sayiina.

"Is it me, or have you also noticed Tarkan's voice becoming shriller in his defense against the merchants?"

"I agree with you. I see a lot of anger directed at Tarkan. Who's to know which side of the argument will win over."

Once the arguments had ceased, Hasad and Tarkan stood alone, speaking privately. Hasad nodded, then approached Ragnar and Sayiina. "Tarkan would enjoy your company for tea after the meal tonight." He then bowed respectfully, waiting for their reply.

Ragnar was surprised at the request and looked at Sayiina with raised brows.

"Tell Tarkan we accept his invitation," she replied equally and returned his nod.

"Excellent. I will inform him." Hasad then returned to his position at the front of the camel train and to Tarkan Ozturk.

"I wonder what this is all about. Something tells me our talk around the table will be very revealing."

Sayiina nodded and smirked.

At seventy years old, Imam Husayn was the most knowledgeable and studied cleric of the Koran in all of Iran. This also explained why he was chosen to lead prayers in the largest mosque in Tehran. He had a substantial following of powerful and wealthy men who, when in need, would go to him for counsel. Willingly, he gave his time and advice to secure favor for himself and his family. After all, he had a large family with many wives and children to support.

Some patrons left behind helpful offerings of coins. Others gave up dark secrets and information about themselves and others. All this was used to enrich and strengthen his influence over the people of Tehran. Outwardly, he showed the people of the Islamic faith a calm, thoughtful, and wise demeanor. Very few knew of his dark side, as he was a vengeful man if ever an injustice was done to him or his family.

Word had reached his ear from a trusted source that a small caravan was approaching the city from the east, not two days away. He sat alone on the floor of the candlelit mosque, considering all options available. The timing was right for the caravan he had been patiently waiting for, and nearly two years had passed since a particular caravan owner had seduced his youngest daughter while passing through Tehran. Right now, his spies were watching their movements, and if this caravan were foolish enough to try to circumvent Tehran, they would quickly have unwelcome guests. The son of a camel would pay for his disgraceful behavior. The imam concluded his thoughts with a prayer to Allah for revenge.

Ragnar and Sayiina entered Tarkan's tent just as Sorbon Sherzod was leaving. They nodded to each other in recognition, and as always, the leader looked grim. Inside, Tarkan and Hasad stood waiting.

"Welcome, Ragnar and Sayiina, my honorable friends," Tarkan began. "Please be seated. Make yourselves comfortable here."

Ragnar noted there were more than enough silk pillows littering the floor of his tent. More than anyone would need. Tarkan poured out four cups of tea, giving one to each.

"You are probably curious why you have been invited for tea this evening."

"Aye, for sure."

Ragnar watched as Tarkan's eyes looked down and away to avert direct contact.

Hasad did not look away.

"There is a lot of discontent among the merchants and myself, as I am sure you are aware," Tarkan admitted. "Do you know why?"

"Only that you do not wish to stop in Tehran, and they do," Ragnar spoke.

"If I do not stop in Tehran, I will lose the merchants' support. If I lose their support, I will not have a caravan. More importantly, I will lose my honor and reputation so close to our journey's end. No merchant will do business with me. I need advice from an outsider's perspective, such as yours."

"Really? What don't we know?" Sayiina queried and raised one brow quizzically.

At her question, Tarkan paused, then began. "Almost two years ago, I made a poor decision in life while passing through Tehran. I worry considerably about it now, and perhaps my karma has changed for the worse. I believe someone in Tehran wishes to do me serious harm. I cannot go there. The risk is too great."

Surprised to hear this, Ragnar offered a suggestion. "You have Tajik bodyguards available to you. Use them as a shield."

"The Tajik numbers are too small against what will come for him," Hasad said in Tarkan's defense.

Sayiina pressed, "What did you do so terrible to create this powerful enemy?"

Tarkan hesitated at Sayiina's question, and the room went silent. No one spoke as the growing tension was suspended.

"I have a problem with a woman's infidelity and her family." This time, he kept eye contact with them.

"Seriously, Tarkan, are you telling us a woman is preventing you from entering Tehran?" Ragnar asked just for clarity.

With questioning eyes, Ragnar held his laughter in check and disbelief. He then sat back and waited for a response.

Tarkan's facial expression went first to embarrassment, then snapped to anger. The hand holding the teacup was shaking when he placed it down, something Ragnar had never witnessed until this moment. Perhaps it had always lurked beneath his calm veneer until provoked.

He looked to Hasad for an explanation, who sat staring ahead.

Hasad had seen Tarkan enraged before.

A slightly calmed down Tarkan continued. "Not just any woman." He seethed at the injustice done upon him. "But the daughter of the most powerful Imam in all Tehran. This wicked, shameless woman threw herself upon me until I consented. There was nothing I could do but submit. I'm sure it was a trap she set. I didn't learn of her position in society until after bedding her."

Tarkan raised both hands, palms up. "I need advice. What would you do if in my position?"

Sayiina shook her head in silence. The thought of a woman holding Tarkan Ozturk's life and means of support in her hands was real karma. One he could not run from.

"Well," Ragnar started, "as I see it, you are in a tough situation. The merchants will abandon you if you try to go around the city. Word will quickly reach the imam, who will see to your end. Not a good path for you, Tarkan.

"If I were you, my best advice would be to go to Tehran and seek out the imam. Hear him out. Be patient. Do not reply in anger. Let him vent his outrage toward you as a good father would.

"When he is finished, show him you are a man of honor. Say to him you wish to marry his daughter. This will shock him and take the wind out of his anger. It might be a winning solution. The merchants would be satisfied, the Imam's rage would be sated, and, of course, his daughter would be happy once again. That is my best advice for you."

Motionless and dumbfounded, Tarkan sat with unblinking eyes. A small bead of sweat appeared on his temple when he choked out, "That is your best advice, infidel? I should never have shared my dilemma with you.

"Hasad." Tarkan's voice was now shaking. "What is your opinion of the northerner's words?"

At first, Hasad stared at Ragnar, emotionless; then his face lit up. "I think his advice is brilliant. All our troubles answered at once. Yes, I like it." A slight grin and a spark in his knowing eyes gave his acknowledgment to Ragnar.

"What?" Tarkan shrieked. "You side with a nonbeliever?"

"Yes, I do, Tarkan. We will all be dead men—you, me, the Tajik mercenaries. Perhaps the merchants will survive the imam's wrath, but no one loyal to you will live. Ragnar's advice is good, and as the Chinese say, 'you will be able to save face.'"

Ragnar and Sayiina stood to leave.

"Thanks for the tea, Tarkan. I hope my advice is helpful to you," Ragnar said.

Imam Husayn sat on a high-backed chair, much like a king on his throne. While he wasn't royalty, he was indeed a powerful man. The chair was placed beside an elevated platform, where he held prayers inside his mosque. On either side of him stood large personal bodyguards, each armed with a scimitar on their hip.

Husayn was raging inside, waiting for a specific Turkish merchant to arrive—Tarkan Ozturk of Constantinople. The very name caused him to seethe. Word had reached Husayn that Tarkan requested an audience, so he granted it. The man could speak, but not before his personal retribution, and he would not escape alive. If he wanted to live like a dog, he could also die like a dog.

The front door of the mosque opened, allowing Tarkan access. As is customary, he first removed his shoes and then faced the wrath of the Imam sitting before him in judgment.

"Imam Husayn?" he asked.

"Tarkan Ozturk?" was the stone-cold response.

Imam Husayn ordered one of the guards to bring his daughter Leila to him. After a moment, the guard returned with a young lady beside him, her head bowed.

"Is this the man?" asked the imam.

Leila lifted her head and locked her gaze on Tarkan, who stood motionless. "Yes, Father."

"You are dismissed," he told her.

Now, the imam stood and faced Tarkan, expelling his long-held wrath toward him. "Do not speak, you dog. You are a snake's poison, a man with no honor. The reason I let you breathe is that I do not wish to spill your blood on the floor of this holy mosque."

Tarkan remained silent and perfectly still during the barrage of insults hurled on his character. The beads of sweat on his temples betrayed his nervousness.

"Do you know how much dishonor you have brought me and my family? I cannot even give her away; you have taken her maidenhood. No man will want her this way. You are a disgrace, a disgrace to your family, I say!"

The imam stomped and ranted, and still Tarkan remained mute, although his clenched hands were wet from stress, not knowing his end. The imam was feeling frustrated with Tarkan's calm and voiceless manner. "What do you have to say in your own defense?"

"I came here to say I wish to marry your daughter, Leila." Tarkan bowed with respect.

"Huh?" was the imam's stunned response.

Tarkan saw all the rage leave the Imam the moment he said those words. His shoulders slumped forward when the revelation took hold. His face changed dramatically, from angry furrowed brows with compressed lips to delight with a big, toothy smile.

"Do not move," he ordered Tarkan. "Stay right here."

The imam spun around quickly, walking to a door behind his guards. When passing them, he said, "If he tries to flee, kill him."

Soon, he returned with Leila beside him.

"My daughter and I accept your offer. It is an honorable decision, and you have restored yourself before me. I will perform the ceremony myself right now. My guards will be witnesses. Agreed, future son-in-law?" Imam Husayn smiled shamelessly, maybe even more than Leila.

Caught off guard by the imam's brazen request, Tarkan stammered. "Of course." Then he turned and gave Leila an assuring smile.

Ten minutes later, the ceremony was complete. Imam Husayn leaned over to them and whispered, "I want grandchildren. Do not fail me."

Ragnar and Sayiina wandered through the makeshift market established by the caravan merchants. They had acquired a lot of exotic merchandise while on the long journey back from China. Beautiful bolts of woven silk in many colors. Spices of the Far East. Figurines and tableware made of fine porcelain, a highly sought-after commodity. Precious and semi-precious stones—rubies, jasper, lapis lazuli, and powdered antimony. The merchants' wares were gathering attention, situated near a large mosque, and the buying and selling were lively and high-spirited.

"I think some, if not all, merchants of this venue will have heavy purses at the end of the day," Sayiina remarked offhand.

"Aye, lass. Tarkan made the right decision. He probably didn't want to, but the ultimate price exceeded the risk. I wonder how he's dealing with the Imam."

Just then, he noticed Tarkan walking down the mosque's front steps. A young woman of petite stature followed close behind. Ragnar steered Sayiina in their direction and stopped before him.

"I take it your meeting with the imam was successful?" Then Ragnar looked at the young woman standing beside Tarkan.

"It was very successful. Once again, all is well, and my good karma has returned to me. This is my new wife, Leila," Tarkan said proudly. "She will be traveling with the caravan to my home in Constantinople. There, she will meet my family and be the newest member of my harem."

"Congratulations, Leila," Sayiina said.

"Thank you. I may be his newest bride, but I will soon be his best."

Sayiina laughed at her reply. "Boldly said. I like outspoken women."

Tarkan was surprised at Leila's response.

Ragnar joined in. "An excellent choice, Tarkan."

Now Sayiina intervened. "Perhaps Leila can ride alongside me on occasion. We wouldn't want to bore you with women's gossip. We lowly women could bond with the few days remaining on our journey."

Ragnar noticed a look of suspicion cross Tarkan's face. Sayiina never spoke this way of "lowly women and women's idle talk." But, not wanting to upset his new bride, Tarkan replied abruptly, "Of course, of course. But first, I would buy my bride a wedding gift in the market."

He took Leila's hand and quickly walked away toward the market, ending their conversation.

Watching them leave, Sayiina commented, "Tarkan will be challenged with his new young wife in the coming days. I don't think she is a shy, submissive woman. I like her."

"Aye." Ragnar chuckled. "She's a spark. Maybe you see a bit of yourself in her. I mean, when you were her age."

"What?" Sayiina snapped. "Are you saying I'm old?"

Trying to look innocent, Ragnar replied, "Nay, lass, uh, I'm saying you're in full bloom. And that's just fine by me."

The port city of Trabzon cradled the eastern shores of the Black Sea. It was a sweeping, picturesque vista before Ragnar and Sayiina, who had advanced half a mile ahead of their steadily approaching caravan. Stopping atop a high bluff gave them a bird's eye view of the harbor below and the lay of the land. There, they could clearly see the docks and ships resting at anchor.

"We're near, Sayiina. I know these waters."

"How far?"

"The question is, how long will it take to arrive at our destination, Norway? First, we must buy passage on a sailing ship crossing the Black Sea. Hopefully, on a ship that will continue traveling up the Danube

River. We can cross over Germany on horseback, then sail again a short distance from Denmark to Oslo, Norway. It might sound far to you, but it isn't compared to the great distance we've already journeyed."

Sayiina looked behind, watching Hasad approach and stop before them.

"So, now you make your way from our caravan?"

"Aye, we'll cross the Black Sea by ship. Thank you for guiding us safely. We'll find our way from here," Ragnar replied honestly.

"You two, although infidels have everyone's thanks and respect. All asked me to express this. You have unusual karma, having traveled so far unscathed. I think Allah is protecting your steps."

"Where is Tarkan, our fearless leader?" Sayiina queried. "Does he not wish to say farewell?"

Hasad's eyes met Sayiina's steady gaze and question. She witnessed a look of disdain from him for Tarkan.

"Those two words do not belong to the caravan's owner. He is too preoccupied with his new wife. No, the title 'fearless' belongs to the Tajik Brotherhood. I think you already know the leaders. Farewell and safe travels, Ragnar and Sayiina."

Hasad then turned away, riding to the head of the caravan. He gave a hand signal for everyone to move onward.

Salar and Hamasa broke together from the caravan and rode up to their position.

"We will also say farewell as friends, but not goodbye," Salar expressed. "You are of our brotherhood for life. Wear your Tajik armbands with pride. Few deserve them more than you. May Allah protect you."

"Fair winds, brothers," was Ragnar's reply.

"It was a great honor to team with you in our *buzkashi* victory, Sayiina," Hamasa said. "Not any woman could have ridden my steed, Alexander, and win the king's game. I look forward to another team match with you."

"Thank you," Sayiina replied. "And I accept your invitation here and now. I am sure there will be many more victories for you. I want to tell you and your brother, Salar, you are courageous in many ways. In

Yakutia, my people would say you have great warrior spirits. Stay true to yourselves and your people. Your karma will do the rest."

Then, with bowed heads, both brothers touched their hearts, lips, and foreheads, speaking as one, "May the evil eye be far from you."

"Aye, and you as well, friends," Ragnar and Sayiina replied.

The brothers then turned and rode back to the caravan.

"Do you think our paths will ever cross with them again, Ragnar?"

"I don't know, Sayiina, but I will never say never."

Just then, a gust of wind whipped up behind them. "Let's make our way down to the harbor, lass. I feel a turn in the tide is waiting for us."

CHAPTER 31

Ragnar led the way down from their location, overlooking Trabzon Harbor. They'd said their farewells to the caravan in their own ways. Now it was time to part company.

"Let's go right to the inner docks, Sayiina. I want a close look at the ships moored there."

"Of course. Are you looking for something or someone special to set sail with?"

"I'm seeking a sailing ship set apart from the others in appearance. I'll know it when I see it."

When they arrived and dismounted, they led their horses on foot up and down the many docks. A glance up told Ragnar it was near noon, and the sun had not quite reached its zenith. The whole area was a beehive of activity, loading and unloading the varied ships' cargo. Sailors of many nations yelled and cursed at each other in their native tongues. Creaking rope lines moving through block and tackle were pulled by baying mule teams. They did the heavy lifting of loaded pallets from the ships' holds onto the docks.

Occasionally, a woman's voice called out to sailors passing by from shadows between warehouses, attempting to entice them, then hustle their coin from them. Overhead, gulls circled, crying for their next meal. They chased scraps of food tossed overboard from a ship's galley to the waters below.

Ragnar was very familiar with this, and a flood of memories reclaimed him.

Following closely, Sayiina asked, "Is what you're looking for anywhere to be found here, Ragnar? This whole area smells awful. It's a gathering of fish, manure, sweat, and urine, all warming under this day's noon sun. I want higher ground soon or to be away from here. Perhaps we could leave and return in a few hours to look again."

"Aye, I understand everything you're saying. Let's walk just a little farther down this pier. I want to see if anything is moored behind those two big carracks rafted together. If nothing is there, we'll come back later."

Approaching the carracks, Ragnar discovered another vessel tucked in and tied off in the rear of them. It was a large sloop, maybe a 60-footer. Sitting alone on the last piling at the end of the pier was an old white-haired man smoking a pipe. He didn't look their way. Instead, he stared across the harbor while lazily exhaling smoke from his nose and pursed lips.

"I'm looking for the captain of this sloop," Ragnar started.

"Aye," the old man responded.

"Aye, do you know where I might find him?"

"Aye."

Ragnar turned to Sayiina, raising his right hand. His index finger lightly tapped the side of his head, indicating possible senility. In return, Sayiina shrugged.

"And where might he be?"

"You're here, mate. I'm Captain Lyndon Norton, but most of the deck swabs call me Cap'n Lyn. Who are you two?"

Ragnar hesitated, staring down at the old sea dog sitting comfortably. Not the usual uniformed ship's captain. No, Captain Lyn was old school. His knee-high breeches, made of red canvas, were held up and in place by a length of rope tied about his waist, with a white woolen shirt under a gray Kersey jacket with tin buttons. Black low-heeled shoes covered sockless feet. He looked like any other sailing man with a completely unpretentious manner about himself. Ragnar liked the cut of his jib.

Sayiina caught Ragnar's look of surprise when a large black raven cawed overhead, then perched on the sloop's railing.

"Is the black bird a friend of yours?" Ragnar inquired.

Captain Lyn shifted. "If I be superstitious, I might be asking the same of you, matey. You might be bringing a bad omen my way! What business do you have with me and my ship?"

"We're travelers. My name's Ragnar and my mate's name is Sayiina. We need passage across the Black Sea. I see your sloop has been stripped down. Do you also trade along the Danube Riverway, by chance?"

"Aye, not a square sale on her. She's all lateen-rigged. Built for speed, not comfort, and aye, the Danube is our destination."

"Can we book with you? We have the coin, and I can help; I know your ship rigging."

"I'm sorry, but I don't need more deckhands. You'll have to find another ship."

Just then, Captain Lyn stood, his attention attracted to two sailors approaching quickly. Together, they carried a third man on a canvas stretcher.

"Cap'n Lyn," the two sailors cried out, stopping before him, trying to catch their breath. "We may have lost 'Fair Winds' Mike!"

"Damn! What happened here?"

"Dunno, Cap'n. We found him lying in his blood outside a brothel in town. He's still breathing, but he ain't moving. Might've been back-stabbed, judging by the heavy bleeding there."

"Damn and double damn. Better get him aboard." Cap'n Lyn spun on his heel to Ragnar. "The injured or dying man is my sail master and a damn good sailor. You say ye know the sails' rigging on my ship?"

"Aye."

"Then you and your mate can earn passage, but not your horses. My holds're full. There's a farrier on the east side of the dock who might buy them. Make yourself ready. We sail at four bells."

"Aye, Cap'n Lyn. A night sailing. Perfect."

"Aye," was his only reply as he returned to his ship.

Sayiina took a serious look at Ragnar.

"Perhaps the raven is watching over us, Ragnar."

"Aye, lass, you might be right here."

Ragnar glanced down at the ring he wore, the aptly named Eye of the Raven. He knew he would have to share the power of the Yakutian talisman with her soon.

Sayiina stood next to the stern railing near Captain Lyn. He leaned on the ship's tiller, skillfully guiding them points west across the Black Sea. Her palms were wet, and she gripped the rail hard in the rolling waters.

Up ahead, Ragnar moved nimbly between the main sail and two foresails while constantly directing the deck hands, who adjusted rope lines with full sails. He was trying for maximum speed tonight and displayed his formidable knowledge of safely capturing the cool night sea wind around them.

"Your mate knows what he's doing, I'll say that. We're moving at a goodly clip. 'Fair Winds' Mike might learn a thing or two from him if he lives, of course. Damn, brothels are full of thieves and murderers. No honor among them, I can tell you.

"Ragnar," Captain Lyn called out. "Belay your lines to a cleat. Let's parlay a moment together."

"Aye, let's."

"What would you like to parlay about Cap'n Lyn?" Ragnar asked, standing at the same stern rail beside Sayiina and putting his arm around her shoulder.

"Aye, mate, I've been watching your ways working the sails. You're good at your craft. Where did you learn them?"

"I've been a sailor all my life."

"No, I mean, where'd you get your start working the sails?" the captain said, continuing to work the tiller.

"Oh." Ragnar paused, replying with caution. "A long time ago, I apprenticed with the East India Company. Just a boy back then. Why do you ask?"

"I'm just trying to get the cut of your jib, if you know what I mean."

"I do," Ragnar replied with a slight grin, recognizing a mariner's choice of words.

"I, too, used to work for them years past. I signed on as a fourth mate on deck the *Royal George*. Just twenty years old and pretty green around the gills then."

"How long was your tenure with'm, might I ask?" Captain Lyn wanted to know.

He then pulled out his pipe from a jacket pocket, tapped the bowl with a finger, and sucked on its stem.

Sayiina watched the man's bushy, furrowed white brows as he tried to remember another time and place. He stared into his pipe bowl as if looking for a lost memory.

"I stayed an "Indiaman" till I was awarded papers as sail master. Then stayed on for a few more years and quit when my contract ended. I didn't like being a part of all the slave trade the company was involved in. Over the years, I've mostly contracted out my services. My last five years at sea were as sail master of the *Phoenix*, a three-masted Russian-built brigantine, working the fur trade with China on the far side of the new world."

With that, Ragnar leaned back on his elbows and rested on the railing, waiting for a response. Sayiina slipped her arm around his waist for steadying support.

"I once knew a Norwegian sail master long ago, also named Ragnar."

Ragnar's back stiffened, hearing Cap'n Lyn's words. Sayiina saw Ragnar's eyes open just a little wider and steadfast.

"He loved a good shanty when anchors aweigh. Can't rightly recall his last name. Damn good sailor, though. Sailed us well and smartly when fighting pirate corsairs off the Barbary Coast. I'm probably still standing upright because of him. Never heard tell how he fared at sea."

Cap'n Lyn continuously guided the tiller, occasionally looking at his pipe. He didn't speak directly to Ragnar, more to the ship's sails and the night sky.

Ragnar was astonished. All he could say was, "Really?"

"Aye. He was one of those men who left a lasting impression in my early years."

"Olaffson. Was his last name Olaffson?" Ragnar quickly pressed him for his answer.

Now Cap'n Lyn turned, looking straight at Ragnar. "Aye, that sounds the way of him. Do ye know of him?"

"That is my name, and my father's is the same. Did you know him?"

"Not too much. We sailed together for only a while on the *Royal George*. My station was to look after the powder monkeys who supplied the gunners. He worked the sails. You be his son, then?"

"Aye," Ragnar replied quietly. "He died before me. Shot dead by a Corsair musket, fighting in North African seas."

"I am sorry. He was a good man. It's not by chance we've met Ragnar Olaffson. With respect to your father, I'll take you and your mate as far up the Danube as I can. Aye, it's fate and destiny's waters we now sail, Master Olaffson. Arr!"

CHAPTER 32

The Cossack hetman riding out front raised his right hand to halt the twelve soldiers he was leading. They were perched above, silently watching the movements below of a man, a woman, and a large black dog. He was confident their position had not been compromised as the trio stalked along the edge of a moor. There, they stealthily approached a stand of reeds and grasses, hoping to flush out waterfowl. No doubt this night's meal.

He ordered ten of his men to dismount and quietly block their return path. The strangers were not to be harmed, only to be held at gunpoint until he arrived. He noted they were not armed with rifles or pistols. The woman carried a great bow similar to those of the Tartars, only more prominent, with two sheathed knives in her waistbelt. The man wore a cutlass across his back with long knives strapped to his hips. It was evident from their garments they came from elsewhere. But their movement in the hunt was very familiar. They moved precisely like him.

The hunters below stopped and crouched. Their prey was close at hand. The woman cautiously notched an arrow and pulled her bowstring taut. At her nod, the man touched the shoulder of the dog, who instantly shot forward, leaping headlong into the rushes. As a result, half a dozen geese were flushed away from their nests and into a frenzied flight. At the same time, the woman stood, releasing an arrow. It found its mark, piercing a bird with such force that it pushed it sideways, where the protruding arrow struck a second goose in flight dead. It was an almost impossible shot, with the hetman nodding in appreciation of the skilled archer.

Vasyklo Medved knew above-average skill when he saw it; if this were not by chance, he would know more of them. He was a hetman of the Cossacks and had hard-won his position fighting Tartars on the steppe borderlands. His mastery of the Ukrainian shashka had earned him renown by many on the battlefield. In his meaty hands, the long, curved blade almost came to life. His sweeping arc was a blur, leading to death. Fleeing enemies would not forget him.

Carrying the two fowl, Ragnar and their newly adopted harbor dog approached Sayiina.

She stood still, turning her head sideways to listen behind. Raising a hand sharply, Sayiina indicated for him to stop, then whispered in a lowered voice, "We are being watched."

"Are you certain?"

Ragnar drew his cutlass from its sheath, grasping the hilt tightly. The dog gave up a low growl. Sayiina slowly turned away from Ragnar in anticipation of trouble and waited.

Ten heavily armed, hostile Cossack soldiers emerged from the forest, preventing their return passage. With serious intent, every soldier pointed a loaded rifle in their direction. The dog growled again, baring its teeth. Its ears flattened, and its nose wrinkled. It was a primal warning everyone present understood.

"Stay the dog, Northman," one of the Cossacks ordered. "Or I will kill it now."

Sayiina took a step forward, and all rifles moved to her position.

Ragnar spoke calmly to Sayiina, knowing the situation was a tinder box. "Not here. They have the advantage."

"Why do you prevent us safe passage?" Ragnar asked.

"We wait for Hetman to follow, and now so do you."

Grimacing, Sayiina whispered, "Cowards; I hate Cossacks!"

Soon, a horse and rider came forth from the forest. The men parted to allow passage and then closed ranks behind him. The man halted a few feet before them and dismounted.

Ragnar witnessed a supremely confident man approach. Everything about him spoke leadership. He was large, with broad shoulders and muscular arms, much like Ragnar's old friend at sea, Yuri Kozachenko.

The tail of his dark top-knot hair was tucked in the back of one ear. He wore calf-high leather boots, loose-fitting breeches, and a sleeveless woollen-lined leather vest. Ragnar could see the only weapon on his person, his shashka, a 3.5-foot-long, slightly curved sword. Lethal in the right hands. His face reflected a fierce image of combat and war. But his gaze was penetrating and revealed intelligence gained from experience.

"I am Vasyklo Medved, Hetman of Ukraine. These Cossack men are my bodyguards," he said in a distinct, rough voice. "Who are you, and where are you from?"

Although it was a question, Ragnar sensed it more like a command to answer. Before he could reply, the dog leaped forward with teeth bared to strike the hetman's throat. More remarkable than the creature's assault was the speed with which the hetman drew out his sword. In one motion, his sword blade flashed in a defensive arc, cutting the dog's jugular and then throat. He then deftly turned, allowing the dog to fall. The swiftness and deadly accuracy of his sword were impressive. Behind him, his men were laughing at the display of strength and violence. Blood ran down the gutter of his shashka blade.

Outraged at the sight, Sayiina instinctively withdrew one of her knives but stopped when the tip of the hetman's sword pressed her neck.

"Sheath it!" he demanded of her.

Hearing the hetman's tone of voice, Ragnar moved closer to Sayiina's position, ready to strike.

"Stay your sword, Northman; I did not come to kill you or your partner. I came here to learn of you. But if you continue to attack me, you will die. So, I ask you now, is this the ground you wish to fall upon?"

Ragnar relaxed his grip on the cutlass slightly but held his ground. "No."

Sayiina cautiously sheathed her long knife.

Vasyklo lowered his blade but continued holding it firmly. "Good. Tell me who you are and where you are from."

"I am Ragnar Olaffson. My last home was Petropavlovsk, Russia."

"And what is your profession?"

"I am a sailor and have been all my life."

Vasyklo paused, thoughtful. "You look Nordic, not Russian, and the blade you carry is exactly right for fighting in close quarters, as on a ship."

He then turned his gaze to Sayiina, studying her closely. "Your kind, I don't know. Tell me, who are you?"

"My name is Sayiina Teresova. I am from Yakutia." Then she proudly added, "My profession is hunter/tracker," glaring at him, full of resentment.

"You have skill with your bow. Are all the women of Yakutia like yourself?"

Ragnar noticed it was a compliment, but Sayiina did not hear it that way.

"No, they are not."

"I have never heard of Yakutia before. Where is this place?"

"Yakutia is far east of here, eastern Siberia, and north of China."

A slight smirk crossed her face, and Vasyklo detected it. "Do not take me for ignorant, woman. I see a lot of hatred in you toward me, yet we have never met. I ask myself, why would that be? So, you have revealed the answer to me.

"I know many young Cossacks of my country work in Siberia, enforcing the czar's rule. An unpleasant task that some people would resent, even hate their brutality. You, I believe, have been a victim of their hand. Something you cannot forgive or forget."

Sayiina remained silent, staring at this man who was schooling her in leadership. Her continued silence only strengthened the sting of his words. Now motionless, she strained to suppress her memories of the Mongolian jail and Marko Dragovich's cruelty to her.

"I am not your enemy," he continued. "But I am trying to decide if I let you go your own way or make you my prisoners."

Ragnar quickly interjected, "If you say you are not our enemy, why would you make us prisoners?"

"Out of necessity, Northman. If, as you say, you have traveled successfully from Siberia to here unscathed, that tells me you two are very resourceful. I cannot allow you to aid the French."

"Why would we aid the French? They mean nothing to us. We're trying to reach Norway." Ragnar was frustrated, not fully understanding. "What aren't you telling us?"

Vasyklo realized instantly, with Ragnar's question, that they were unaware of the war footing of many European countries. "How long have you been traveling together?" he asked, raising his eyebrows in question.

"Seven months, perhaps. Why?"

Vasyklo chose not to respond to Ragnar's question. "Has it always been just the two of you?"

"It has, except for traveling with a Turkish merchant caravan."

"Are you aware you are traveling through a theater of war?"

"We've spoken to no one for a while now as we've been sailing up the Danube River. We make our way north across the country to the sea, then to Norway. Neither of us is interested in any war."

"Your passage, by a stroke of incredibly good fortune, is leading you undetected between two opposing armies here in the heart of Germania. The French are in the west, and Russia/Austria is in the east. The czar calls all available soldiers to his aid, and my men and I are advance scouts for the Russian army, which is only one hour away. We are here seeking to find the French army's position. This forest is full of French spies doing the same. I see you both wearing the colored armbands of the Tajik mercenaries. How did you come by them?"

"We earned them," Sayiina said proudly, lifting her chin with confidence.

"I know these men. Strong, hard, and fearless in a fight. They are not easily impressed. So how did you accomplish winning this badge of honor?"

"By killing their enemies." Ragnar stepped forward, showing no fear of Vasyklo and his men.

"Very good. It must have been a remarkable battle, and you can tell me the tale at a later date. I have decided on your fate."

"We are not part of this war. We make our way," Ragnar challenged.

"No!" was Vasyklo's harsh answer. He slammed a balled fist into an open palm. An angry hetman now commanded their situation.

Ragnar and Sayiina remained very still, untrusting the situation with these Cossacks. Any misstep might be their last. The hetman was intelligent but explosive, and any of his loyal soldiers would follow his lead. They had little choice but to listen.

"You two have wandered undetected into a war zone. At these times, people have to choose a side. There are no other options. You are either an ally or an enemy of Russia—your decision. You also have extraordinary survival skills to travel so far, mostly alone. Because of the Tajikistan colors you wear, I can honor this with safe passage.

"Now that you've learned so much, you will not be allowed to fall into French hands. These men behind me are all excellent hunter/trackers. Aid us with your skills to defeat the French, and you will be free to travel. If not, you will be imprisoned or shot as French spies. That decision I will leave with Field Marshall Kutusov."

"That's not much of a choice," Ragnar protested.

"Hard times require hard choices, Northman. You choose."

Ragnar called Sayiina aside, away from the hetman. "We're so close to our destination, and our fortunes have turned for the worse, Sayiina. I believe the hetman will honor the Tajik badges we wear, but can you work with these men? I don't see any other choice."

"There's no real choice, and I'll fight to my death before I enter another jail cell with a living Cossack in it. I will aid them, but if anyone touches me, I'll kill him."

"And so will I," he agreed.

Both turned and walked back to face Vasyklo Medved. Ragnar began speaking while Sayiina listened, watching the soldiers' movements with keen eyes. "We will aid you and Russia and expect you to honor your safe passage words. One last thing—she is my mate, and no one touches her."

Vasyklo laughed loudly, and some of his soldiers did too, on hearing Ragnar's brave words. "Boldly spoken, Northman, with so many of the finest swordsmen facing you. Welcome, but I should warn you: if your fierce mate attacks their pride, they will defend themselves from her."

It was a crude remark purposefully made in jest for all his men to hear.

Sayiina understood and wasn't shamed at all. She knew all about men and said mockingly, "Do all Cossack men think only with their little heads first and their big heads last?"

Ragnar was pleased with her response. It was met with more laughter and some fellowship.

"Da," the hetman said. "Now, we ride back to our battle camp and await further instructions."

Field Marshall Mikhail Kutusov read the dispatch on his field desk. He was standing inside a large tent, considering its contents. Looking up, he dismissed the courier and turned to his Cossack hetman.

"Austria's General Mack has surrendered to Napoleon, and I am sure we will be his next target. We are outnumbered with both men and cannon but not surrounded."

"What are your orders, Field Marshall?"

"Retreat north with tactics." Kutusov replied, "We have few choices. The little emperor will have to find us before he can engage us. We still have time to use evasive maneuvers to wear down his army. There, we can join General Buxhowden in the city of Znaim. As always, Russia and I are indebted to you to act as our rearguard. There is no finer cavalry alive than Cossack horsemen. I will also require the most accurate surveillance reports from your rear scouts. I suggest you send half a dozen of your best close to enemy lines. Every time the French change their march, send back a courier to alert me. Timing is everything for us."

Ragnar eyed the Cossack hetman exiting the Field Marshall's tent. He and Sayiina stood around a nearby fire with some of his Cossack guards. Their talk was casual; some wanted to hear about their travels, but all the talking stopped when Vasyklo Medved entered their circle.

"I need six volunteers to go as close as possible to the French lines."

"What is required?" Ragnar asked.

"To inform the field Marshall of French troop movements."

"Aye, count me as one."

"Myself as another," Sayiina added.

"This is dangerous work, Northman. You will be shot as spies if captured."

"We will keep our word, Hetman, and assist Russia however we can. Without risk, how can there be our reward of freedom?"

"Well said. Then we understand each other."

Turning to Sayiina, Vasyklo said, more challengingly, "You claim to be a hunter/tracker. Prove it to me."

Unmoving, fearless, Sayiina stared back hard into his dark eyes. "You will soon know how good I am."

"Good," was his cold reply. "Four more."

CHAPTER 33

When Colonel Villeneuve received an appeal for an audience from one of his better scouts, a certain Lieutenant Marcel Mayer, he agreed immediately. It was not uncommon, but the tone of this lieutenant's voice suggested urgency was at play.

The lieutenant stood before him, and he listened quietly, occasionally asking questions for clarity. He noted the lieutenant wasn't a particularly big man but lean and hard. His peers respected Mayer for being a competent scout and for his intuitive reports. He had correctly assessed the enemy's position on more than one occasion. On the whole, he was a very able and proven French officer.

When the lieutenant finished speaking, the colonel was in disbelief at the man standing before him. He closed his hands together and rested them on his desk. At first, he lowered his eyes, then raised them with doubt.

"Do you want me to believe that Field Marshall Kutusov, the head of the Russian army before us, relies on field intelligence from a woman of unknown origins who might be a clairvoyant or, worse, a Russian witch?"

"Yes, sir. I know this may seem strange, but she rides with Cossack spies. These advance scouts are close to our battle camp on the ridges above, where I, by chance, observed them this morning. Just knowing Cossacks would never allow a woman to ride with them as an equal, her presence was startling. These are elite soldiers."

"You are sure it was a woman?"

"Yes, Colonel. My first thought was she might be a prisoner. There was another spy as well. He looked like a northerner with white hair.

They were familiar with each other, and their body language suggested kindred."

"Again, repeat to me what you observed in every detail.

"From my hidden position on the ridge, I watched the black-haired woman as she dismounted and walked casually to the fore of the mounted scouts. She first looked over the valley onto our armies below; she knelt on one knee, bowed her head, and concentrated. Then, she simultaneously closed her eyes and touched the earth with her right hand. After a moment, she stood and spoke to a nearby Cossack soldier. He only nodded, turned, and hastily rode east, away from the scouting party, toward the Russian army. The woman mounted her horse, and now five spies watch our troop movements below."

"Lieutenant Mayer, give me your interpretation of what transpired."

"Honestly, colonel, in my years of scouting, I have never seen anything like it. My words may sound impossible, but . . ."

"Speak up, Lieutenant; you have no reason to halt now."

"Yes, sir. I would surmise we are being tracked, not hunted. The Russians know our position as we know theirs. I believe this woman is being used because she has the gift of 'sight.' It is the only explanation possible. She can read from the earth when our armies use a feint against Field Marshall Kutusov."

"Impossible!" the colonel exclaimed loudly.

"If I may, sir?"

The now-exasperated colonel replied, "Go ahead, Lieutenant."

"If Field Marshall Kutusov continually and successfully proves to elude us, this might be his hidden hand."

This remark had merit, and Colonel Villeneuve acknowledged it. "Well spoken, Lieutenant Mayer. Can you find these spies again?"

"I think so, sir. They keep to the high ground and follow our movements."

"Good, continue to follow them, but do not be found out. If you see this woman, repeat the same motion and inform me immediately. Field Marshall Kutusov is a seasoned and wily soldier. As you know, we are in pursuit of his army now. They retreat north, but we have to catch them. I hesitate to take your observations up the chain of command because they are too imaginative. If he continues to evade us with maneuvers, I will take it to General Montebello for his decision. Is there anything else you wish to report?"

"No, sir."

"You are dismissed, then. Just remember, I am not ignoring your report. I need time to weigh its validity."

"Yes, sir."

Field Marshall Kutusov was flanked on his left by his Cossack hetman. They stood inside his command tent, patiently waiting for the Cossack scout to catch his breath before reporting.

"Napoleon's Grande Armée moves north, directly toward us. I have seen this. But there is something else."

"Say it," the hetman demanded.

"The Yakutian woman says they intend to distract the rear of our army with an assault on our left flank."

"What?" Kutusov exclaimed loudly. "Are you saying Napoleon intends a feint, and you report this to me? How did you come by this information, Soldier?"

At this point in their exchange, Vasyklo Medved interjected with the best diplomacy possible. "Field Marshall, we have employed two new scouts with unusual skill sets. They are neither Cossack nor Russian and will aid us in return for their freedom to travel. I believe one is Norwegian, and the other is a woman from Yakutia. She is an exceptionally skilled hunter/tracker."

A calmed Kutusov listened to his hetman, then turned his attention to the scout. "First, you need to answer my question, Soldier. Tell me what I need to know. I repeat: how did you come by this information?"

The scout spoke out boldly. "The woman is gifted with the third eye. She always seems to know impending danger forward or behind her position. That is all I can say."

"You are dismissed, Soldier." Field Marshall Kutusov remained silent while watching the scout leave.

"Your thoughts, hetman, on your forward scout's report."

"The Yakutian woman is different. I did not consider her a seer, only exceptional. But knowing the distance they have traveled confirms her ability to see danger advancing toward them and how to evade it."

Kutusov contemplated the hetman's words. He stared at the palm of his right hand, then at the back of the same hand.

"Can you mount 4,000 of your Cossack cavalries and be ready to protect and strike our enemies on their left flank in two days?"

"I can arrange this."

"Then do it, and be prepared to strike at Napoleon's feint. Wipe them out, then meet up with our rear guard. We will push hard to cross the Danube River. Make it so, Hetman. Your Yakutian scout will have one chance to be the eyes of the Russian bear. If she fails us, you remove her from your ranks."

Vasyklo nodded in acknowledgment, then exited the tent.

The day was closing in the west, and Vasyklo Medved sat calmly astride his restless horse. On this small hilltop, he overlooked a flat, open plain. Behind, two of his mounted bodyguards moved nearer, one to each side, then stopped. Napoleon's still-distant Grande Armée approached as a flowing ribbon across the land, growing larger by the minute.

"Are all the men informed and made ready?"

"Da, Hetman."

"The French army will soon rest for the night. We will watch for a break in their line when moving toward us tomorrow. Field Marshall Kutusov will push his army hard north, crossing the Danube. The French will not be expecting our counterstrike to their feint. We will strike them down with our shashka, like scythes reaping grain. Tomorrow will be a Cossack's red dawn."

One full day and still no signs of the Cossacks, the northerner, or the dark-haired witch. Lieutenant Marcel Mayer knew their trail but not their location just yet. They were good at not being found out, but as his father had taught him as a boy, the successful hunter is always patient. The forest would reveal them, even if only for a brief moment. He knew they would follow alongside the Grande Armée above and near the forest where he was now. He was tired of trekking on foot. Below, he could see the French army had come to a halt, more than 50,000 men strong with artillery.

So, he decided to stop searching for the day, sat down, and leaned his back against a large oak tree. He witnessed many campfires starting up for the night. However, this would not be for him, as a fire would attract too much unwanted attention. He reached into his shoulder bag, withdrew a saltless biscuit, and bit down on it. It was bland and stuck to his teeth, so he sipped from his wineskin to wash it down. He would drop down into the valley tomorrow to replenish his meager provisions.

"When this war is over, I will quit being a soldier and learn to cook good food." He then took another sip of his wine.

A shiver ran down his spine. He laid his rifle across his lap and waited. He knew it would be a long, cold night with hopefully no snowfall. He said a prayer while covering most of himself with fallen leaves and made the sign of a cross over his heart. At midnight, he fell asleep with a gnawing hunger in his belly.

The snort from a horse's nostril and muffled voices snapped his eyes awake from a fitful, predawn sleep. Marcel remained motionless, afraid to disturb the dry leaves concealing him and be found out. Slumping against the tree gave cold comfort to his aching back muscles.

The voices continued, but he couldn't quite make out the words. They could reveal their position to him, though. He ever so slightly turned his head and gazed at the location of the voices. There they were. Five Russian scouts sitting astride horses, not 50 yards ahead. They were on the same ridgeline overlooking the valley and surveying the French army below.

Suddenly, the woman pivoted in her saddle, peering intently in his direction. Fearful, he shut his eyes so as not to make contact with her and slowed his breathing in hopes that his rapidly beating heart would slow down.

"What is it, Sayiina?" Ragnar asked.

"I'm not sure. For a fleeting moment, I thought we were being watched."

"Really? The area looks clear, but we don't have the time to sweep it. We need to get ahead of that army below. Determine the strength of the assault on Kutusov's left flank and get word to him quickly. Let's keep moving forward for now."

Just then, the valley below came alive with the sounds of trumpets, clamoring soldiers, and neighing horses. Marcel opened his eyes to gaze over the scene. From his position, it appeared there were two battalions of 1,000 men each, with cannons, breaking away from the main body. Napoleon was making a move to distract the Russian rear and slow down its march, thrusting northward.

Marcel thought, *Is this the maneuver the witch woman foresaw?* He chanced a glance back their way, but they were gone.

Hetman Vasyklo Medved was the tip of a spear. The blade and shaft were the 4,000 strong and fully armed Cossack soldiers at his command. They only waited for his signal to unleash a furious assault on two fast-approaching French battalions.

Nothing could have ever prepared the French for what was coming against them. He scoffed at this little ruse of theirs. He knew they were hoping the Russian army would stop and defend itself. His orders to cut deeply into their ranks and then quickly return to act as rear guard is what he would deliver. Many shashka swords would earn the name 'song' after the slaughter today. His fingertips touched the hilt of his sword at the thought.

The tree-lined valley he had chosen would serve well for cover and surprise. The French would march straight into it as the path of least resistance for their wheeled cannons. Once both battalions were inside, he would signal the first wave hidden within the treeline to attack their left flank. The surprise counterattack would shock them into a forced defensive position with arms. There would be no time for a heavy artillery bombardment. He would lead the second wave, striking at their front cavalries' ranks. Their charge would be to wither their officers and create chaos among the foot soldiers.

He had faced French soldiers many times in battle. If they did not hold the advantage on the field, there was more flight than fight in them. He rode alone to the top of a hill in full view of the unaware French army. He raised his sword for his mounted Cossacks to attack in force.

The thunderous sound of 2,000 heavy horses shook the valley floor. He wasn't surprised when the French stopped and wheeled to face their greatest fear, screaming wildly for aid.

Some front officers rode back to bring order to the ranks but were the first to be cut down. This first counterassault slammed into the side of the second battalion like a scimitar cutting through flesh. He immediately raised his arm to signal the 2,000 swords behind him to charge their attack straight as a spear into the heart of the officer cavalry. His assault was like a reaping whirlwind blowing through a valley of death.

Field Marshall Kutusov and his Cossack hetman waited in his command post for the arrival of his rear scouts. These two leaders represented the heart and arm of this Russian army, so far from their native home. Kutusov turned to his hetman.

"Your victory has bought us a lot of time that we desperately needed. Well done, Hetman. The little emperor will think twice before trying a ruse again."

Just then, a Cossack guard outside their tent announced the arrival of the scouts. "Hetman, they are here."

"Allow them to pass."

Ragnar, Sayiina, and three Cossacks walked in and presented themselves before the two leaders. Ragnar spoke first. "You asked for us?"

"I did," Kutusov replied.

Sayiina, for her part, looked at an elderly and portly man. Not what she was expecting to see. Moreover, he was blind in one eye, as it was opaque.

"You five have done us a great service," Kutusov said. "I was told and am now convinced that you are a gifted woman. Tell me your name and your home." His voice was stern yet fatherly toward Sayiina.

"My name is Sayiina Teresova. I come from Yakutia."

"Da, your home is the Russian frontier. I know of it, but I have never been there. You have traveled far."

"Yes."

"Are you so different from your people in Yakutia, Sayiina Teresova?"

Sayiina grasped his two-edged question. She always wanted to belong but could never fit in, yet she was Yakutian in her heart. "You seek truth and not flattery."

"Of course."

"Da. I am not gifted like you think I am. I am not a true seer. I can sense approaching danger and feel a shifting change. What those changes are, I can only suggest. It's personal and who I am today and will be tomorrow."

"Well explained, Sayiina of Yakutia. I like unafraid women who know themselves. I would ask you to continue to ride ahead of these men and aid our cause."

Sayiina shook her head slowly. "No, I don't lead these men. I don't ride before nor behind; I ride alongside them to aid Russia."

It was a challenging response worthy of a Cossack. Vasyklo Medved looked over to Kutusov in a questioning way for his response. At first, Kutusov did not speak.

"Most people would refer to me as 'General' or 'sir.' Now you choose, Sayiina of Yakutia."

Staring at her, he waited patiently.

"There is only one man I submit to, and he stands here beside me now. I will call you 'General' out of respect, not 'sir' for submission, my general."

Again, Vasyklo Medved was impressed but would not show it here. There would be another time and place of his choosing to speak to her. Hers was a worthy response.

"Excellent." Kutusov was satisfied with her answer. "Continue to bring your reports to me or my hetman as soon as you know something. Along with your intuition as to how the French may proceed. Your insights are equally important to me. I believe not all battles are won on the field. Our enemy is deceitful, and at this time, he has more soldiers than us. We can wear down his army by staying ahead of him. Our Russian infantry and militia are very strong. Our Cossack cavalry is the best. Together, we can defeat Napoleon's army. I ask you to remain the eyes of the bear as we retreat north."

"I will do this, my general."

"Good." And Kutusov gave her a rare smile. "Go and get some hot food and replenish your supplies. Our army moves early tomorrow morning, I am sure, the same as the French. We are in a foot race, and I intend to win."

Ragnar, Sayiina, and the Cossack scouts turned and departed the command tent.

Kutusov watched them leave before speaking to his hetman. "The Yakutian is a gift we will continue to exploit. She is fiercely proud yet shows me loyalty to our cause and her mate. I like her attitude of 'nothing is too formidable.' Yet they scout for us in dangerous proximity to our enemies. I want to hear her next report as soon as it arrives, Hetman. We still might slip through Napoleon's grasp."

Both men now studied their temporary map, discussing options before them.

Outside the tent, Ragnar suggested, "Why not eat first, then get our rations before returning up the ridge?"

"I'd like that."

One of the Cossack scouts turned to them. "Follow us for food. We eat better than the others." Then he gave them a knowing wink.

He led them to a large cauldron where a group of Cossack horsemen stood. They both sensed the aroma of cooked food spiriting in their direction. Their Cossack guide grinned. "Bear stew. We have an old farmer's saying in my country of Ukraine."

"What is that?" Ragnar pressed him.

"A man is what he eats."

"Aye, then tonight we are all bears."

"Da, and one very hungry she-bear," Sayiina chimed in.

CHAPTER 34

Lieutenant Marcel Mayer had lost sight of his enemy but was confident they would soon be found. They would reveal themselves to him again. He only had to follow the march of the French army below. He sensed the woman was intuitive, but her 'sight' wasn't perfect. She had failed to discover his location at the base of the oak tree a few days prior. She had a weakness. It was small but still something he might be able to use to his advantage.

He moved in a crouch along the forest ridgeline, using it as camouflage wherever possible. This excursion had taken almost all his provisions, and he would soon need to resupply. Marcel was confident the Russian spies were near, and his resolve to find them was strong. He also wanted to be updated on the most recent marching command to the troops.

He stopped to view his terrain maps, which showed he was close to a town named Dürnstein. It lay across the Danube River, with the great city of Vienna farther east along its shoreline. Standing and overlooking Napoleon's Grande Armée, his heart swelled with national pride. He wanted to join their march, even if only briefly. He determined, or maybe it was his intense hunger that decided, to break cover and join his countrymen. Sprinting unfettered from the dark, oppressive forest gave him a feeling of unchained freedom released into the light of day. There was no direct path, only a gently sloping field of waist-high grass. He was elated, much like a boy without a care running home on a country road.

Had he exercised more prudence, he might not have caught the attention of five Russian scouts sitting quietly astride their mounts not far behind. They, too, were observing the French army moving below, close to Lieutenant Mayer's last position.

Ragnar leaned over in his saddle, asking Sayiina, "Is he the one you sensed had been following us?"

"I think so. He couldn't have known how close we were to him, or he wouldn't have exposed himself like this."

"I can cut him down like a blade of grass," one Cossack suggested. "My shashka is thirsty."

"Not this time. But his fate will be decided soon."

"We should take advantage of him breaking discipline by moving farther away," Ragnar said.

Sayiina nodded in agreement and then dismounted. Kneeling on a single knee, she touched the ground before her. She sensed the danger below, and then, unexpectedly, a more distant danger appeared on the northern side of the Danube River. There, she set her gaze. "What lies north across the river?"

One of the Cossack scouts dismounted and produced a field map. They all positioned themselves around it to see what it revealed.

"What did you see, Sayiina?" Ragnar asked with some apprehension.

"I sense two forces at work. Napoleon's army below chases General Kutusov, but one army has already crossed farther ahead on the river's other side."

"The field marshall needs to be warned," one scout said.

"Aye," Ragnar agreed. "Let's move and inform him of an advanced army close to his position."

Mounting quickly, Sayiina agreed. "There's no time. We must ride with haste."

Field Marshall Kutusov, with Hetman Medved, waited for the rear scouts to arrive. Their timing couldn't have been more opportune. The plan of the Russian's northern retreat entered a new phase since they'd now crossed the Danube River at the town of Krems. Now, the combined Russian and Austrian forces were 40,000 men with artillery and cavalry. Although outnumbered by the Grande Armée, they were in a stronger position. Kutusov was well aware that his Russian conscripts of farmers and farriers were better in a defensive mode and fearless if forced to attack. He said as much to his hetman when the command guard posted outside interrupted him.

"Enter and report."

The five rear scouts walked in together, but it was Sayiina who spoke first. "My general."

"Ah, the eyes of the bear. Speak," was his hard reply. "What have you seen? Also, report your insight."

"The Grande Armée is pursuing you with vigor, but I have detected a smaller yet lethal danger waiting on this side of the great river."

"Where?" he demanded.

"They're near and to the west. I don't know the lay of the land, my general. This force is positioned at the river's edge, is what I see."

With Sayiina's report, he calmly spoke to his Cossack hetman. "Send a dozen of your scouts west immediately. I want to know their location and strength quickly."

"Da," Vasyklo Medved replied, then exited the command post.

Kutusov now turned his gaze to Sayiina and the scouts standing before him. He addressed them equally. "Well done, soldiers. At this time, I can only offer you a hot meal and rest tonight, along with my gratitude for the dangerous work you do."

The three Cossacks nodded in deference to Field Marshall Kutusov and departed from the tent. Ragnar and Sayiina remained, glanced at each other, and then at Kutusov. He looked up from his maps and asked, "Is there something else you want to tell me?"

Ragnar spoke first. "Although tired, we'd like to be part of the scouting team riding west."

"Really? You have earned a rest from action. If your information is accurate, you will have much-deserved respect from the soldiers of this army and me. We do not flee the Grande Armée from fear but retreat to regroup with others. Then we will fight on our terms."

"We do not doubt Russian fortitude, something we've learned first-hand on our travels. We believe being in the right place at the right time will often bring favorable results. Call it karma. My mate, Sayiina, is gifted and may be useful to our struggle."

Kutusov looked hard, first at Ragnar and then at Sayiina. Then, he burst out in laughter. "You know you're not real soldiers. You don't have the needed discipline. Strong, fearless, and opportunist is what you are.

"Yet here you stand before me. What are you? I see you as soldiers of fortune. Am I wrong?"

"No," Ragnar replied. "But without risk, there's no reward. We want to be free to follow our own paths."

"Yes, I know this. My Hetman has told me, but I will determine the time and place. To win your release, you must prove to me you earned it."

"Aye," Ragnar acknowledged. "Your assessment of us is accurate. We're not real soldiers. We're more swords for hire on our journey. We excel in danger where others would fail. Sleeping this night in camp is not our way. Use our skills, and let us accompany the scouts riding west. We want our freedom."

"And to make a difference," Sayiina added.

Field Marshall Kutusov listened carefully to these outsiders. "You wish to ride back into the fire with no rest?" he replied in disbelief.

"Aye," they said as one.

"I was hoping to have you well-rested for a specific task I have in mind. But I see you are eager to prove yourselves once again.

"Da, join the scouts but return alive. This Russian army needs good soldiers, even foreign ones. You are dismissed."

Ragnar and Sayiina turned and left the command tent.

"That was a good appeal you made to the general," Sayiina said.

"I've spent a lot of time dealing with Russians, Sayiina. Not all are blockheaded, as others might think. For myself, it's not what I say so much as how I say my words. Kutusov knows this."

Lieutenant Mayer was surprised to learn he was reassigned to the newly formed VIII Corps. His duties continued as a forward scout but under the new command of General Gazan. He was still free to roam, but unlike before, he wasn't just following the Grande Armée. His new orders were dangerous, and he knew it.

This division of 7,500 men, comprising infantry and cavalry, was at the forefront of the VIII Corps. He was on foot before them. Cossack scouts would be everywhere. It was hazardous terrain to trek through undiscovered.

He moved in his fashioned stealth mode, occasionally creeping on all fours. Marcel stopped beside the beginnings of a local vineyard. Breathing deep to control his nerves, he sat back on his heels and scanned across five acres of unpruned grape vines. Marcel caught the sounds of men nearing, and he remained dead still, holding his breath. A squad of ten French infantry fusilier-grenadiers on patrol revealed themselves. He sighed in relief, knowing he was not alone, then relaxed his position.

Unseen, they continued marching past the vineyard when suddenly, a dozen armed Cossacks stood before them. Like himself, they had concealed themselves in the vineyard. Each leveled a musket with deadly intent toward the grenadiers, who, when surprised, abruptly stopped their march.

Three grenadiers, in self-defense, withdrew pistols and were immediately shot dead by the Cossack enemy. Not knowing their fate, the French soldiers looked behind for a possible escape, even an impossible chance. However, any thoughts of fleeing were instantly suppressed when twelve more Cossack soldiers revealed themselves, blocking their only way of escape.

Knowing Cossacks were the best at ambush, Lieutenant Mayer witnessed the trap his compatriots were in. Why they were all not executed outright on the river's edge caused him to pause. Instead, the grenadiers were now surrounded and reluctantly surrendering their weapons. Several Cossacks approached them and bound their hands behind them. They would be made prisoners and most likely interrogated to divulge their knowledge.

He had heard stories of how the Cossacks' use of their *nagaika* was very persuasive, and he shuddered.

Lieutenant Mayer was in shock at what he had just witnessed. How was this trap possible without foreknowledge, so far ahead of his division? His eyes widened, and an unknown fear gripped his chest. He realized the black-haired witch was nearby, and only she could have sensed their presence. With terror, he fled back into the forest but, in doing so, revealed himself to her. There, among the Cossack soldiers, she stopped and turned to stare at him. Her eyes locked on his for a brief moment, and he knew he was her next prey.

Mayer ran for his life.

CHAPTER 35

Lieutenant Mayer ran back to his division as if a horde of taloned demons pursued him, reaching for his very soul. He did not look behind where the Cossack ambush had occurred, fearful that in doing so, he would see them in pursuit. He ran like never before, with no regard for personal safety and concealment. He wasn't sure how long he'd been running, but each stride had at last delivered him to his battalion camp and sanctuary. Now utterly exhausted from the ordeal, gaunt and weak, his knees shook when at a complete standstill.

On arrival, his first impression was of men, horses, and wagons preparing to march. Confused by so much activity, he sought the leadership standards among its ranks. It was his duty and moral obligation to report the ambush resulting in the fusilier-grenadier patrols' capture.

When he saw the standard of his old regiment pass, he spotted Colonel Villeneuve on horseback and called out his rank and name. In return, Colonel Villeneuve responded and reined in his mount to pause. He turned to see the source, which was Lieutenant Mayer, who was running up to him, first saluting, then speaking in a fatigued voice, "Sir, I need to report."

"Now is not the time, Lieutenant; we are on the march."

"Sir, my information is very urgent."

Colonel Villeneuve looked down at this young scout. His voice and poor posture showed exhaustion or near collapse. These were trying times, and men in all capacities were pushed to their limits. Seeing Mayer's condition, he moderated military protocol with a tempered voice, demanding, "Report, Scout!"

"Thank you, Colonel. The black-haired Russian witch and two dozen Cossacks have killed and captured a full squad of fusilier-grenadiers ahead of us, sir."

"What! How far ahead?" he demanded.

"I am unsure," Lieutenant Mayer stammered. "An hour away on foot?"

"What did you see, Lieutenant?"

"The Cossacks were waiting in ambush. It was a trap set inside a vineyard."

The colonel was astonished at his report. "I only sent them out two hours ago. This is not good news. The grenadiers know our strength and position, and soon, their harsh inquisitors will learn it as well."

"Yes, sir. There is only one explanation I can surmise. The witch could see their coming and readied the Cossack trap in advance."

"Well spoken, Lieutenant. This needs to be taken up immediately with your division commander, General Gazan. Stay nearby. Rest on a nearby wagon. Your presence will be required soon."

Lieutenant Mayer nearly collapsed but found solace on a bed of hay close at hand. The stress of his ordeals was leaving him, only to be replaced by an intense headache. Most of his strength was depleted.

He had just one more task ahead of him: reporting to General Gazan. Opening his wineskin, he raised it to his parched lips and drank deeply. He craved rest but knew there would be none given here. These were the trials of war all men endured, and he wanted to be a survivor. His drooping chin snapped up at the sound of Colonel Villeneuve's voice.

"Lieutenant, follow me. General Gazan will speak to you regarding our discussions of Kutusov's scouts and the 'seer' they use to their advantage against us. Hold back nothing from him of your insight. Remember, knowledge is power."

After telling his story of the ambush to General Gazan and the other officers present, Lieutenant Mayer stood silent and at wilting attention. He had completed his orders. The next decision would not be his to make but would be made higher up the chain of command.

"Lieutenant, your observations are opportune," General Gazan said. "In fact, I believe you are correct with your insight. Russia would not be the first army in history to employ clairvoyants in their ranks. This army is stronger and better, so we do not need these talents to defeat our enemies. What else have you observed of her?"

"A white-haired Northman travels everywhere she goes. I believe he is her protector."

"I mean, Lieutenant," the general asked purposefully, "does she have a weakness?"

At this question, Lieutenant Marcel Mayer closed his eyes, paused, and opened them with clarity. This was at the heart of the final decision not yet made. "I believe she does, General."

"And?"

"Once, near her position, I was lying under cover of fallen leaves, and she did not see me. She sensed I was close but couldn't sense where."

"Excellent. Can you exploit this weakness?"

"Yes, General, I believe I can. But I will need assistance. With half a dozen fusilier-grenadiers, we could also set up a trap and capture them."

"No, Lieutenant, set your ambush and kill everyone but the woman. We will use her talents against our enemies," he added with cruel intent. "If she does not comply, we will kill her as well. After all, it is war," he said casually and dismissively.

"Yes, sir!"

Lieutenant Mayer was caught off guard by his general's cruelty toward others. This was a weakness of his leadership. He turned to depart the command tent when Colonel Villeneuve spoke up. "Follow me. I will assist you in scripting six good grenadiers for your orders, Lieutenant."

"Yes, sir."

Lieutenant Mayer's father had always taught him that the measure of a man's strength was not always in his arm but instead in the strength of his resolve. Today, he would be tested. He and six grenadiers were all lying under blankets of fallen leaves for concealment. They positioned themselves in the fashion of a horseshoe near the edge of a low-lying bluff. This gave even the most casual observer a clear view of events unfolding below. It was a position no advance scout could resist to see an enemy's strength and position. He had chosen it for these very reasons.

No sooner had they concealed themselves than the French VIII Corps came under attack. Thunder from heavy cannons filled the air, and the ground shook.

But that was not their fight for today. Theirs was a more subtle task of capturing an enemy outside the battlefield at all costs. They had steeled their nerves all day long, knowing the battle raged below. They were also aware that battles paused at each day's end. Dusk was near, and Mayer sighed in relief at its coming. Snow fell around them, and the war continued.

He was about to rise but stopped. Falling snow, dark trees, and dusk had concealed their soft approach. What he thought to be an illusion was the witch and her posse slowly entering his trap.

Sayiina, Ragnar, and two Cossacks cautiously rode to the bluff. She leaned over her saddle to speak to Ragnar.

But Ragnar, watching her movement, spoke first. "What is it?" he whispered. "What are you seeing?"

Her brows were creased with intently focused eyes. "There's a lot of negative energy here, but it could be coming from the battle below. I want a better view from the bluff to clear my thoughts and learn of our enemies' position."

"Aye then. There's still time for us before we lose all daylight. We also have a full moon tonight to guide our way back." He then turned to the Cossacks to indicate their next location with a hand signal.

Cautiously, Sayiina nudged her horse forward. Everyone followed her lead. In a few moments, she halted, surprised to see the battle still raging so late in the day.

The snow had ceased, and the same wind, now breaking the clouds apart, also swept her raven hair before her. Sayiina shook her head to stay the negative thoughts running through her mind. Now conflicted, she couldn't quell an inner notion tormenting her of better judgment over risk. When she dismounted, and her feet touched the ground, a powerful shiver ran up her spine. Not from fear, but danger. She yelled to Ragnar and the men behind, "We're in a trap! Ride away now!"

Her warning cry came too late, as six heavily armed grenadiers rose seemingly as one from the very earth and surrounded their position. Without a word spoken, both Cossacks were shot dead. Ragnar was hit by three musket balls, one in each shoulder and a third in his left thigh. He fell from his mount, grasping his wounded leg with both hands. In so doing, his hand touched his ring, the Eye of the Raven.

Sayiina screamed at her enemies, "You bastards!" Then she quickly knelt by Ragnar's fallen form. Blood spread from his wounds, crimson oozing through his clothing. She couldn't tell if he was even breathing, and again, she cried out in a blind rage, facing the men who had done this evil deed. "I will kill you all."

A frightening aspect crossed her face as she stood, withdrawing both Yakutian knives. Baring her teeth, Sayiina hissed as a viper might before its deadly strike.

Lieutenant Mayer and the fusilier-grenadiers drew out their swords and very cautiously advanced on the she-witch.

Overhead, the clouds parted, revealing a full moon. Its shafts of light pierced the darkening night on the bluff. A gray mist drifted downward to envelop the unfolding scene.

From an unknown location, Sayiina heard a deep voice utter a single word: "Stone."

Immediately, Lieutenant Mayer and all six grenadiers were rendered helpless and motionless. Sayiina wheeled around to where Ragnar lay unmoving, seeing a dark specter floating above him. Horrified at the image, she thought a reaper had arrived to take his soul. She positioned herself in an offensive *Panthera* crouch and hissed through her teeth. "Touch him, and you die, demon."

"You are brave, Sayiina of Yakutia, and a worthy mate for this man. But I have not been summoned to harm, but rather to heal."

The black-capped specter descended to kneel beside a stilled Ragnar lying on the ground. He reached out with his left hand, passing it over Ragnar's wounds. In doing so, each rifle shot rose from his body, and the open wounds closed behind.

Sayiina saw Ragnar resume his breathing. She gasped in disbelief, having witnessed a miracle. "Who and what are you? Are you a god?"

"No, I cannot bring back the dead. The two others are dead. Ragnar was dying, so I was able to help him return. I am a shapeshifter, one of only two in this world. Your shamans in Yakutia are aware of me." He stood to face her.

Sayiina took a step back when he revealed his true self to her.

"Your mate has in his possession a powerful talisman in the form of a ring. In times of dire need, he can summon me for aid. Tonight, he called when he touched the Eye of the Raven under a full moon."

Sayiina was trying to understand what she was being told. She looked around at the standing and motionless grenadiers surrounding her. Their taut hands were gripping swords, ready to strike. Ragnar was breathing easily and, for the moment, at rest. She then turned her gaze to this black angel of mercy. Nothing seemed natural, as if she were in a waking dream.

She asked the shapeshifter, "How do you know my name?"

"I learned it when you were imprisoned in the Mongolian jail."

Astonished, Sayiina's eyes widened in disbelief. "You were there?"

"Yes, I was summoned then."

"That would explain our escape from hell. Can you also free us from this place? Please, would you take us elsewhere, away from this war, somewhere safe?"

"I can," he replied calmly, "but you must never return. Your lives will be worth nothing if you abandon the Russians and their cause. If you are still certain you want to leave here"—he effortlessly lifted and carried Ragnar—"hold on to the sleeve of my cloak and do not let go."

"What will happen to the French soldiers here?"

"The energy that holds them will diminish in a few hours. They will awaken confused, thinking you disappeared before their eyes."

Sayiina felt lightheaded when touching the shapeshifter's cloak. A breeze passed over her face, the same breeze now lifting her body above the treetops. She looked down and saw the world turning below. Where they would descend, she did not know. Her world was surreal and fantastic when they slowly descended outside a field barn.

"Where are we?"

"Northern Germania. There is a nearby town named Bremen. You will be able to secure provisions and travel from there."

Sayiina stood on firm ground and regained her sense of here and now. She spoke to the shapeshifter with a new understanding of his power and the relationship with her love, Ragnar. "Thank you for aiding us. Do you have a name?"

His pale, chiseled face watched her. "Kane."

Now slowly fading from her sight, she heard the specter say, "Fair winds, Sayiina."

As a Yakutian, Sayiina understood there was both a natural and spiritual world all around her. Kane was someone who could cross over both, a heavenly soul touched by the hand of God. She wondered if she would ever meet him again.

Her attention turned to a stirring Ragnar. He was moving and trying to stand. She instantly knelt at his side, reassuring him he was safe and away from war. She looked deeply into his eyes, watching him regain his strength. Ragnar returned and held her gaze. He was very much in love with this woman.

"What happened? I thought I'd died in the forest. Where are we?"

"Very near a town named Bremen, northern Germania."

Ragnar nodded as if searching for a forgotten memory.

"I also thought you'd died until a guardian came to your rescue. You were shot in both shoulders and your leg. How do they feel now?"

He sat up, touched his shoulders, and then his leg. A puzzled look crossed his face, quickly replaced with knowledge.

"You know of Kane, lass?"

"I do. When were you going to share this with me? You carry a talisman so powerful you can summon a shapeshifter for aid."

Ragnar felt scolded by Sayiina and a little foolish now that she had discovered his secret. In his weak defense, he insisted, "I was going to tell you when the time was right. It's not like I can just call for him, only under the direst circumstances. And even then, there is no certainty in life.

"I only learned of the ring's power while watching Marko's cruelty upon you. Helpless, I felt my very soul was being torn apart as I cried for help. By good fortune, Kane answered my call."

"Aye," Sayiina agreed. "If not for Kane, I would be dead by Marko's hand in that hellhole." She bowed her head to the suffering memory. "I, too, have a secret that I want to share, Ragnar."

They both stood, embraced, and she whispered in his ear, "I am with child." She pulled back, then watched for his reaction.

Ragnar beamed, a grin creasing his weathered face. "A gift from God, lass; I am beyond pleased for this good news."

Sayiina sighed, thankful all was right in their world together on this journey. She touched his cheek and kissed his lips, grateful for this man in her life. Sayiina's spirit was lifted with joy. "Kane has made our journey possible, Ragnar."

"Aye, lass, he has made a difference by allowing us to continue our course home."

It was an early November morning, and the air was cool and crisp. Blue sky and not a cloud in sight. A beautiful start to a new day. Ragnar put his arm around Sayiina's waist. "I feel good. Let's go to this Bremen. I actually think it's a friendly harbor if my memory hasn't failed me yet. My father may have taken me there when I was learning to sail."

"Really?"

"The name sounds familiar to me. Perhaps we can book passage to Norway from there."

Sayiina listened as Ragnar spoke. She loved the sound of his voice. Strong, confident, and self-assured. He was unlike the other men who had come and gone in her life. Now, she desired a home to raise their family and was confident he would provide it.

With their arms around each other, walking down the road, Ragnar lifted his face to the warm sun.

"You keep unusual friends, Ragnar," she scolded in jest.

He laughed. "If you mean Kane, yes. But be careful, lass. I consider you my 'best' friend."

Hearing a truthful irony in his reply, Sayiina smiled broadly. "Good."

www.ingramcontent.com/pod-product-compliance
Lightning Source LLC
Jackson TN
JSHW020913040425
81989JS00003B/59